Loving Enemies

~ Barney and Myko ~

Southern Japan
1944–1946

Arthur H. Barns

THIRD EDITION

Loving Enemies
~ Barney and Myoko ~
Southern Japan
1944 – 1946

Copyright © 2011, Arthur H. Barnes

ISBN: 978-1-60414-448-2

Library of Congress Control Number: # 2009921013

Third Edition

Published by Fideli Publishing Inc.
www.FideliPublishing.com

Cover Photographs: The U.S.S. Zellars DD 777 on April 12, 1944, painted by SKIP RAINS, Napa, Calif. artist noted for native American paintings at the Smithsonian; Myoko in Cloak and Garden, modeled by Miye Bishop; and the author in uniform, 1945.

About the Author

Arthur H. Barnes was born in Ventura, CA. He earned a B.A. in professional arts from Brooks Institute, Santa Barbara, CA. and an M.A. degree from Pepperdine University, Malibu, CA.

While serving in the US Navy (1944 -1950) he survived a Kamikaze attack and earned a Purple Heart; and he served in Okinawa, Japan, which experience provided the source of many of the details and flavor of this story. He worked at the Data center of the Edwards Air Force Base, CA., in the Major Company for 27 years.

He lives with his wife Alvena in Bellingham, a most beautiful city 22 miles south of the Canadian Border and overlooking the San Juan Islands. He has been married from 1950 to the present, and dotes on one "fabulous" grandson.

Other books by Arthur H. Barnes

In The Service of Our Country:
The Ship and Her Men of the USS Zellars DD 777, 1998

The Longest Way Home, 2002

Beyond The Darkest Shadow, 2005

Lonely Horses, 2006

The Sword Maker, 2009

Acknowledgements and Thanks

To Miye Bishop for giving beautiful form to the character on the cover;

to the friends who critiqued my book and responded to my request for their honest reactions;

and to my wife Alvena, who stood back always and encouraged me to write, even though she thought — because each novel was so different from the last — that her husband might be slightly crazy.

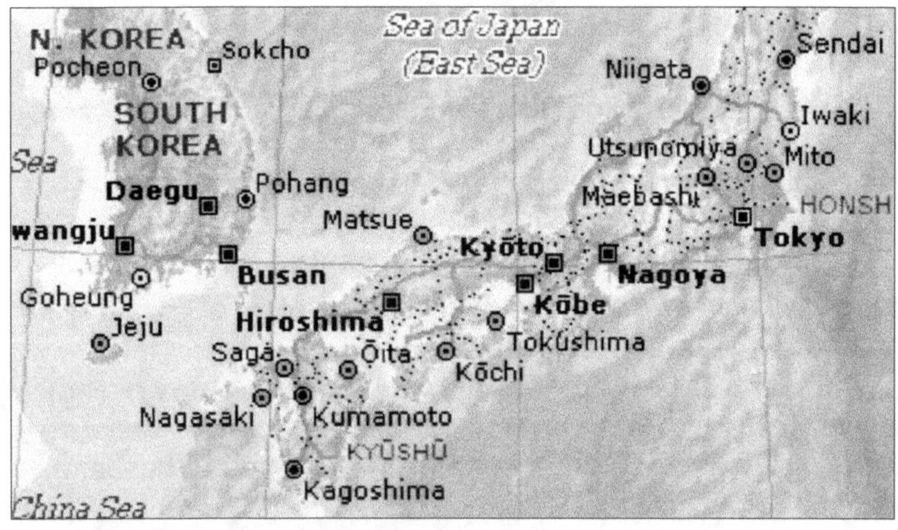

Above: Southernmost Japanese islands.

Below: the island of Kyushu, showing the town of Fukuoka and the area (in solid red square) of Barney's landing and Myoko's house and garden.

Table of Contents

Author's Note

The author wishes to clarify, for all readers, the use of certain terms used in this novel.

During the second World War Japan attacked the United States and necessitated hostilities as its enemy. In light of the resulting destruction, and of its combatant behavior as reported, it was natural and inevitable that derogatory terms, such as "Jap", would have been employed to refer to this enemy by Americans, especially in the heat of battle. The author has therefore, in certain situations narrated in this book, employed this term in order to convey to readers the realities and emotions of those times.

The author wishes to assure readers that in no way does he wish to offend by the use of the term and begs to have his intentions understood as stated here. Rather, he joins with the entire world in praise of the Japanese people for their progressive culture and desire to bring about peace and a measure of harmony to our still troubled world.

— Arthur H. Barnes

PART I

The Mission

October–November 1944

October 4, 1944: 0500

Wafts of gentle salt spray combed over the bow planes of the Seawolf as she moved quietly, but very determinedly, toward the island of Kyushu, the southernmost major island of the Japanese homeland. The objective, a strange but seemingly easy one: put a special person on a selected lonely stretch of beach south of the city of Fukuoka, Japan, with required supplies, Continue on your assigned patrol, pick him up in 14 days and rush him back to Pearl Harbor.

Standing the 04:00 to daylight watch as lookout was one of the most calming events Barney had had during the past week, since he had come aboard the submarine. As the salt spray mist lightly coated his face and jacket, he had time to think about the place in which he now found himself. The spray evaporated and turned to fine salty residue as Barney's thoughts and feelings went back to several weeks ago.

He had been a very satisfied sailor on board one of the newest and best 2200-ton Sumner class destroyers that the Pacific Fleet had seen to date. The ship had been charging around several of the latest recaptured islands firing shore bombardments, and on several occasions had shot Japanese planes out of the ever-blue sky. Barney felt that if one had to be in a war, this was the best duty one could hope for. To date the Navy had been very rewarding for him and he was sure that would continue. Recently he had been promoted to Petty officer 2nd class and given the duty to train several new seaman strikers in the fire control gang. Life was great! Then totally unexpectedly, BOOM! A PBY Catalina flying boat landed close by, and its crew ushered Barney aboard the aircraft and whisked him away without any explanations.

A day later, he had found himself standing in a room deep inside a cement bunker, somewhere in Pearl Harbor — in front of some very determined-looking men, who had not identified themselves — and heard one of the wildest propositions that he could have imagined.

Barney had learned good basic Japanese as a high school student, long before he imagined a war in his own future. Just after World War Two began, his family had been transferred to El Centro, California. Even though most of the Japanese had been relocated to other areas, at least one family had not, and Koji Washuri became a best friend to Barney.

After school, basketball practice, or just leisurely throwing a ball through the hoop, was fun. Often the two of them would wander off through the many citrus orchards, tossing rocks and talking about many of the main events of the times. One of the most memorable events was, as they wandered through the grapefruit orchards during the ripe season, when he and Koji would select ripe-on-the-tree fruit, peel and section them and enjoy them together. Now, just remembering the shared grapefruit made his mouth water.

Rarely was the war with Japan a part of their conversations, simply because of the deep friendship and respect that was developing between them. It was a good way to learn trust and to share each other's culture. When Koji first invited Barney to his home Barney was captivated by the fact that his parents did not speak one word of English, yet they were very gracious with visitors who came to their home. Koji's father owned a large vegetablc farm near El Centro and took great pride in his contributions to help feed the country. He was a very proud American.

Barney badgered Koji to teach him the Japanese language, so that he could be a better friend both to Koji and his family. For the next two years Barney spent many hours at it, and became good enough with the Japanese language that when in the Washuri home he used their language all the time. It became a game to see how often they could trap Barney in some of their conversations. And that was why he had found himself standing in front of those few very stern, difficult-looking men.

A flash of greenish light from the bow of the submarine quickly jerked Barney back to the present. The light was the sea being churned as it broke over the diving planes, causing a brighter than usual luminescence from the salt water phosphorous as the sub moved toward its destination. Losing one's concentration from lookout responsibility was not recommended, and getting caught would mean one heck of a chewing out by the officer of the deck. Even at that early hour of the morning it was very important to keep sharp eyes and ears for anything 360 degrees about the boat. Barney had volunteered to stand the last watch before dawn because it gave him the longest amount of time to stay topside and take in as much fresh air as possible. Although some in the Navy considered submarine duty the best, Barney was not too crazy about being submerged with so much water all around him.

It was difficult to keep his mind on his duty as lookout; however, he began to go over the details of his new and weird objective. The three men at Pearl Harbor had given him some real lectures — God, Duty and Country speeches. They impressed upon him that what they were about to ask him to do would make a most significant difference in the outcome of the pending invasion of the mainland of Japan. Even with the best in photographic intelligence, the war planners did not feel very sure of the many potential obstacles that would face the invading troops as they made their way ashore. And somehow that is how Barney fit into this wild scheme of coming events.

The objective seemed simple enough. The submarine was to put him, enough food, and other supplies (including a special radio) onto the Western side of one of the main islands of Japan. Supposedly there were high cliffs with some cave-like enclosures that he could make into some kind of hiding place. His primary objective would be to search by night for any military-type installations and study the roads to determine if they would support the heavy tanks and other equipment that would come ashore during the invasion; further, to study what the civilian population was like. He was to observe what they were doing most of the daylight hours and anything else that might be of interest should the U.S. decide to use that particular area for landing troops. Do not try to fight or engage in any way the Japanese people that you might be forced to meet. If caught he was to simply state that he was a survivor from a sub that had been sunk (which turned out to be a sadly prophetic statement) and that he had made his way ashore, hiding out in the heavily forested countryside.

The target area was to be somewhere south of the city of Fukuoka, a place Barney had never heard of, and one of which little knowledge was available. It was on the western side of the island of Kyushu, the southernmost island of the bigger islands of Japan. Maps, tracing materials, pencils, a small but very high-powered spotting scope, and a high quality camera with several lenses were all the equipment that he would need.

The time frame for the gathering of all the information was set for two weeks. Into Barney's mind crept the thought of how he would accomplish all that he was being asked to do in so few days. Waves of fear of so many unknowns seeped into his thoughts and caused a very bitter, acid taste. The muscles in his stomach twisted and convulsed, manifesting his fear. Even if everything that had been planned went perfectly, Barney knew that this was still not going to be any fun. It would not be a holiday. If he was this apprehensive about what he was about to do, what would it be like once he reached the beaches of Japan, alone, and with no one to talk to? *Damn, how did I get into this mess?* He almost started to blame Koji for teaching him the damned language.

The very early shafts of light were just creeping over the placid Pacific Ocean as the officer of the deck yelled, "Clear the bridge, lookouts below, dive, dive!" and the scramble was on. The stories of depth charging, diving so deep that the hull would cave in, and other wild events had caused a subliminal, but strong, fear that had not been a part of destroyer duty. Barney had not cared to look into what a submarine design was like. Therefore, he was not very well acquainted with how it was able to cruise submerged, nor with the fact that it had two different kinds of propulsion systems: one for surface cruising using diesel engines, and a second one using electric motors for submerged cruising.

The huge battery compartment was one of the main concerns of the crew due to the constant need to have maximum power available at all times. One never knew when the boat would be forced to run submerged for long and hazardous hours. The electrical power system did not create any odors and made very little noise when in use. The big diesels with the ever-present smell of diesel fuel, along with the other odors of human sweat and cooking, caused Barney to cherish the moments of topside lookout and fresh air. Ed Larson, Chief of the boat, often reminded him that the smell of an unventilated, closed-up boat did take some getting used to.

It had been some nine days since leaving Hawaii. As the night closed around the lone travelers in what seemed like a very small sea-going system, the skipper, showing a different attitude and a deeper concern, announced that they were now in enemy waters and for all hands to pay closer attention to their duties. The enemy could be expected to show its face at any time. It was also time to let the crew in on the reason a non-sub passenger was aboard.

The attitude of the crew toward Barney became more congenial and he often heard the crew saying, "Someone on the boat has lost all his marbles and is just plain nuts!" He was beginning to agree with them, but a commitment was a commitment and anyhow, how could he get off this damned sub? He couldn't go over the hill, so to speak.

For the next three days the different specialists of the crew: radioman, for communications; the boat's exec, for accurate plotting of potential targets;

and the captain, for general reinforcement, went over all the details for this hair-brained expedition. Much of what they recommended were items that Barney — and the men who got him into this fix— never thought of. He was very grateful and it gave him a small measure of confidence in his task.

A new concern, one that was beginning to plague Barney the most, was how the guys were going to find him and get him off the damned island when the time came.

October 8: 2300

Delivering Barney was not the only chore that the Sea-wolf had on her schedule. After putting him ashore the sub was to conduct a normal war patrol to the north end of the island of Hokkaido, return through the Nemuro Straits, on down the eastern side of Hokkaido, then reenter the Sea of Japan through the Tsugaru Straits. They were to sink everything afloat and be at the rendezvous site exactly 14 days from the day he was put on shore. All the whatifs a person could imagine became a part of his every thought. *This is enough shit to scare the devil himself,* was his total emotion. One thing for sure was, no one could pile any more on him; there was no more they could think of, or somehow they would have done it.

Black is really black sometimes, but tonight could not get black enough for the chore that they were about to perform. The sub, cruising barely submerged with periscope raised up the maximum height, was attempting to find the exact series of cliffs on which to discharge the lone passenger.

The time was 2300 hours and with all the junk that Barney had to haul up the 300-foot side of an unknown cliff, there would barely be enough time before daylight to do all this stuff, find a hole in the cliff side and say all the prayers, both in Japanese and in English, that he could think of. Quietly, the skipper announced: "Surface, landing party to the conning tower, gun stations will be manned and for God's sake be fast and quiet." To the surface and the black of the night they went. Small gurglings of seawater could be heard as it was being dispelled from the ballast tanks.

There were slight movements of personnel as the men went to their stations for the quick topside activity. A soft hiss of fresh air enveloped the crew as the conning tower hatch was opened and all were naked to the world of hostile Japan. The sub was on the surface only a few hundred yards from a very ominous dark shore.

Breakers could be heard loud and clear from the direction of the landing site. *Was this the right place? Couldn't we look a little more, maybe longer or something — to make sure you guys are putting my scared ass on the right beach? Boy, oh boy, what a way to find out if Koji had taught him the correct words in Japanese.* These were just some of the more pressing thoughts going through Barney's mind. *Now it — REALITY — was about to happen.* These thoughts were completely scrambled inside Barney's head. It was spinning and loudly screaming: *This is not the thing to be doing at the tender age of not quite 20, and, will I be around to reach 20 after the next 14 days?*

A small black inflatable boat was put over the side, and all the gear that he would need — or thought he would need, to do what he was supposed to do — was piled in the center. The second-class bosun, Carl Benson, was ready to row Barney toward the sound of the angry sea that was breaking on the darkened shore. A small slightly protected cove turned out to be the landing site. It offered enough protection from the breaking surf so that off-loading the equipment and foodstuff was not complicated, and it took only a few minutes to stack everything on the rocky beach. Benson gave Barney a strong grasp of the arm, almost bruising his hand in a good luck, see you in a few days or nights handshake. Then he hastily retreated back into the darkness of the night and the submarine.

Barney stood on the beach just as Benson had left him, staring out into the direction of the sub. It seemed like hours before he heard the soft whistle of the air being forced out of the sub's ballast tanks as it returned to the security of the darkness of the undersea.

Alone! Not in all of his life had Barney dreamed that anyone could be so alone, and feel this deserted and lost. *How could the US Navy do such a thing to a young guy like me? One hell of a predicament to be in! Oh well, I'm here and there's only me to get all this stuff up the side of this hill and daylight will come all too soon.* Barney knew that he had to have everything out of sight and be in some kind of hiding place that would allow him to gather his thoughts and try to make the best out of this commitment. More what-ifs. *What if there is no path up the steep cliff? What if I can't find a hole in the cliffs so that I can get out of sight? What if I'm seen?* And so on. "First things first," Barney said to himself, and first was to get some idea of the small inlet in which he now found himself stranded.

Creeping slowly toward the face of the cliff, stumbling over beach stones, it took him about 30 minutes to get his bearings. One very narrow, and what looked like a seldom-used trail zigzagged upwards to who knew what or where. He decided to make a non-carrying exploratory trip to the top and find some kind of very temporary shelter. The soil was wet and slippery, and careful placement of each step was mandatory in order to keep from sliding back to the bottom of the climb. In the darkness, it seemed that each change in direction of the trail was about 12 steps, not including the stumbles and slips. After at least an hour, the top of the climb suddenly flattened out and Barney found himself staring into a very dark and slightly terraced valley. He could barely make out any details of the area. Deep shadows across the valley made it appear rather steep and rocky.

Off to his right the terrain dropped out of view and to his left it rose gently over what appeared to be another shallow valley. Along the edge of the cliff, as far as he could see in the darkness, were large clusters of some kind of high vegetation. Barney's first thought was if he could get all his equipment and stuff to the top he could hide in the biggest cluster of whatever the tall growth was. Sliding and grabbing handfuls of dirt, he made his way back down to the beach. It took him three trips to gather his food and equipment and stack it near the closest vegetation.

This backbreaking effort had really done him in and he fell out of breath upon the edge of the cliff, gasping for air. Now he was free of the beach. The fear of being seen or caught made his skin prickle with sharp sensations much like electrical shock. *If I could just fly, I would get the hell out of here right now,* he thought anxiously.

Barney first went to the cliff side of the cluster and found that the vegetation was a small forest of giant bamboo. It grew so close that no way was found to allow crawling into the inside of the mass. He thought that if he could move deep enough into the bamboo, he would be out of sight and secure for the coming day. Backing up, he next tried the landside of the bamboo and found a very low crawl space where two of the clusters came together. This would have to do for the time being. Being careful not to drag any of the packs, so as not to leave any trace of entry, Barney put the packages in their respective piles, covered them with a thin canvas and laid down atop the smallest pile. Everything else would have to wait.

He was totally exhausted and could not even think clearly, let alone logically, about what he must do next. A jumble of all his emotions and fears gathered together causing a few tears and a frightful few hours of sleep.

October 9: 0630

A misty, damp daylight with thin shafts of light penetrated the thick foliage. Barney had been awake for some time. He was not sure if he had really had any sleep. Everything seemed so far removed from anything real, that it was not easy to get himself underway toward the reason he was where he was. He first crawled to the ocean side of his cover and looked out onto a very quiet and most beautiful sea. How could this be a place of war and killing when everything was so peaceful and had such great beauty?

Moving away from the direction of his storage space, he found that the clusters of bamboo were not very wide and grew along the fringes of the cliff. The widest part was no more than 30 feet. This would not offer much of a place to hide in for long. Crawling along the edge and moving farther away from his temporary hiding place he saw a rather sharp turn in the cliff. An outcropping of large boulders and short bushes looked like it might provide some kind of protected hiding place.

Barney stayed very low so no one could see his travel to the new place. He found a fairly good trail that disappeared over the edge and appeared to go down toward the ocean level. Trying to be as hidden as he could, Barney explored down to about the halfway mark, where he noticed another narrow path going to his right and slightly upward. The new path climbed over several large boulders and disappeared into the far side of the cliff. Behind the group of boulders was an area that, with some extra digging and moving of smaller rocks and soil, could be made to offer as safe a hiding place as he could expect to find for the duration of his stay.

Back he went to begin the task of hauling his supplies. He made the exchange in two trips and set about the digging and building of his nest. As the first day's darkness settled about him, he began to feel somewhat secure in his small cave-like dwelling. He had dug some eight feet into the hillside and created an opening big enough to stand up in. This also offered him, somewhat hidden from view, a place where he could look out to sea and observe any seagoing traffic, should there be any.

Barney's first food, if that is what one could call it, was good old C-rations of franks and beans. He had never before had the distasteful experience of this poorly thought of concoction, and the first taste did nothing to make him think better of it. He ate it cold and found little satisfaction in the feeling that he'd had a meal. Tomorrow morning early, before the sun came up, he would begin his observation of the land, make his maps, take whatever photographs he could, count the people, and write down all the information that he was there to collect.

Barney was saying to himself: but wait a minute — in order to be somewhere of importance where there will be places of interest — airfields, roads, military installations and areas of large population — I'll have to be there by daylight and in a concealed place. Not knowing what he should expect, Barney laid out all of his different materials and food supplies. Taking care to have only the items of greatest need, he put together a small package that would not draw attention should he pass by other night travelers.

The men at Pearl had supplied him with what they perceived as the best way today's poor peasants would be dressed in Japan — and even though the fit was OK, Barney felt like the only frog in a very small pond. Black, overly large sleeves and baggy pants legs, a sash much like a thin rope for a belt, canvas shoes with smooth soles and a loose-fitting pullover shirt cloaked his real identity. Underneath he had regulation Navy issue underclothing. No one could say what the local farmer wore under his pants and shirt, but unless anyone got too close, it would make little difference what Barney had underneath. Additionally, he had been allowed to bring one set of underclothes and five pairs of black socks. Hours went by while he waited and rested.

October 10: 0400

After wrapping the native clothing about himself and picking up his meager pack, Barney eased himself out of his hole and began the spooky trek into the darkness. As he made his way clear of the bamboo thicket, the first decision was which way to turn. According to his impression of the lay of the land, his instinct was to go to the left, up over a small rise that looked like it would drop down toward a valley. In the darkness there was no way to tell anything or if he was about to meet anyone. Walking away from the hiding place toward the low hillside, he followed a well-used wide footpath running from right to left. It was a main travel route from somewhere to some other place. He turned left into who knows where, or to whom.

The dark night was very quiet and for some 45 minutes Barney did not hear or see anything as he made his way down the path. He could have passed close by people and dwellings and not known it. The first indication of life was when he turned a sharp bend in the path and came upon what appeared to be a farmhouse sitting on the very edge of the path. Frozen in the center of the path— with a strong taste of stomach fluids in his throat— Barney eased to the side of the path and steadied himself from the surprised reaction. Turning his head from side to side to better tune his hearing he listened and watched the house for any signs of people. Remembering that the Japanese were supposed to be dog-less gave him a little reassurance, since no noise came from the farmhouse.

Keeping close to the dark side of the path he began to creep past the house, and went some 100 yards before his breathing returned to a normal rhythm. If this was what his travel was to be like, he would never get to any place of importance before daylight. Putting his head down and trying to walk as he thought the local people would walk, he simply took off down the path at a fast clip.

Barney had been on the path for some two hours and had not been disturbed by any of the countryside. The farmhouses were becoming routine and he was seeing them more often. There had to be something to see in front of him. Guessing as to time, he felt that it was about two hours before first light would be upon him and he had to be hidden somewhere. He speeded up his travel and some 15 minutes later a hilly area opened up.

A large open plain with many dwellings filling the landscape came into view. He guessed that he had not more than an hour to be in the open, and therefore a hiding place became mandatory. If he kept to the right all trails would stay close to the up-hill side of the plain, offering the best opportunity to find some kind of lookout. Moving still faster he skirted most of the dwellings and finally found a narrow, well-used trail heading to the area that he had in mind. Shrubbery, much like the kind he was used to on California hillsides, began to cover each side of the trail and there was an outcropping of large stones close by.

Breathing became more labored as the pitch of the trail increased. To the east a very faint of first dawn was beginning to show. Time was running out for finding a secure shelter. Just as Barney was about to dive off the trail into the weeds and brush, he came to a narrow seemingly unused trail that lead off to his left. This seemed to offer the best place to hide. Some 50 yards up the trail was an almost vertical downward turn that had a small spring running at the end of it. To his right was nothing but small trees, scrub brush and a lot of big boulders. No trail went to the higher location so up he went, out of sight and well hidden. Taking off his small pack Barney collapsed at the base of the largest boulder and rested.

October 11: 0600

Sunlight was full in Barney's face before he started to take stock of the strange surroundings. A very large city lay to the north of him — many smoke stacks were spewing dirty plumes into the early morning air. This could only be the city of Fukuoka, Barney's target city, the place where he was supposed to gather all the information that he could find so that the authorities at Pearl could plan the invasion that was sure to come soon. Farther off to the right, at the upper end of the plain were the sounds of aircraft engines being run up. There had to be some kind of airfield, or maybe an aircraft factory.

Observing the area in the direction of the sound of aircraft, he viewed a wide plain to the outskirts of the city. It was all gardens or farmland. The plots were so small that there seemed to be millions of them. Some smaller industrial complexes were scattered at the edge of the city. Some of the buildings showed heavy destruction from American bombings. Then there were residential dwellings for a great distance to the main part of the city. Scattered throughout the main downtown area were many factories and a large open harbor. As Barney scanned the harbor he noted that it was filled with many small cargo and transport ships. Looking farther out to sea there was a vast anchorage pier extending as far as he could see. On the very far horizon was the faint outline of tall mountains.

First things first. He needed to take inventory of the primary supplies that he was given, list them in the order of their importance and use some kind of counting plan so that he could keep track of numbers and amounts. The most pressing problem was his own security within his hiding place. Looking about the area, he found that by some blind luck it was well enclosed with trees and very low shrubbery. The boulders offered the ability to move about and change the field of observation. Confidence was fast being restored to the hidden spy — well, a temporary spy.

Shifting his view uphill and to the back of his outpost made him feel good about his hiding place. As far as he could see above him, no houses or other man-made objects were in view. Now all he had to do was settle in and begin the careful observation of the large community that was spread out below him.

Number one on his list was, of course, the amount of military and defense installations. Number two, all roads and large open spaces such as parks and bombed-out areas. Special attention was to be given to the main roads and the attempt to determine if these roads could support heavy tanks and trucks. It appeared that the American Air force had not done much damage to some of the inner-city area. Many of the larger manufacturing facilities had been blown to pieces. The dock area showed the most destruction and there were no dockside warehouse buildings left standing. After glassing with his high powered spotting scope for several hours, Barney noticed for the first time a large structure far to the south of the main city. Setting his scope so that it gave him the best view, he concentrated on the far object. Some smoke stack activity was all that he was sure of. Making a note to himself that this was something that would require a different location for a good look, he returned his attention to the main part of the city.

It took Barney all day to just map the main roads and open park areas, list the most significant parts of the factories and determine what seemed to be the population centers. He didn't know why but he made note of the time of day and in which direction the people were traveling each hour of his observation. Somehow it seemed important to know when the population moved from one place to another as the day passed. This could be significant as he compiled all of the data and made a summary at the end of the day. People, and the estimated number going to one area, and then another, allowed for a good approximation of the most significant activity of the major part of the population.

As darkness prevented him from good visual information, he realized that lunch had completely been forgotten, and hunger pains brought him back to his lonely hiding place. His food plan or meal agenda for the next three days was all in the C-ration packages. He had packed enough to last for what he felt would be a first-time journey, an evaluation of the area, and the return to his home far away from home. Something called beans and ham sounded like it would satisfy his taste buds and not make him too homesick for a reasonable meal. He could not take a chance of even the smallest fire to warm the mess in the can.

The greasy taste left by the cold food was almost too much for him to swallow, however hunger and the desire to stop the pains in his stomach forced him to finish the can and turn to the hard biscuits and then the chocolate bar. Even the chocolate had an old taste to it. When he had finished this part of the C-rations, the only item left was a small packet labeled lemon drink. Now that complete darkness had settled about the country, something hot seemed the natural thing to make— like a good cup of Navy coffee. One of those big white mugs that only the Navy seemed to have, would do just fine. He settled for the yellowish powder, mixing it in his canteen. It was the foulest stuff that he had ever tasted. After several attempts to drink it, he poured the remainder in a hole and covered the hole over. With the empty feeling gone from his mind and stomach, attention had to be given to what was next.

Barney was sure that the most important target was the air facility to the north of his hiding place. He had to find out what was going on and the kind of base it was. He needed to leave the secure place that he was now in and stick his neck into another potential noose. It had to be done, if the information was to be complete and reliable. (He guessed that it would take four hours moving along at the same speed that he had traveled getting to his present spot.) First he needed to get some sleep, and a small amount of time to regenerate his courage before any travel could be undertaken. The only blanket-like item that he had brought was a ground cloth that offered little warmth or protection from any elements, but it was waterproof. This is what he wrapped around his body, then leaning close into a recess of the boulders, he dozed into a very weary, but alert, rest.

October 12: 1205

Sometime around midnight his internal clock went off and told him that it was time to move. He had packed all of his mapping and food material so that all he needed to do was shake the sleepy cobwebs from his head and cautiously move out. First, he tried to remove as many traces of his visit as he could in the darkness so as to prevent detection, and then he made his way up over the boulders and down to the lower branch of the trail. He felt that by following or backtracking to the wide path he would continue to keep to the high ground and on a northerly heading. This should bring him close to his second destination, the air base. Also, at this late hour, his chances of meeting other persons on the path would be much less. Shaking his whole body and assuming a stooped profile of the typical old Japanese man, off he went into the darkness of the third night on enemy soil.

The lay of the land was almost flat for several miles. Then the path began to tilt upward and climb through gentle undulating foothills, not enough to make the heart beat faster, but enough to let his leg muscles know that extra work was required and a measure of pain would follow. The uphill climb also made Barney more cautious and slowed the forward progress a small amount so if anyone should be met unexpectedly, he would have time to react in what he hoped would be a positive manner.

He continually went over the lecture given him at Pearl Harbor: Do not let yourself be detected. It's very important that you get in and out without letting anyone know you have been there. For his own self-image and longevity, he would do his best to carry out this part of the instructions. The path swung to the left and around a narrowing vestige of farmlands, then up a small hill, and back down toward a lower valley. In the distance was the target he was aiming for, the airbase. Even in the darkness, there was a definite outline of the base.

Running from north to southeast was the longest of three runways with the other two cutting across almost in the center of the installation. In the half-moon light the runways shown like silver paths in a flat land. Toward the foothills, like huge grounded balloons, were several buildings that looked like hangars. In the darkness it was impossible to see where the personnel structures were. No noticeable activities could be seen, but the place was big — very big.

Observing the lay of the land, Barney considered that it would be most difficult to find a secure hiding place, since everything was so open and free of trees or vegetation. He needed a place that would allow clear observation of all parts of the base and of the surrounding areas that lay below him. Looking as hard as one could in the darkness, Barney had to almost circle the whole facility before he found some meager cover. At the northwest end of the base area, but not on the grounds, was a sort of refuse dump. It was full of old pieces of concrete, whose thickness said that they had come from the runways, and many other odds and ends. In this mess, he found a hollow that permitted enough space to back into and crouch down far enough to be out of sight — but, should anyone come prowling, it would be impossible to stay hidden. But hunker down he did, and with no visible light to see by (daylight was some time away) there was time for a few badly needed ZZZs, and maybe a thought as to what was next. Snoozing came first.

October 12: 0615

As the damp dawn was seeming to take forever to offer enough daylight to see by, Barney came wide awake. It could have been the sound of airplane engines being revved up and the early morning activities of the base getting underway. He was close enough to the main part of the base to identify officers from the enlisted men and to form a good judgment of the different activities that each group was engaged in, such as plane handlers and mechanics. The fuel trucks of course were the easiest.

Their officers and men seemed just like the American officers and men. The officers were all yelling at the enlisted men and the enlisted men were doing all the work. The great difference noted was the tone of voice. The officers had a very definite kill tone in their commands and the enlisted men acted as though they would be killed at any moment if the officers were not fully satisfied with their response. Ruling through extreme fear was their means of getting things done in a hurry.

Back to the job. Placing blank mapping paper on his lap, and setting up the spotting scope, Barney was ready to bring down his own brand of havoc on the little yellow bastards. First he counted the number of aircraft, the different types of fighters, and then bombers, (twin engine and single engine). They did not have a large number of bombers and the fighters seemed to be older and well used, a mixed bag of all types that he had seen during training for aircraft recognition. The fighters were scattered all over the base, a few here, and some farther away. From the U.S. Navy reports that floated around in Pearl, the enemy was not supposed to have many planes left. The base below seemed to dispute that information, for on one side of the field he counted at least 250 very useable and seemingly ready to go aircraft. Counting the personnel was something else. The little men seemed to be moving all the time, and always at a slow run. Mumbling to himself, he said, "let's see, about 50 on the flight line, 20 driving the refueling trucks, another 120 to 140 working on the airplanes, dozens cleaning up the leftover debris from the last visit of the good old Navy Carriers and U.S. Air force, and maybe 60 officers doing the yelling." By the count of aircraft, he assumed that there were an equal number of pilots. Now, who else?

The base must have some kind of security force (not many in sight), and the cooks, medical, and other staff should bring the number to about, let's see, a rough guess of 950 men altogether. That is what he wrote down.

The sun was at high noon when Barney was satisfied that he had all the data that he would need about the airfield and his attention turned to the different ways to get to and from the base. Where are the roads and what kind? How wide and from what direction? It took another hour to detail all this information on the map layout, and then he just leaned back staring out to the far horizon toward the city of Fukuoka. What next?

He had been on the Island of Japan for three days and so far what he had done seemed easy. Behind and above him there was a loud-rattling movement and his heart went clear out of his body. At that moment he would have bet that there was not a drop of blood in his whole system. Frozen was not the word for the feeling that he had. He could not, nor dared not, try to see what was making the noise. Sitting very still and taking whatever was forthcoming was the only thing he could do. He died tiny pieces at a time. Some 20 minutes later the rattling stopped and the faint sound of someone moving away could be heard. Paying very careful attention, Barney could now see a two-wheeled cart going back toward the main part of the base — a cart rolling on what looked like bicycle wheels, no wonder he had missed the sound of its coming.

Crouched in the trash pile, Barney had no choice where he was until it seemed safe to begin his return trip. Most of his rations were gone and he had forgotten to bring the special Kodak camera. Just after dark a misty drizzle settled into the valley. This was good in one respect and bad in another. The misery of the rain would cause most other travelers to be inside, making it much safer for him to travel. The cold damp rain also made it more miserable for him.

As complete darkness enveloped the area, guessing that it was near 10:00 o'clock, groaning with pain from having been cramped in one place, Barney stumbled up the short slope and onto the muddy path. The whole return trip to his original hiding place was without incident. As the morning began to clear he slumped down in the cave he had fashioned, pulled the ground cover over his wet, chilled body and fell asleep.

According to the position of the sun, it was near noon and his damp clothes made everything more miserable. He had to take the chance of being seen from the sea in order to dry out. By placing the wet garments on the boulders facing away from the ocean, chances of being seen would be slight. He stretched his naked body out on the ground cloth and took full advantage of the warming rays of the sun. Some two hours later, feeling almost new again, he took time to think over all that he had seen and done, make additional notes, and to plan his next venture.

If he was to record everything that he had to, he needed a plan. Barney decided to look at the areas in the sequence of their position within the plain of the valley, starting with the air base, then the city north, the central part of the city, and then the southern area where most of the factories were located. The last part of this objective would be the far southern area where he had seen the still unidentified large complex.

For ease of travel, he decided to reverse the direction from his first adventure and investigate the southern part of the city and the unidentified complex.

So as not to leave anything out and maybe leave behind important items such as the camera, he checked each item on his list. Missing the need to photograph the air base would mean a trip back if he was to have the best record. Due to the wide area that he wanted to cover, Barney planned to be gone at least four days. That would mean a total of eight days in this very unfriendly land — a little bone-chilling when he thought of the amount of time left before he was to be picked up.

As dusk settled about the cliffs, Barney was determined to have something warm on his menu for dinner. Gathering the few twigs and dry limbs available in the brush just above his hiding place, a small, almost smokeless fire was started. Opening another can of C rations, he set the can in the edge of the tiny flames and sat back. Very little smoke came up from the blaze and he felt more comfortable than at any time since he had arrived. Even with some heat the rations were still barely edible. His last water had been used to make the so-called lemonade, and that led to another problem — finding good water to drink.

Not having any road maps or ideas of the travel patterns, paths and trails, Barney had no concept of how to get to his next place of observation. The path that took him to the high side of the valley and the air base was in the wrong direction. Following the path a few miles from his present place, then onto the main path for about eight miles, would get him to the top of the ridge where he could see the beginning of the wide valley. Then he would have to find another path off to his left, to the south, that would take him in the direction he needed to go. He made a mental map of the few places that he had seen, gathered up his material, and cautiously departed his lair.

His first check point was the farmhouse that had caused him his first real measure of fright. This was located at the bottom of the last rise before he could see down into the open plain. Some 100 yards past the farmhouse he found another path that he had not noticed the first time. It was as well worn as the path he was on and went in the direction that he wanted to take. Almost immediately the path twisted and turned as it went up a rather steep hill. The first trees of any size stood out in the darkest of shadows like giant goblins with arms outstretched to grab him. He cautiously made his way up to the crest of the hill, and to his relief the whole city was spread out before him.

Moving to his right, off the path and under the trees, he could pick out the best way to approach the southern part of the city. Some of the wider paths and the roads could be seen or conjured by the way the houses and larger buildings were lined up. To find a way that would get him close to the area to be observed was not going to be easy. In fact he could not detect any place that would give him a reasonable hiding place in which to do his thing. Getting closer was his only choice and off he went down to the lower part of the hill and into who knew what.

Barney decided if he was to get the information that was needed, he would have to play Japanese and simply go down into the people-places and see directly. If there were other people on the street it would pose a real problem and almost assure that he would be caught. Again, as he entered the housing area, he slumped over in an old man's posture and deeply bent his head so that no one could see his face and the fear that was on it. Within nine blocks he met no one; then turning into a wide street he came upon three old men, looking like what he hoped he looked like, and carrying on an intense conversation. So as not to draw extra attention to himself, Barney mumbled "konbanwa," the Japanese greeting for the evening and shuffled on his way. The old men never left their discussion.

Cold nervous sweat was like a river as it ran down his neck and back. His thoughts were to make one big, slow sweep of the area and hopefully wind up far to the south of the main population and in the direction of the still unknown southern complex. Several more times he met small groups of older men sitting outside of what looked like business places, and he went through the same greeting routine without any further need to do more than a Japanese hello. For the first time he began to realize the need to speak the Japanese language.

By guess alone, Barney felt that he had covered the right amount of the city to be where the best observation could be made and a recording of the important activities would be possible. The street that he had been moving on was a wide, almost three-lane passage, which had to go somewhere important. The one thing that he had noted was the Japanese didn't waste space and this was some kind of main thoroughfare. Several streets farther he found a section of the industrial, or factory area, that had taken one hell of a bombing, with all of the buildings showing unbelievable destruction. Some of them were nothing but piles of rubble. If he could find a bombed-out structure with several stories still standing, it might do for his hiding place. He found several with one corner standing and others without any floors but none that he could use. Making a broken sign post a landmark, Barney began a walking circle of 10 blocks to his right, then 10 more blocks to his left. Still no luck.

He was beginning to cuss the U.S. Air force for being too good at their job. They could have saved at least one almost blown-up building that would offer a place for him to hide!

The only thing left to do was to take another part of the city and repeat the 10-block search pattern. Not in the two sections that had just been searched, but on the right side of a small hill that he had not noticed before, stood a partially destroyed concrete structure that had most of what he was looking for. The building had been some seven stories high, overlooking the southern direction and had nothing but destroyed buildings scattered around it. Picking his way over the loose broken pieces of stone and cement, keeping as quiet as he could, Barney found several broken staircases that led to the higher floors. Trying not to disturb any of the rubble so as not to make a noise was not easy. The next two floors were much the same, but from the fourth floor and on up, the destruction was much worse and did not allow an accessible way to the next floors. Barney felt stuck and was about to give up when in the farthest dark corner, he saw what turned out to be some kind of elevator mechanism with several cables hanging down from the above floors. Pulling on the strands to see how well they were anchored above him, he decided that the cables were from a small dumbwaiter. The cables were so small that to get a good grip on them was difficult. In his pack he had wrapped the camera and several other items into an old green G.I. towel. Cutting the towel in two pieces, he used one piece for the camera; the second piece provided him a means by which to grip the small cables.

He didn't stop climbing until he was as high as the cables went. What had been the top part of the building was gone and what looked like the sixth floor had a big hole and two corners of the overall structure missing. Fortunately the remaining corners were in the back part of the structure and offered the most security. Barney had little of the night left; daylight was less than an hour away and he had to be hidden from everything and everyone.

Crawling as low as he could get, Barney took inventory of his new surroundings and the view that they offered in all directions. He found that the view to the south and west (the one showing most of the southern parts of the city and the industrial complexes) gave him the greatest picture of the details that he needed. He would have to be very careful. The view to the south was well protected by the fallen front corner of the building and the associated rubble from the blown-out walls. This expanse was of the diminishing town limits and had the few factory buildings that were still standing. The real value of the southern exposure was the observation it afforded of the main highway and some lesser roads leading into, and out of, this part of the city. Barney didn't know anything about other towns or cities farther south, therefore he had no sure idea where these roads went. It was obvious that the main road was the one he would have to take in order to get to his next place of interest, the large far southern complex. Like the day before, a soft mist began to fall and the cold bit into his tired, hungry body.

Barney was afraid to move any of the pieces of broken cement to make for more comfortable and secure protection, so he snuggled down as tight as he could with mapping materials, camera and spotting scope, ready for a day of extreme caution.

In the darkness he had not been able to see the dockside road that joined the main highway almost under the building in which he was hiding. In the early morning, a group of heavy trucks came chugging from the dock area onto the main highway and headed south. Each truck was heavily loaded with military personnel, what appeared to be construction equipment, big timbers, some telephone pole-like pilings and a derrick with which to drive pilings with. There was an overall greater military presence in the area but most members looked like ordinary soldiers. He guessed that there might be some three to four thousand that could be seen from his perch, which meant there might be many more that could not be seen. It was a guess at best anyway as he made his notes on the mapping sheet.

Taking some pictures and drawing the main details took him all day and at nightfall he was ready to cover up in his ground cloth, take a deep breath, and get some needed sleep.

October 14: 1500

The next day was much the same — until late in the afternoon. With great fanfare and much noise, a long convoy of trucks, wagons and marching men came boiling over the southern landscape heading into town. From his hiding place it seemed as if all of the soldiers in Japan were marching below him. With near abandonment Barney held the camera above his head and snapped several shots of the activity. One item that caught his attention was the age of the soldiers. Except for the officers, all of the troops were very young; they looked about 13 or 14 years old. There were a few very old grizzly-looking relics bringing up the rear of the columns. A note of this was made and another couple of photos taken. Maybe the folks back at Pearl could make something of them.

Barney began to take inventory for the two days he had been in the building and decided that there was no advantage in sticking around any longer. Besides, the longer he stayed in one spot, the more possibility that he would be discovered. Making sure that he had everything in his pack, he put his arm on a slab of the concrete and dozed off.

Two long hours passed before he started the downward slide on the dumbwaiter cables. Complete darkness had set in and he felt safe in taking to the streets, as he had done getting there. Bowed head, baggy looking dress, a slumped over profile, a couple of grunts as he passed by others walking along the street gave the impression that he was just another late traveler.

Small groups of three to five persons and several single walkers were scattered along the roadside with plenty of spacing between them. This made it easy for Barney to slide into a position along the road and offered the least opportunity of being noticed. Plodding along, he looked no different than any one of the other nightwalkers. The farther they moved away from the city, the fewer the people and, seemingly, the darker the night. It was impossible to tell how long he had traveled before he came to a branch in the road. The one he chose was to the right, for that was the way the big complex should be located. This road continued on the flat for some six miles and then it began to climb steeply up hill. Also, he had run out of other travelers and had the road to himself, except for an occasional small truck barreling down the dusty road. As he looked back in the direction from which he had come, he could see that the climbing road was quite high above the town. Some trees and high brush grew in a scattered fashion along the uphill side of the road. He crossed a narrow suspended footbridge that spanned a deep but narrow gully, continued up hill for some 20 yards and then slowly began a descent to a swampy-looking valley below.

Fully lighted on the far side of the valley was the complex that had caused him concern. He could see from his present position that all the fuss was a large shipyard that had great activity going on. He had miles to go before he would be close enough to observe and take pictures with any detail. Barney began to look off to his left for some signs of a hiding place.

He was almost at the entrance of the shipyard before he saw another well-traveled dirt road going around to his left and up a very dark series of hills. Taking as many precautions as he could he climbed the steep slope, zig-zagging back and forth directly above the lighted complex. The road came to an abrupt end, and on the point of a hill stood an awesome looking big ass gun.

There was no one within sight or sound. That alone made the scene somewhat eerie. To one side of the cannon was a dirt bunker with wooden doors and some kind of heavy leather hinges. As dark as it was and as strange as the place appeared, he did not want to do much investigating. If no one was about now, someone would be later, and sure as hell anyone coming up that dirt road would make enough noise to alarm him.

October 15: 0515

Daylight was beginning to show on the far horizon and Barney was standing out in the open. He had less than an hour to be out of sight and, he hoped, to be able to observe the activities stretched out below him. A narrow and what looked like a seldom used trail crossed the hillside just above the gun emplacement, but really didn't go anywhere. A second trail ended in an area used as a latrine. The trail to the right ended in a large cluster of low brush and was least used. So somewhere above in the shrubbery had to be a temporary hole, rocks, dead stumps — something to hide behind for the day until he could find a more secure place.

Crawling on hands and knees through the underbrush, he headed upwards. As he climbed he saw several large clumps of shrubbery which could have been used. He was not satisfied because they were too close to the damned gun and left him with a feeling of too much openness; he decided he did not need the extra pressure. He crossed two ravines that twisted up the hillside and meandered off in a direction that did not give a view of the shipyard. He continued farther up the hillside. The sun was about to break the crest of the near mountains as he bent to the left of some low-growing clusters of bushes. Just above the bushes was a slate rock ledge, which offered a total panoramic view of the whole valley and the shipyard. During the day, he would have to camp under the edge of the vegetation to be out of sight from below. More importantly, should anyone visit the gun emplacement, he would be safely hidden from their view. As the daylight became brighter and the sun was full in the morning sky, details of the surrounding area and the places that he needed to photograph became very clear.

After an hour of simply looking, Barney had to make some kind of plan in order to get the most out of his stay. As it turned out the shipyard became secondary in his thinking. Much farther south, farther than he had been able to see before, was a massive army facility. This would take closer looking into. For the time being the roads leading along the valley, the traffic moving along the roads, and the shipyard and its activities would keep him very busy.

A morning meal of the hardtack biscuits and the lousy chocolate bar was all that he could stand of the C-rations. Now the mapping and counting activity began. Small groups of soldiers marched both ways down the main road. That seemed to be all that was going on as far as the roads were concerned. In the shipyard complex most of the activity was repair work. Barney counted seven destroyers under battle damage repair. He also observed two cruisers and one small aircraft carrier. The aircraft carrier was listing a great deal to starboard and had very little of the bow above the water line. Someone really gave that son-of-a-rising sun a going over.

The number of personnel working at the yard could be a source of fighting men, so counting or estimating this potential seemed important and was noted. The ship's big guns could be another factor, and the number and guessed-at caliber were added to the note. On his map, he drew the direction of each ship as it was tied to the dock. It was obvious that some of the guns could not be trained onto the land target, and that might be important.

Land-based gun emplacements were next. Not too many of them could be seen from Barney's perch. The southern part of the base swung out into the giant bay and undoubtedly had some important defense measures established there. He made a guess because there was no way he would venture out to that part of the bay, for he would be sure to be caught. Through his spotting scope he watched the repair crews going about their tasks and was amazed at the slow pace and lack of effort of the workers. He surmised that with the events of the war going against the Japanese, their motivation was being seriously diminished. Another item that he noticed, and had seen throughout the city, was the lack of wood, construction timbers and such. All of the scaffolding was done with giant bamboo poles laced together and was as high as the structures being worked on. Oh well, the Japanese were little guys and didn't weigh much so it might be OK. Barney mumbled to himself, which he was doing a lot of lately, "you wouldn't find me on such a rig."

Barney felt pleased with his efforts so far as he made preparations to fold everything up for the night. It looked like a nice clear and not too cold night. Again, by backing as far as he could against the slabs of slate stone, he made a sort of fire pit the size of a gallon container and warmed his can of dinner. As he had anticipated, the night was comfortable, and Barney had his best night's sleep since leaving Pearl Harbor.

October 16: 1540

The next morning had been no different from the day before — trucks that looked the same, soldiers that looked the same, marching at the same speed, and the yard workers in about the same hurry, going about their jobs.

Compiling all of his notes, making some corrections where he had changed his mind about the count of personnel, and taking several photos of the shipyard finished off the rest of the day. It was still light. Looking at the sun, he estimated the time to be near four o'clock. As he began gathering up his equipment and getting ready to move down the hillside, the noise of a truck coming up the dirt road to the gun emplacement scared him crazy. A ton of what it's overcame him and, even though he was well hidden, the hiding place became very small. There was no place to crawl into, or back down into. All he could do was move to the back of the ledge, slump down into the rocks as best he could, and stop breathing. From the sound of the men below it was apparent that the gun crew was about to conduct a routine training drill with the big gun. There was a lot of yelling as they went through their exercise of make believe — shooting the American Yankee dogs who were about to invade their sacred homeland. After an hour-and-a-half it became quiet again and Barney stuck his head out far enough to determine what was what. The gun crew was gone and the door to the bunker was slightly ajar. He continued to observe all of the surrounding area to make sure that no one would be coming back, until he could not see any more due to darkness.

When he knew everything was clear and it would be safe to move, Barney slowly, and as surely as he could, left his rocky shelf and crawled down to the gun emplacement. Entering the edge of the gun site he again made sure that no one was left for lookout, or maybe to clean the cannon. There was no cover over the gun and everything was exposed to the elements. This allowed Barney to have a good look at the darned thing. As it turned out, it was an old piece, but in good working condition. The gears were well greased and the metal parts cared for. The gun sight was an open-ring affair and the pointer and trainer mechanism was all manual, but it looked like it could shoot. The bunker was a simple dirt cavern cut into the hillside with cement block sides and a wood and dirt cover for a roof. Opening the makeshift door far enough so that he could see inside, Barney found two stacks of six-inch heavy projectiles and the powder cases to go with them. Although it was dry inside, it seemed like a poor way to store ammunition if they expected it to function when needed. It was hard to tell what kind of ammunition types they were. However, with the position and obvious intent of the gun, they had to be for any type of sea-going ship that might come over the horizon within range of the thing. On a dirt shelf lay the fuse-setting wrench, some odds and ends of oily rags, and several cans of heavy grease. In the corner next to the door stood the cleaning ram and a six-inch round wire brush used to clean the inside of the barrel. *Not much to work with for screwing up the works,* thought Barney, *but what if I could remove all of the powder from the powder cases? The damned thing couldn't go bang and hurt someone.* After looking at the powder cases he decided that to get to the powder he would have to do a great deal of damage to the cork that held the powder in the cases. However, this would make it easy to tell that someone had tampered with the powder, and the hunt would be on. There had to be something else that he could try that would cause them grief.

Examining the spanner wrench used to set the fuses, Barney found he could unscrew the fuse mechanism and dump out all the powder from each projectile. At least, should the gun be fired, and by luck should it hit something, there would be no shell explosion, thereby causing only a minimum of damage. This was the best he could do, and he set about carefully dumping out the explosive black-looking pellets onto his ground cloth for later disposal. He would have to find a good place so that if the powder was found it would not point to a specific type of ammunition.

When the road activity had diminished to almost nothing, around nine o'clock, Barney began his way to the main road, and again assumed his Japanese posture. The army camp was at least a five-hour steady walk farther south. He had no urge to hurry, because the last thing he wanted to do was to draw attention to himself by doing so. The older and more tired he appeared, the less potential for being stopped. Somehow it seemed much easier to simulate the old man routine now— he did feel much older and, God knew, he was beat to death with fatigue.

October 17: 0400

As he had thought, it took him five hours before he encountered the first indication of life and a military establishment in the neighborhood. It was the screaming of some kind of a superior chastising a lesser man. "An officer giving hell to an enlisted man," Barney said to himself. Barney could not help but think that if any one of the men back at Pearl had treated him like that, he would have told him to stuff it... From what he had heard, if a Japanese soldier tried to talk back, the next noise he would hear would be a bullet behind his ear.

The noise with the troops inside the compound must have been a changing of the guard, because it was four a.m., and shortly after the outburst everything quieted down. It did create an extra caution, telling Barney that it was time for another day's hiding place.

This time everything was different. Regardless in what direction he looked, he could not find high ground, broken buildings or a forest to escape into. His only choice was to continue following the road, but in a more hidden manner. Anyone out late in the area that he was in would automatically be stopped and questioned. Just one look at Barney's face, and the next thing would be a bullet.

The southern end of the base was less active and appeared to be little used. This allowed Barney to be a little, but not too much, braver. The only place that he could see that might be used as a shelter was a stand of tall trees just outside the fenced section of the southwest corner. The foliage of the first trees was not as thick as he would have liked, so he chose a second line of trees that offered the most limbs and leaves to cover his perch.

Climbing up the slick trunk was difficult and exasperating. Selecting several of the strongest branches from which a platform could be made, and using other smaller branches to make it inconspicuous, took the balance of the darkened morning hours . By daylight he was all set for the next 12 to 14 hours.

There was no way he could stay perched in such a restricted position for any length of time. He found it impossible to lay his mapping paper out so that he could draw the details that he needed. Written notes and a few ground-level photos would be all that he could hope for. Such was the day. What he observed was not worth the climb up the trees. He was too far removed from the main part of the base. Tonight he would travel down the road south as far as the darkness allowed and then return to his first hiding place, the blown-out building.

The routine of reviewing the day's sightings and making sure he had everything, trying to leave no trace of his having been there, was completed and he was ready to go. The road was nothing more than an extension of the base area and ended at some kind of training grounds.

Retracing the same steps along the road, Barney did not even sit down as he passed both the army base and the shipyard. The main thought was how to find the same roads and paths he used getting to where he was at the present time. He found the bombed-out building without too much of a problem, for the road ran directly in front of it. He could not remember all the turns and streets that he had used before. Several times he came across men sitting in front of shops and residences, deep in conversation, and they paid no attention to the hunched over passerby. It was well after midnight before he was able to identify the main path leading back to his lair. Being some 20 miles away meant that he would have to almost run the rest of the way in order to be out of sight by dawn. With no other people in sight, he set out walking swiftly, the way he thought a fast-moving Japanese would look so early in the morning.

October 18: 0700

Daylight was on him and he was still some three miles from his objective. He had to keep on moving. There was no apparent place to hide and he was not meeting any other traffic anyway. As he approached the turn-off point to his hiding place, he had his first real good look at the close-in area near his cave.

The place that he had landed on the first night was a short, but deep, ravine that went back from the beach for about 300 feet. The side to the south, at the top of the ravine had what looked like California red oak trees, only shorter. Past the trees and close to the edge of the cliff grew more of the giant bamboo. A very beautiful and tranquil-looking beach scene. Almost hidden in the lower recesses of the undulating small hills that lead to the ravine, some 50 yards from the edge of the cliffs, was a small thatched-roof dwelling. There was about 50 feet of space in front of the structure, then the main path that Barney had used to go north. Across from the path and slightly to the north was a two-tiered series of small farm paddies. The upper tier, the larger of the tiers, had what looked like rice growing. The lower tier, which was split into thirds, had nothing growing in the top one-third. A deep green low-growing vine was in the center part, and what was obviously cabbage had been planted in the bottom, or most southerly part. The soil and grounds looked well cared for, in fact they looked like a beautiful flower garden. The empty part, the top of the lower tier, was in the process of being recultivated. No one was in sight.

Getting to his main retreat was all he could think of at the moment, so down the narrow trail to his cave he went. Tired and feeling very physically as well as mentally depleted, Barney laid out all the data that he had gathered on his last trip, divided the material into assortments of importance, spread out his ground cloth and was immediately asleep.

He was awake before the sun was completely out of sight and just sat in the opening of his earth dwelling, enjoying one of the most peaceful, beautiful and quiet sunsets that he had ever seen. *In sight of such a grand display of nature's bounty,* he thought to himself, *why is such a beautiful country destroying itself in such a useless war?*

With the deep feeling of melancholy that had set upon him, Barney began to reflect on all that had happened to him since joining the Navy in 1943. Regular boot camp at Farragut, Idaho, a hurried-up trip to San Francisco's Treasure Island, a lot of basic seamanship training, then a week at Point Montara, along the coast south of San Francisco, for real live gunnery practice. There, along with many other sailors and officers, he learned to use the types of large and small caliber guns that would be on board the various types of ships on which most of them would be serving. Montara was much like the scene that was spread out before him now.

Between boot camp and the Treasure Island tour, he had used up the better part of a year of the war and he had not seen one slant-eyed enemy. In early 1944 it all changed; he was sent to sea on one of the best destroyers in the Pacific fleet, a fast graceful 2100-ton Fletcher-class ship. That was the first time he had been on salt water, but it was for only two weeks of sea duty, to let a young first-time sailor get a taste of the open ocean and a touch of seasickness. The training cruise was to San Diego with many drills and live gunnery exercises on the way. He learned to stand several different duty watches and even had a watch at the helm, steering the 2000 tons of steel and men through the night. This had been a real thrill and an experience he would not forget.

Returning to Treasure Island, he had found himself assigned to an older-type destroyer, one that had seen real battles and also had a good reputation. The captain was an Academy man who had been to sea since the first day of the war. There was much more training, but this time it had been to learn all one could learn about his permanent duty station. Shortly thereafter they had sailed for Pearl Harbor, and Barney could still feel the sting of tears that had slowly run down his cheek as they entered the harbor where the remains of the Arizona and several of the other battle ships still showed the results of December 7,1941. Soon after entering Pearl, he was promoted to fire controlman third class, and what a great feeling that gave him. It meant that he must be doing things the right way, the Navy way.

At sea under normal steaming conditions, he had the after-steering watch and at general quarters, the quad 40MM gun director.

His concluding thought about his Navy experience to date was, The US Navy is one damned fine place for a young crazy guy like myself to be.

A light far off on the horizon brought Barney back to the cave and his present situation. He looked out to the light and ship and wondered what kind of boat or ship was showing the light, and which way it was going. At this distance, he could not tell. Where might the damned thing be going? It had to be Japanese. Regardless, it would not interfere with the evening at hand.

He had been nine days on Japanese soil. Barney was not sure of any other cities that were in the general area of Fukuoka, yet he knew that somewhere over the mountains was a city called Nagasaki and to the far north of Kyushu was another large seaport called Kita-Kyushu. It was not the intention of the men at Pearl that he should try to venture so far from his original landing site, still he felt that he should at least determine the types of roads or highways that might lead that way. He wasn't about to jump up and take off to find out, but there was a need to get as much information as he could about routes to and from the Fukuoka area. Later he would think about it. Right now, he must review all that he had done and seen so that no holes would be in his search.

Noting on a slip of mapping paper the key elements of his search so far, the only item that concerned him to any degree was that he had not had his camera when he was at the airfield, so that would be a must to do. He had to have good evidence of the number and types of aircraft and their disbursement around the airfield. That would be his next number one objective. Trying to look logically at the best routes to other areas that he felt must be included in his search, large main roads that invading troupes, vehicles, big guns, tanks and support equipment would be using once ashore. It was important to have the best information that he could obtain.

Since the Island of Kyushu was the smallest and most southern of the main Islands of the Japanese empire, should an invasion occur on Kyushu, Barney knew that a lot of defending traffic would come barreling down all roads and the wider ones would be used most. Therefore he had to learn as much about these places as possible. Saying to himself, "the airfield is north and what seems to be the most important highway is also north, I could do them both as one trip."

With a cold shudder, "it could also be a short walk to a firing squad!"

How much time would such a journey take? Just to get to the airfield and to the dump where he had been hiding had taken a long night. When he had finished taking his pictures, he would still have to wait for darkness before another move could be made; then how far down the road should he go? "Don't know — never been there before," was his self-comment. He would have to do his best to find out what was on the other side of the hill and as many of the other hills he deemed important. One other item he was sure of, that was a quiet night's rest.

This time, with hunger eating at his bones, he found a C-ration with spaghetti and what was supposed to be meatballs. Maybe the meatballs were the balls of an old bull because in all his life he had never eaten any meat that tasted and smelled like this. He also noted for the first time a round tablet that was labeled, "heat." A small packet of heavy wax covered matches was also attached. If the darned thing would work, it would make heating his food much safer. Also in the rations was another small can of very oily peanut butter and this might make the hardtack taste better. Same old chocolate bar and two pieces of hard Chiclets chewing gum —these items might have been in the other packages he had used; he had saved all the leftovers. He would check later. One other item was beginning to bother him: lack of a bath. He had not had any soap and water on his body since the day before he left the sub, and the smell of his unwashed body might announce to passersby that a stranger was in their midst and draw unwanted attention. He wondered if the Japanese sweated — surely they are people like me. What a crazy thought he had just had. His next thought was a simple one, and just his speed: he could slip down the path to the sea and take a saltwater bath in the surf... no soap or towel, but it couldn't help but make him feel and smell better than at present!

Gathering up his one pair of spare underclothes, he eased out into the last of the fading light and made his way down the trail. He had no problems with his romp in the cold surf and, as he had hoped, he felt terrific. He first used his soiled t-shirt to somewhat dry his body. Barney next washed out the undershirt and shorts in the surf — not cleaned, but refreshed. He returned to his cave without any problems and made his bed as close to the opening as he could. This allowed him to look out into the night and dwell upon the remaining days of his covert stay in the land of the rising sun.

October 19: 0520

He was wide-awake when the sun began its creep across the morning sky. Since he could not travel in daylight, he planned to use the day to package the items he felt would be necessary for his longest journey so far. Barney knew that in order to make all the miles, he would have to do some daylight traveling and he expected to find areas with little or no foot traffic that would make such travel less dangerous. No big bundles that would draw attention; and his hat needed to be reshaped so as to better cover all his face. He could use some kind of make-up to add to the bent-over old man appearance. He remembered from the movies the way good make-up was used to do just that, but the artist had everything on hand to do such crafty things.

His first thought was the soil inside and outside his cave. Maybe if he mixed it in different ways — as a thin mud — and then let it dry to a crust, it would work. After several attempts with the dirt idea, he gave up: as soon as the mixture dried, it would flake off and leave a dirty surface. He set the idea aside for the time being and thought about the farmhouse. Maybe it had something that would work. He had not noticed anyone around during the brief look, maybe no one was there at certain times and he just might have a closer look.

This would be another and different risk. Therefore, he would have to give it some real serious thought. Back to the needs for tonight's journey. When he was sure that all the items had been placed in a small pack, bound tightly and tested for comfort, he set it aside near the mouth of his cave and tried to relax.

At mid-afternoon, the thought of exploring the farmhouse crept back into his mind and he decided to have a look. As he crawled to the opening of the big bamboo and started to move toward the open area just above the house, he was set back into the bamboo with a jolt. Bent over in the way all Japanese seemed to be when busy, was the figure of an old farmer at work in the unplanted part of his paddy. He had his old straw-looking hat pulled down over his face so far that Barney could not see any of his features. His size, about 100 pounds and maybe about five foot in height, added to Barney's estimate of age. He looked old, really old — maybe 80 years. The farmer was tilling the muddy soil with a long-handled tool much like a garden cultivator, only the tines were some eight to ten inches long. The old man would swing his implement down into the muddy soil, then pull it toward himself, whack the clump of dirt that he had just turned over, break it up and then repeat the same backbreaking effort over and over again. Barney thought to himself that turning the soil over like that, doing an acre would take two forevers and probably kill him. As Barney continued to watch, he was amazed to see that the old man never stopped or slowed down, one hack after another, and before long he had dug up a sizable part of his paddy.

The longer he watched the more Barney was amazed and the more he admired such hard, backbreaking effort. Barney guessed that he had been in the clump of bamboo watching the farmer for over an hour, and was about to retreat to his den when up the path, hidden from view by the farmers shanty, came three somewhat mean-looking and noisy Japanese soldiers. The loudest and most belligerent one was a short, stocky, extra mean-looking devil; the kind that Barney had visualized all Japanese soldiers to be. As they came along the path close to the farmer, the mean bastard left the trail, bounded over to the farmer, began to yell a lot of profanity and threatened the frightened old man. The farmer just cowered as the ill-tempered Jap, using his swinging arms and gun, gave the poor old farmer a real verbal bashing. Barney could not figure out what the farmer had done to deserve such an abusive tongue-lashing. He could hear most of the words and understood all that he could hear, and knew that the abuse was uncalled for. What a mean son-of-a-bitch!

Barney retreated back to his hole feeling sorry for the little old man.

Back in his cave, Barney again thought about how he could disguise the appearance of his exposed skin so that it would look as old as he was trying to act. Poking in the ashes of the small cooking fire of several days ago, "ashes" he said to himself," just plain old ashes." When wet, the ashes formed a somewhat sticky mess and they had a gray color to them when dried. Maybe, just maybe they would work.

The first attempt was not too good. Although when the stuff dried, it did stick much better than the plain mud, it was stiffening to the skin and left a tightly drawn look. What next? How about some of the oil from the peanut butter? That would give a little lubrication to the mixture and might solve the stiffening problem. Barney added part of the oil to his formula and stirred with vigor, let it set a few minutes — it worked like real Hollywood makeup. He mixed as much as he had oil for and stored it in one of the empty C-ration cans. He guessed that he had enough for four or five applications. Now he was ready to start his night's adventure into who knew what.

The return trip to the airfield was uneventful. No one bothered to stop Barney or make conversation with him, and he was able to find the same hiding spot that he had used before. For picture-taking Barney decided to take up his observation position directly opposite the building area of the airfield. This would give him a wide-pan view of the total area, including the entire base, showing all the parked airplanes, and more important, the three runways and taxiways. Not far from the edge of the base perimeter stood a tall group of trees and some old bombed-out buildings. If no one was around, this could make a fine protected shelter for the day.

Barney had circled around the site and had been standing in the shadows of the closest pile of building rubble for some time. He wanted to make sure that he could photograph all that he knew would be important to the American planners. He was so intent in looking at the base that he did not hear any noise until he was addressed by a sharp, demanding voice. Barney's heart jumped into his mouth. Keeping his head bent low and moving in his old man crouch, he stuttered out a weak "hello" and said that he was looking for some free firewood. The person came from around the corner of the building and let Barney know that all the wood and any other material was in his keeping and that he would cause great bodily harm to the old man if he didn't leave. At this point Barney could care less. Regardless, he had been discovered, and that would not do.

Shuffling slowly toward the Japanese man, he made all of his moves as though he was decrepit and about to fall down, which caused the other man to step out where Barney could get a good look at him. He was very old-looking and was dressed in rags. His stature was that of a fairly strong person but not too wise about what could happen to him. The tattered old Japanese started to reach out for Barney's arm to try to force him along and out of the area. Barney first feigned stumbling in the direction that the other man was attempting to move him. This allowed Barney to move to the man's right side and as he did so, to lash out with his closed right fist and hit the scrounger in the center of his throat. At the same time he grasped the old man with his left hand in the same place to shut off any attempt to scream or cry out. As the man slumped to the ground Barney grasped the back of his head and twisted his neck completely around until he was sure that no life was left in the old man's body.

As Barney released the deadweight and looked down at the bundle of death, a horrible and revolting feeling came over him, one that he could never have imagined. Barney was glad that it was the other guy's body that lay at his feet instead of his own. A bitter bile came up into his throat as his stomach rebelled at what he had done. Killing someone in a battle was not the same as choking and breaking a person's neck with your own hands. Every fiber in Barney's mind and body was rebelling at his act of causing this person's death. This would be something that he would have to resolve later, for now he had to remove all evidence that either of them had been in this place.

Without a shovel or some kind of digging tool it was impossible to bury the remains. The only other choice open to him was to make the death look natural or as if there had been some kind of accident. An accident around blown-up buildings would be more acceptable and could be considered the results of a bombing if the old geezer was found some days later. Inside of the most damaged building, among piles of blasted remnants, concrete, bits of wood, and some metal pipes, Barney placed the corpse in as twisted a manner as he could. Several large broken blocks of concrete were laid on top of the body to make it look like death came from a bombing and gave the overall appearance of the body having been flung across the rubble. If anyone did not investigate too closely, it could be wrongly assumed by what means the old man had died. As quickly as he could, Barney took his pictures and got the hell out. There were still lots of daylight and it took him an hour before his heart began to settle down to a near-normal beat. He would breathe hard far into the night before he could feel free of the reaction of having killed someone — anyone, even an enemy.

Barney had three more days to finish his assignment, to make sure he had all his records and to be ready to be picked up. He had an urgent wish that the pick-up time was now.

It was a long trek to his next stop and he had no problem finding a good secluded hiding place; some kind of old mill that looked like it had been used for grinding rice flour. Rice hulls and some old sack material was all that was left, along with many signs of some of the present inhabitants — rats or mice. A loft and a small room that must have been used as an office was on the upper level. By standing up the broken-down door and wedging in some of the old sacks, Barney was able to make it varmint-proof. Some hardtack and peanut butter was all he cared to eat for his breakfast and he drifted off into a fretful sleep.

During the day Barney had awakened several times from bad dreams, always related to killing someone. By late in the afternoon he had had all he could take of sitting still. Picking up his gear, he made his way back onto the highway and, as he had done before, bent low and started to walk north. He had forgotten all about the ash make-up; turning around he went back to the old mill, knelt down in one corner, took the can containing the ash mixture from his pack and slowly applied the old liquid wrinkles. Now if it didn't rain, he would feel and look older and be more secure in the fact that for his purpose, he was an old Japanese man struggling down the road on his way home.

He had walked five or six miles when he noticed another large army camp some distance from the main highway. He moved over to the edge of the road as though to rest, took out another hardtack and munched as he took in all of the details that he was able to see. It was too far away to photograph so he didn't even try. Much of his enthusiasm for the present trip had gone away since yesterday. Barney walked until midnight and then just turned around and began an uneventful return trip.

As the morning sun came over the far mountains, Barney made no effort to hide. Everything had gone well so far and no real traffic was about. He did not want to stop and it was great to walk in the warm morning sun. At noon, according to his hunger pains, he passed the same airfield, found the hiding place that he had used before (the rock pile), sat down on his ground cover, pulled the ends around his shoulders and went to sleep. He slept until after dark and began what he hoped was to be his last night's walk on enemy soil.

October 21: 0530

He was back in his home cave as dawn broke in all its bright colors. Exhausted again, hungry, and just plain miserable, he sat down at the mouth of his hiding place feeling more disheartened than he had ever been.

Barney began reviewing all that he had seen and been through for the past several weeks, since he left his beautiful ship and became embroiled in this spy shit. He wondered if this trip would be of any real help should his country invade this part of Japan, how many people on both sides would die in the process, and how much of the unusual and beautiful country would be turned upside down and destroyed.

As he looked far to the south and then to the north, there was not a boat or living person in sight. All that he could survey was nothing but the very best of what this great earth was composed of, nature's sheer greatness, beauty everywhere; something that God and nature had taken millions of hard years to create. Soon man was about to tear it asunder with giant guns, earth-shattering bombs and thousands of angry combatants trying to destroy each other to the last man.

A really great world we are living in, he thought. The problem was to try to keep on living. Getting comfortable, Barney closed his eyes, tried to barricade his mind against all unpleasant thoughts, and slowly went to sleep.

He was awake in the the late afternoon and started the process of assembling the special radio antenna, putting all his notes and film in one package so that all the data could be handed over to the sub's commander as soon as he was aboard. He wanted to be rid of all that this adventure had been, and his hope was that when he passed on these materials his feelings would return to normal — if they ever could. He made a checklist of items that he had to take back with him, and another list of the things that could be buried and left behind. Not one thing, not a C-ration can nor a piece of foreign paper could be evident; even the footprints to and from his place of hiding had to be covered up. All was ready for his first radio call to the sub. *Come and get me the hell off this place,* was his only present thought. Now he could just sit back and wait.

When Barney had agreed to undertake this task, the Pearl Harbor people had told him that he should not do certain things or show specific items. One item that they insisted that he not wear was a watch. He had never carried one here — it had been left in the cave with all his supplies and foodstuff. Barney kept his eyes on the minute hand as the hour of

1100 struck. He turned the battery power switch to the radio to on and broadcast his first come and get me message.

"This is quiet man, this is quiet man, silent man; please acknowledge, silent man, please come in." Barney waited the prescribed five minutes before he repeated the radio message. There was no return message. The receiver just sat there and gave out a low hum. The agreement was to make three radio calls on the night of the pick-up date; if there was no response, Barney was to wait until the next night and at the same hour make the same radio call. If there was no answer on the second night, he would repeat the call on the third night. He made the last call of the night, without response.

Disheartened and deeply disturbed, he closed down the radio for the night and found a steady stream of tears running down his much-troubled face. This was one disappointment that he had not planned on; he hadn't even thought about such an event happening. But he knew that a submarine could run into many kinds of trouble and so might be delayed. He and his emotions would just have to wait until tomorrow night. The sub was sure to be on time tomorrow, he assured himself. Even though it was near midnight, Barney was not about to get any sleep. If he could, he would sleep during the day. In the morning he was sure to have everything sorted out and would be feeling better about missing the first night's rendezvous. Sometime before dawn he fell asleep.

He did not awaken until almost noon. There was nothing for him to do for the rest of the day so he simply stared out across the deep blue ocean and daydreamed about his present predicament. This turned the events of his Navy life back to the first time his ship had entered Pearl Harbor with the battle ship Arizona's devastated superstructure rising out of the quietness of her graveyard under the waters of the harbor. It now seemed to Barney that the torn and twisted metal was like a hand pleading for the pain to stop; the pain of blasted bodies from the ship and the now-dead crew. No one, absolutely no one, could keep back a few tears of grief, and even hate, all at the same time, as they passed this monument to all men who go to sea in iron ships to defend their country.

During the many long days and nights of training at Pearl, the blasted and sunken ships along battleship row had reminded all of them of why they were learning to go to war and kill other people, the yellow so-and-so's (and many other good-sounding sailor words). Barney reflected back to many unforgettable nights at sea, standing the helm watch as the sun made glorious early morning displays, moving at night in convoy with many other ships: aircraft carriers, battle ships like the old Tennessee, more cruisers than battle ships, still more destroyers than cruisers, all staying in their respective positions by the magic of radar. What a great feeling knowing that he, Barney, was a small part of such a great armada — just a small part, but one he felt was very important.

He almost shocked himself out of his present pattern of thought by remembering his reaction to seeing his first shore bombardment of a small Island that was covered with graceful coconut trees growing on one of the whitest sandy beaches that he had ever seen. It had been the first real tropical paradise he had ever been to that had not been overrun like Hawaii had been. It was very tranquil and beautiful until the first 16-inch shell fell upon its white sandy beach. The island had been completely covered with swaying palm trees before the first shots were fired, and some two hours later, every tree had been blown to toothpicks. The soft sandy beach was nothing but huge shell holes, burning equipment and fuel supplies. As his ship had stood off the beach for several hundred yards and pumped five-inch shell after shell into the mess, he had felt a small measure of revenge for what had been done at Pearl Harbor.

The first battle at sea had been a real eye-bugger also. It had been an unexpected night action with many ships from both sides, American and Japanese, toe to toe and head to head, steaming at high speed through open seas throwing high explosives at each other and often not sure who was who. It had been learned after the shootout that American ships had mistaken some American ships and fired at each other causing great damage, and the enemy had had the same experience. What a crazy way to fight a war!

The calls to the sub that night were a depressing repeat of those of the night before. Trying to block his mind to the alarming thoughts bombarding him, he fell asleep only after a long silent struggle.

October 23: 0615

He had missed the sunrise again, and had awakened to the fact that the sun had been up for a good while; he felt its warmth against his face. It was a good feeling, the sun, but he should be somewhere on the ocean, on his way back to the Island of Hawaii. He felt no joy in the beginning of this day, October 23, 1944. All feelings stood still and again Barney found tears of frustration and loneliness dampening his face. For the rest of the day Barney could not get himself started toward any kind of mind diversion that would distract from missing the pick-up schedule.

Barney went back to his first night of arrival and recounted the days that he had been on this horrible journey, to make sure that he had not made some mistake in counting the number of days that he had been here. He did it again and again with the same results. He was on schedule as had been agreed upon, and something was not as it should be. He would just have to wait until tonight. Leaning back against the largest boulder just outside of his cave entrance, he finally settled down to thinking about eating instead of dwelling on something that he could not do anything about.

He soon shifted his thoughts to the little old farmer just over the rise from his hiding place and found himself wanting to stroll over and have a long talk with this most interesting old man. *That would be something else,* he thought, *really giving myself away to the enemy.*

For fifteen days, Barney had had no one to talk to and now it began to feel like almost the most important need. The old man most likely would be scared out of his wits, charge over the hill and inform anyone he could find, even the bastard of a soldier who had given him such a bad time. What about that damned soldier? The more Barney thought about the dirty guy, the more he became angry with anyone hurting innocent, helpless people, especially a little old man who was doing nothing to hurt anyone.

Trapped, that is what he felt. He was beginning to wonder what the different emotion was that had crept over him and his conclusion was: fear — he was trapped inside the cave, at least until it became dark enough to be outside and maybe climb up the bank onto the same level as the old man's farm house. Maybe, just maybe, he would not feel so alone if he could at least remind himself that another life existed.

As he sat in the mouth of his hiding place, he began to take stock of all the different emotions and changed feelings, ones that he had never had before. Where did they come from? What made them turn out this way? And, why did he feel such a one-sided friendship, and maybe even a kinship, toward the old farmer? What had made him feel hurt when the son-of-a-bitch Jap soldier threatened the farmer? Why had he wanted to go over and kill the little asshole? Deeper yet, and an act that really puzzled him, was the killing of his enemy in the bombed-out buildings near the airfield. What was bothering him was the thought that in order to survive, one had to put all of the pieces into perspective — all the struggles of the real world of man — how barbaric some of them could be, and what a person must do to other people when forced to protect himself, such as killing the old man at the airfield. On this one subject, Barney reflected, thank God I'm young enough, smart enough, and hopefully will live long enough to learn as much as I can about mankind and what men consistently do to each other. It is not an easy or friendly world right now.

The hardtack and peanut butter was most difficult for him to swallow. It was from all the throat-tightening events of the past nights and days and had nothing to do with the stickiness of the peanut butter. He mixed the last of his water with the lemon stuff and finally washed down the choking mess. Another item — even though the sub was to pick him up for sure tonight — he would have to refill his water supply. This would give him an assured reason to venture out early tonight and get away from his locked-in surroundings. That made him feel much better about the day.

Night came ever so slowly. It seemed that complete darkness would never occur in order to allow Barney to move out and climb the cliff to refill the water container. He wanted to seek out the old farmer again and maybe just say "hello." Finding the trickle of the stream where he had previously obtained good refreshing water in the dark required a sneaky walk to the far side of the old man's paddies. The water supply for his farm came out of a shallow spring in the side of the hills just above the largest paddy. Barney filled his container, reluctantly returned to the cave and made ready to make his second rescue call to the sub.

On the third call, a tightness in Barney's throat almost made him choke. A slight hum from the radio was all that came out of the darned gadget. Now real fear set in. He rechecked the output meter that told if the signal was being sent, but the meter indicated that everything was working right; the batteries were OK. Was there anything else that he could have overlooked? Rechecking, he could find nothing wrong. He sent the signal a fourth time anyway. A fourth transmission was not in the program. But — at this point, who gives a shit? Barney wanted off this damned place and NOW. As he began to close down the radio, his hands were shaking so hard that he found it difficult to touch the switch. If he had felt fear the night before, what took over Barney's mind and body now was absolute numbness. His ability to think and try to rationalize even the most basic needs was somewhere else. Stumbling to the very back of the cave, he wanted to seek out the darkest corner and bury himself. For the remainder of the night, Barney lay collapsed on the dirt floor of his now prison.

A faint streak of pink sunrise was starting to show in the eastern sky. A lone seagull, awakened by the beginning of a new day, swooped close to the opening of Barney's cave. It gave a short sound that brought Barney out of his destructive stupor, for it sounded as lost as he now felt. Looking out through the opening of his cave, he could not even focus on the far horizon. At last, he realized that he had cowered down in the back of his hiding place and mentally gone into oblivion. Spiritless and drained, Barney began to put the happenings of last night's events into place. He would be trapped for another 18 hours before he could try to contact the sub again. He could not tell if he had slept during the past few hours. His body was not responding to anything — hunger, thirst, the need to take a leak, nor especially, sleep. The world and all its troubles — people, trees, farms and the war — could go to hell. The rest of the day was meaningless.

As the evening approached, he began to have the feeling that tonight would be a repeat of the last two nights and he was about to find himself stranded on the shores of his country's most hated enemy.

After the second attempt to contact the submarine, Barney knew that the third sending of the scheduled signal would get him no response but he sent it anyway.

For the next three nights he repeated the desperate call into the blackness of the sea and received the same hum from the radio.

Tears no longer slowly moistened his face because there was a long and steady stream of the saltiest wetness that he could have imagined. The flow continued until dawn when there was no more wetness left to dampen his face. No one in the whole world could be as alone and lost as he felt at this moment. All the rest of the day he could not move himself to get beyond his painful misery. There was no thought of "what should I do next" or "does it hurt to commit suicide?" or "if I don't get caught or die, how am I to obtain the food and clothing to survive?" None of these important thoughts came to Barney. He was dead for all practical purposes as far as that moment was concerned: dead... dead... dead.

The princess of nature must have been aware of the tremendous pain that Barney was experiencing that evening. As the sun started to descend far off beyond the horizon, a series of the softest and most gentle clouds gathered all along the line of the ocean that formed the far horizon. Colors even more vivid than Barney had seen in earlier evening sunsets swept quietly across the blue sky. It seemed to say this evening is for you; take heart. You are within my keeping and I will not let you be afraid and feel alone. For now I am your beauty, I am your strife, do not despair, we will share brighter moments this day As he gazed about at the sky, the land and the sea, he wondered what had made him have such an absurd notion. It was far too early in his game of survival to think that he was going nuts but that's what it seemed like to him.

All through the night he had continued to dwell upon his situation. By morning, he had only one plan. He would not give up, he would make the most of everything and by God he would survive. Fight, that's what he had to do —just fight.

PART II

A New Life

November 1944–March 1945

November 1944

For several days Barney had left his cave to get water and nothing else. He had now realized that his main concern was food. He had to have some means of stealing, robbing or whatever to find at least a minimum amount of nutrition to stay alive. Several of the many farms could give him a place to start the search. For some unknown reason, Barney could not think of stealing from the little old farmer right at his cave steps. No, he could not do that because the farmer was his friend — even though the farmer had no idea that Barney existed.

In the evening of the fourth day of his stranded state, he had taken stock of the remaining C-rations and some of the items that he had not cared to eat. When he left the submarine, he was given a case of the rations and he did not consume the three meals per day as planned. Of the 24 meals he had used only nine meals and not all of each package. Counting all together he had 15 unopened packages and bits of the other nine. If he ate the remainder of his rations at that rate he would be OK for about 20 days. "Now that's not too bad," was his self-comment. The thought of not starving for 20 days caused him to open one of the last two stew packages, light the little green cooking tablet and heat the not-too-appetizing contents. It wasn't very good but he could not afford to waste one small morsel.

Not this week, but maybe next week, he would leave his lair and travel to the farm house that he had bypassed on his first night's outing. He would find something there and like a pack rat, would begin to build a store of eats that would get him by for a while.

If Barney remembered correctly, the moon had come up near midnight last night. He planned to leave his hiding place at least one hour before the moon was to show itself. This would give him time to make the one-hour hike to the targeted farmhouse before the moon came up, making his travel less noticeable. He would need some light to help him find items that were eatable, dig or cut, whichever fit the crime, cover his tracks and get the hell out. He met no one on his outward trip and as he arrived at his borrowing destination, he took great care to look the field and paddies over before selecting what to take.

As it turned out the food was a young field of sweet potatoes, and the soil was damp but soft and easy to dig. He was very careful not to disturb too much dirt around the mound of vines and he took only a few potatoes from each digging. Altogether he took some 30 medium-sized tubers and stored them in his pack. The farmer also had two rice paddies that were flooded. The rice was far from harvest so there was nothing there for his food storage. At the very back of the farm was a small patch of adult cabbage and another type of green plant that Barney was not sure of. He selected two medium-sized heads of cabbage from one end of the patch and for some reason, went to the center of the patch and took two more. He then tried to remove all traces of his thievery; however in the soft dirt it was impossible. As he left the farmer's vegetable patch, he turned north, away from the direction of his cave home, and walked for a mile or so then turned around and retraced his steps back to the cave. Barney was sure that if the farmer discovered a cabbage patch thief, he could not trace the direction that the thief came from or went back to. Some neighbor might be blamed for the theft, and that was OK as far as Barney was concerned.

The most urgent need for food would be a good protein. The best source was at the foot of the cliffs, in the ocean. If he could obtain some hooks and a strong line, that would be all that he would need. The rocks had plenty of mussels and there were always sand worms under the rocks, so he would not have to worry about bait. Maybe he could fashion some kind of hook that would do for small fish. He had some string from small bundles and he thought it would be strong enough to hold the smaller fish. It would be worth a try tomorrow.

After knotting all the pieces of suitable string together, he had enough to make a usable fishing line if he had the longest bamboo pole that he could find. This would not be easy for almost all of the giant bamboo, even though it was tall enough, was far too big at the base to handle as a pole. Sneaking along the cliff edge of the bamboo growth, he could not find a suitable piece of the stuff. He would have to look somewhere else at another time.

Barney's food supply for the next two weeks was improved by journeying out every other night and gathering all the vegetables that he could find. Each time he ventured out he would select a farm in a different neighborhood. This made his foraging trips long, and in the darkness he did not always find good quality. All his trips so far had been to the north. He had not thought about going south primarily due to the fact that the mean soldiers always came from that direction. In dire need of some meat, he decided to try the southern path the next night and to hell with the damned soldiers.

November 12

The quarter moon was beginning its rise and the night would have a small sliver of moonlight to help see by; this would be of great help in looking for the right piece of bamboo.

Later into the night, he slipped out of his hiding place, skirted the little old man's house and quietly walked down the path to the south. Not more than 100 yards beyond was a sharp bend in the path that went hard left. As Barney started the turn, below him and on the right was a valley of some three or four miles long. It was a narrow valley that began at the foot of not-too-high mountains and ended at the ocean's edge. At the far end of the valley was what looked like a small fishing village. In the faint moonlight it was hard to tell just how many houses were in the town, but enough to show up in the meager light.

The short way to the area where the boats were pulled up on the sand was straight down the path. This did not meet with Barney's desire to keep out of sight as much as he could. If he made his way slightly up the foothills and stayed close to the bushes along the way, he would be nearly impossible to detect. It would take another hour to make the circle but it turned out to be worth the extra effort. As he approached the fishing boat area, he came upon a short dock that barely reached into the surf. This seemed to be the place where the fishermen pulled their boats up on the sand for repairs and, he surmised, to get them out of the water during a storm. The dock offered Barney what he needed most. He found a large pile of drying fish nets and a pole rack full of very fine netting that would make excellent fishing line. He could not take the time to untie the many knots that would be required for a line as long as he needed, so he simply guessed at the length of the netting it would take and cut twice that amount. He could always use the extra line for something else. Besides, he might lose the first line and this would give him a second one.

Further search around the dock area gave him two buckets of about three gallons each for cooking, water-carrying and a number of other uses. Stacked alongside a lean-to shelter were many fishing poles that showed long use — already broken in. Each pole had hooks and lines already made up for use. Again he selected two of the slimmest long poles and laid them on the sand for easy pickup. He was here and wanted to make the most of his visit. He might not have the opportunity to return, especially after the local people missed the buckets and poles. One other item he took before his departure was a length of pipe about three feet long. This he would use to make a rod to hold the buckets over his fire, allowing him to cook most of his food. Barney knew the Japanese ate raw fish, but he had hoped that he could last without having to resort to this custom. As an afterthought, he cut several extra hooks from some of the poles left standing against the lean-to.

Going away from the fishing village would be much easier than his approach had been. He could take the direct route through the farm and paddy formations and even find new foodstuffs to fill his new buckets. The trail up through the paddies led to the main path that went farther south, and Barney guessed that if followed, it would lead to more small villages such as the one he was about to leave. One day —no, one night — he would have to take a stroll farther south and just see for himself. At the top of the rise, almost to the last part of the farming area, Barney found several small ponds filled to the top with water. *This must be the main irrigation water source for the rice and vegetables,* he thought. Then at his feet, absolutely scaring the living hell out of him, was a bunch of Muscovy ducks. If they had been another type of duck, they would have awakened the whole southern part of Japan. Thank God the damned ducks couldn't make anything but a hissing noise. Could he catch one? Hell no, but he found their nests were filled with eggs. If they were fresh, fine, if they were fertile eggs he could throw them into the ocean. From five nests, he took 11 eggs and put them in one of the buckets. The thought of eggs was making Barney hungry and he promised himself a feast when he got back to his cave. Before he left the farms completely, he added several good-sized squash to his cache and rapidly made his way over the hill to his cave.

He felt so much better about everything he had achieved this night that he had to take inventory: two first-class fishing poles with hooks and line ready to go, two buckets that could double as cooking pots, almost a dozen eggs (even though they were duck eggs), and some squash that he was not sure he would like. Now for a good breakfast. Over the past week, he had gathered small bundles of twigs and chips of wood from the beach each time he went down there. Now all he had to do was place one of the C-ration fire tablets into his fire pit, light it, and add small amounts of wood until he had a blaze big enough to cook by. He had to continue to be very careful that the fire made no smoke, or at least as little as possible. The first egg that he broke into the C-ration can was in the first stages of becoming a gosling, almost causing Barney to forget about eggs. The second one was good and even though the egg stuck to the can, it was scrumptious. No salt or pepper and it was still better than any egg Barney could remember. Dawn was still hours away. He wrapped himself in the ground cloth and gently fell asleep. After daylight, he would gather the fishing gear and when it was late dusk, he would try the fishing.

Fishing was not the hard part — getting the mussels and finding bloodworms was near impossible due to the sharp rocks and strong tides. He was soaking wet by the time he had enough of each to try and catch a fish. He just wanted to see something wiggle and fight on the end of his line. By the time full darkness had set in he couldn't see clearly enough to separate the rocks from likely looking fishing spots, but he had four medium-sized surf Perch cleaned. They weighed about two pounds, but they were the biggest two pounds of fish that he had ever seen.

The only way he could cook them was by steaming them in the bottom of one of the buckets. Barney put a number of small round stones in the bottom of the bucket and added enough fresh water so that the fish were lying on the stones but not in the water. He had cleaned the fish as he caught them and he wasted no time building a well-hidden fire. He put the bucket over the fire and watched as the fish began to turn white from the steam and flaked as they became done enough to eat. They were super-tasty all by themselves. He even licked the tiny bones before he threw them into the fire. As the fire died out, Barney leaned back against his sheltered hole, feeling less threatened about being stranded. If he could avoid being caught, he was sure to last out the remaining months or years of the war. God, how he hoped the war would end soon!

All went well for the next three weeks, but Barney started to get lonesome for the company, or sight, of another living person. His only choice was to sneak up through the bamboo clusters, where, by hiding, he could at least sit at the edge and feel a friendship with the old farmer. If he could do that then he would not be alone. He found that the farmer went to the paddies early in the morning, went back to his house at one o'clock, then returned at about four to work until the sun started to set. Something running through his mind reminded him of an old saying that his father had often quoted: from sun to sun, a farmers work is never done. It must be the same the world over.

This started Barney on another series of thoughts. Going back to the days of school, he remembered most of what he had learned about the Japanese country. They were growers of rice, world renowned for their silk industry, great fishermen, ate raw fish, grew pearls and made tons and tons of celluloid toys (mostly dolls) and very fine fly-fishing rods which were split bamboo and were considered the best in the world. But, he had not learned much about the people as individuals. War does strange things besides making people kill each other — occasionally it made one curious about the unknown.

Later, as Barney watched the farmer dig the heavy soil with a cultivator contraption, he began to imagine himself beside the old man holding make-believe conversations like, "do you plan to spend the rest of your life digging this one small patch of ground? What do you think you will plant, more rice or sweet potatoes, maybe some corn?" He had not seen corn planted here, so, "Mister farmer, would you please plant some good old corn-on-cob sweet corn?"

Barney started thinking about what the farmer could plant and it was always different foodstuffs that he was familiar with from home. How come the Japanese didn't grow the same kind of vegetables, and where was the fruit? He just now thought about fruit. So far, he had not even seen a fruit tree. Oh well, they couldn't have everything.

As Barney had watched for several weeks, sometimes all day and other times parts of a day, he had seen very few other Japanese traveling past the small farm. The path running north to south looked like a main traveled route, but no one seemed to use it. He thought, *Who in their right mind would want to go into a city that might be blown to hell any minute by those damned Yankee airplanes? No one; absolutely no one.*

Thinking about airplanes, Barney had seen from time to time the high-flying B-29s swinging away from a bombing raid somewhere to the south. He could not hear any noise from exploding bombs so he knew it had to be far away.

December 21

It was the very next day, just at daylight, when Barney was shaken from his sleep by lots of heavy rumbling from the direction of Fukuoka. As he came out into the sunlight, he could see dozens of the high-flying B-29s starting their high curve away from the rumbling. Intermittent among the planes, diminutive black bursts of poorly aimed flack could be seen.

Turning his attention back to the ground and the sound of the thundering bomb explosions, he said out loud, "some poor bastards are really catching seven kinds of hell." He had no idea what the bomb-load of one B-29 was but he was sure it was many tons. Maybe he would try and sneak back into Fukuoka to see for himself how much damage they had done. That idea he discarded almost immediately.

Within hours, the path alongside the farmhouse became very busy as several hundred survivors, carrying bundles of what must be the few remaining belongings that they had salvaged, fled from the destruction. A few had bloody bandages showing and many others seemed to have had more minor injuries, but all looked very deep in shock. The parade continued in random small groups until late afternoon and then stopped, just like a faucet being turned off. And then it was night — cool, dark night.

Without Barney realizing it, a strong bond on his part had developed between himself and the old farmer as he watched him for weeks more. Barney continually marveled at the care and simple attention the old man gave to each plant in the garden. Each weed and unwanted blade of grass was removed his plantings, stooping here, then there, Barney could not help but feel as though the old man was attending a much-loved child. There was a reverence in the way he cared for the land and all that grew on it. Should the old man continue to care as he now did, the land would last forever.

January 12, 1945

It was one in the morning, as Barney watched the little old man working at the last few feet of the barren paddy that the damned, mean S.O.B. of a soldier came plodding up the trail. This time there was only one other soldier with him. The bastard was walking with his head down and his pace said loud and clear that he was looking for trouble. In Barney's imagination he could almost see foam coming from the little shit's mouth, he looked so wild.

As he approached the old man, the foulest language was directed toward the farmer. He kicked the dirt as he made his way toward the old man. Barney just knew that a beating was in the works. He was totally surprised to see the soldier, as he got close to the farmer, unslung his rifle, and in the most threatening way swing it this way and that, belittling the old man in every way imaginable. Without any warning the soldier swung his rifle, butt first, striking the old man on the left side of his face.

The old man was knocked completely around and he crumpled down into the mud and dirt of the paddy. He did not move and Barney was afraid that he had just seen his unknown friend killed. The soldier again kicked at the soil and, with his companion, went on up the hill and out of sight.

The anger in Barney was so great that he was about to take off after the bastard and somehow waylay and kill him if he could. Barney felt that even though the dirty Jap had a gun, he could kill the S.O.B. He could take the gun away from him and stick the barrel down his throat, pull the trigger without feeling any remorse. But he didn't.

As he watched the lifeless-looking figure lying face down in the mud, Barney thought he could see a small amount of movement from one of the old man's arms, the only part not covered with mud.

No longer was caution a concern for Barney. Looking for any other person that might be moving along the path, and seeing no one, he slipped out of his hiding place and ran to the side of the downed old man. Barney turned him over very gently, looked into his bleeding and mud-covered face with all the compassion that he knew, saying soft words of his Japanese, that he was sorry the old man was hurt so badly. Barney whispered that he was there to help him, and if he could, he would kill the S.O.B. of a soldier that had done this to him. He was sure that the old man could not hear him for he was out cold.

The old man had a deep, long gash just under the left cheek and with the mud jammed into the wound; it was hard to tell just how bad the cut was.

Barney had but one thought: to get the old man to his house — then maybe he could help clean and wash all the mud and stuff off. Picking up the limp body, he stumbled toward the house. Barney had been right about the weight of the farmer; he couldn't have weighed 100 pounds even with all the mud and dirt on him.

Barney had observed the back of the farmer's house but he had not seen inside so he had no idea of the type of furnishings the house might have. As he entered the covered back of the house, he saw a wooden-like bed or wide bench, without any mattress or other kind of cover on it, just board slats. He gently laid the unconscious figure on the bench, making him as comfortable as he knew how, then looked around for the items that he would need to repair the damaged face.

He had to have hot water. He could see any number of pots and other cooking utensils but no stove or means for a fire. After looking into every corner of the place, he noticed an old pot-looking thing that had some ashes in it and was situated in a safe place, so that if there was a fire in the darned thing it could not set other things on fire. This had to be some kind of fire pit for cooking small, one-pot type meals. Earlier he had noted a small pile of coal at the far corner of the room, so he took a few twigs and some dry shavings that were beside the fire pot, lit the pile and watched as a small fire grew large enough so that he could add larger pieces of wood and then the coal. It took Barney almost one-half hour before he had hot water to begin washing away the mess. While the water was heating, Barney had run back to his cave to get the small sample first-aid package that the Navy had provided for him. It did not have a great quantity of basic first-aid items but it was all that he had and it would have to do.

Barney had brought back part of the G.I. towel that he had used to help him climb up the cables of the bombed-out building. He intended to use this as a washcloth to clean out the old man's wound. First he had to clean all the mud and junk from his face. He removed his t-shirt and tore it in half. The water was near boiling so he added some cold water to get it to a temperature, which he guessed would not be uncomfortable, and began to clean around the eyes and mouth. The little guy's mouth was full of mud and dirt. Barney stuck his fingers into the open mouth and pulled out about a tablespoon of the stuff, then began washing the mouth out by pouring in small amounts of water. He was careful not to cause choking. This allowed the old man to breathe better.

The next step was to wash around the wound and then clean the deep cut out so that infection would not become a problem. This he did with all the care and gentleness that he could muster. As the excess water drained down the face of the old man, a real shock set in for Barney. First, the skin was not that of an old man. It was the color of high quality honey; that translucent shining type of skin that can only belong to a woman. He finished washing the face area without regard to the wound, for he wanted to have a good look at the entire face.

Anger began to set in for Barney. He now felt deprived of a great, but unknown, relationship that he had imagined, and he felt very cheated. He just sat back and thought about all the feelings, now lost, that he had built up as the old man was working in his fields. He became angry for having allowed those feelings to build up so strong within him. Barney moved to the back of the patio-style yard and looked out to the sea, trying to bring his emotions under control. Now, it seemed all that had happened before, the problems carrying out his purpose for being here and then being stranded, were somewhere far away. The loss of his contact with someone he had psychologically become very close to caused him hurt and grief. Why couldn't he have stayed just an old Japanese farmer tending his meager patches of soil and letting the devastation of the war pass him completely by?

What once Barney thought to be an old man was now a young woman moving her arms and letting out a faint groan of pain, bringing Barney back to the present. She did not open her eyes or make any other motions. Now Barney's concern returned to the hurt person. *That's right,* he thought, *she is now just a person, not my special little old farmer.*

He turned her face toward him to let warm water run through the wound and flush out all the dirt. He continued doing this until he was sure that the wound was as clean as he could get it; then he ran out of hot water. He refilled the pot that he had used to heat water and started another pot. As the water began to heat, Barney, with his washed hands, gently opened the wound to see the extent of the cut. It was a messy-looking wound and had cut into some of the first layers of muscle tissue. He needed to think what he could do about this.

With the towel that he had retrieved from his cave, he started to wash the rest of the mud and grime from her face and arms. The cut was still bleeding and this disturbed Barney. The cut was so deep that it would have to have some kind of stitches or there would be one heck of a scar across her lower cheek. Barney did not have any items in his gear that would suffice and he was not sure he should look through the house trying to find something. As a kid, he had sewn up a small animal with ordinary sewing thread and needle with good results, but that had been a wild animal, not a woman's face. But, he reasoned., it should be no different with people.

Something had to be done about the cut. No one should have to go through life with a scar like the one sure to result from such a wound. There was no other way — he had to venture into her house and find some kind of solution.

This would be the first time Barney had been in a real Japanese house, and just sliding the rice paper doors open was a new adventure for him.

The first room he entered was obviously the sleeping room. A neat stack of padded quilts and a funny kind of mat was in one corner, with several short dresser-looking tables on each side of the small room. The floor was covered with the traditional Japanese tatami mats. Barney did remember to remove his shoes and walk carefully across to the second room. It was separated from the room he was in with much the same type sliding door as the entry door had been. He was amazed at how easily the door slid open at the slightest touch.

The second room had to be the living room. In the center was a beautiful, dark wooden table that was no higher than a playhouse table would have been. Pillows were at each side as though waiting for a guest to arrive. In one corner stood a tall cabinet with very ornately decorated dishes, several photographs of a Japanese soldier and more of what could be family members. In the opposite corner sat a chest that was of the same kind of wood as the center table. Barney was struck by the simple beauty and neatness of the entire surroundings. He found what he was looking for in the chest — a rather extensive sewing kit. It was full of all kinds of thread and needles. Barney selected several of the smallest needles and a number of the finest white strands of strong thread and hurried back to his patient. She was still lying just as he had left her, on her side facing where he had been sitting. The wound had continued to bleed slowly, so he re-cleaned the area and placed a warm wet cloth over the cut. Then took inventory of all the first-aid material. He had not opened the Navy kit since arriving and had no idea of its contents. The most important items that he first noticed were several packages of the famous sulfa powder. This would be great. Next, was a two-ounce bottle of iodine, some ointment for infection (according to the label), a dozen large band-aid pads, two rolls of 3-inch-wide bandage material and there were some aspirin tablets and regular-size band-aids. Barney almost chuckled at the aspirin. This whole trip had been one big headache and if the whole first-aid box had been full of the tablets, it would not have been one-tenth enough.

Barney could not be sure that the woman was not fully conscious and because he was a real stranger, might be playing "possum". He had to begin at some point to try and communicate with her and now was as good a time as any. As he cleaned the blood from around the cut for the last time and applied the sulfa powder, he began to talk to her in Japanese: "First and foremost, I am your friend. I have been watching you for some time from a hiding place. I am not Japanese as you might think, but a stranded American sailor. Again, I am your friend. I saw what that bastard of a soldier did and I could kill him for doing this to you. I carried you back to your house, this house, and I have cleaned out your badly cut face. Remember, I am your friend." All this Barney said slowly in very careful Japanese. He continued with the gentle commentary and then began to explain that he had to hurt her some more, but just a little bit, and would try and fix the deep cut on her face.

Because of Barney's concern for her injuries, he had not paid much attention to her features. Now that most of her face was clean and he was able to get a good look at her features, he found that this was a young and rather pretty face that he was about to stick a needle into. Somehow the thought of doing so made him flinch with sympathy for the extra pain that he was about to cause. No matter, the stitching had to be done regardless of the feelings of either of them.

Barney soaked the thread in boiling water and, with care, heated one of the needles over the hottest part of the coal fire. He then bent the needle into a curve. From the fire he also made sure that the needle was fully sterilized. Now the hard part. He inserted a strand of thread thru the eye of the needle, and began to repeat the words that he had spoken before: "I am your friend..."

Barney began to explain what he was about to do. "You have a bad cut on your face and if I don't sew it closed, it will leave an ugly scar on your pretty face and that is something I can't let happen." Then he inserted the needle for the first attempt at stitching up the wound. Barney thought he noted some flinching but it could have been muscle response. As he inserted the needle for the second stitch, he stuck the needle in a little deeper than he had intended and he felt a jump that was not in the cheek muscles. If she was not awake now, she was doing a good job of playing "possum". It took Barney a long time to do what he felt was a good effort at doctoring. All during the mending of her wound, he kept a running soft tone, "I am your friend."

When the stitching was complete, he dabbed the closure with warm water to clean it up and then applied more sulfa powder over the wound. His final effort was to wipe the entire cheek with the stinging iodine. Now he knew that she was really pretending; her whole body gave one big spasm as the iodine penetrated the cut. He had to make her believe in his need to make her a friend. Now he was stuck. How could he assure her that he meant no harm, would never hurt her and if necessary, would cut the heart out of the soldier who had caused her harm?

After a few minutes of thought, Barney knew that he had to start at the beginning of how he had come to be at this place, on this Island, and into her life... or was it her coming into his life? He would have to explain to her again that he had been watching her for a long time, and that all that time he was sure she was just an old farmer, working his soil with great love and determination. The farm seemed to be his whole life. He would share with her all the thoughts that he had invented about the farmer whom he had thought was an old, old man, the growing of deep respect at the way the old man had gone about his farming chores, and most of all, what had made the damned bastard of a soldier so angry and hateful toward the poor old guy? Then he remembered that he was not addressing an old man and mentally started correcting his language. His poor old guy had turned into a beautiful young woman. They had both been in disguise.

Boy, did Barney now have some real problems! Problems that he was looking forward to, if he could make this woman understand that he was a good and to-be-trusted friend. He had come to feel he wanted and needed such a person in his life at this time and hoped that whoever she might be, she would feel the same way.

Barney started all over by saying that he knew she was aware of all that had happened to her and it was very important that she listen and try to understand what he was about to say. He further explained that he was going to start at the very beginning of his misfortune (and here he it prudent to invent a little, to avoid explaining his spy mission), and said that his submarine had been sunk off the coast and as far as he knew, he was the only one to reach safety. If that's what you call safety — swimming onto the enemy's home soil. And then he pleaded with her again, "Please try to hear me, try to understand, try to help me talk to you and become your special friendly enemy. Not a real enemy, a person from another place that has great compassion for all the people of the world. Even though America is at war with Japan, your country — you and I can remove ourselves from that terrible conflict and become sensible about surviving until it's all over. And it will be all over in the not-too-distant future. Please, just please..."

He began to relate to her all the details of his finding the cave, slipping out at night to seek food, journeying to the fishing village, stealing (or rather borrowing) some of the villagers' fishing poles, and catching some fish from the surf. The many hours he had spent observing a person he was sure was a little old man who worked in the most backbreaking manner, and of course (in the angriest tone he could manage), "the bastard of a soldier" whom he hated with such intensity. All of this was said slowly, leaving out the true purpose of his being in her country. The need to seek information about the important military facilities, roads, people and most of all, that he had taken the life of one of her countrymen. Again, Barney shuddered at the thought of this remorseful deed.

He had been talking nonstop for some time before he came to where the two of them were now — at her house, and she in his momentary care. Barney, when he next looked at her face, noted that she still had her eyes closed, but now several golden tears were sliding onto her cheeks. Even though she said nothing, there was a sympathetic expression on her face. She would be a friend, and deep inside Barney felt that he had just stopped the war and all was peace once more.

Resting the back of his hand on her swollen cheek, he caught the tears that were flowing down across the injury. It was meant to show his sharing of her pain. She slowly raised her right arm and softly covered his hand as though to say, I understand, and I too, need to have a friend. As she opened her eyes for the first time in Barney's presence, she also, in the softest and most gentle voice he had ever heard, began to share her feelings and concerns for life.

She began by saying that she was very much puzzled by the term "S.O.B", which Barney had exclaimed in English, and asked him to translate it. Barney smiled and explained it was an English insult with no Japanese translation, "son of female dog" being the closest. She again started to tell about the soldier; he was a fourth or fifth cousin of her dead husband. After she learned that her husband had been killed in some faraway place that she did not know, this damned cousin decided to take over for her dead husband. He felt that it was his duty to make sure that she would be taken care of and wanted to move into her house — she had nothing to say about it. He then came with a small bundle of his clothes and belligerently stated that her place was now theirs. "I rejected him with all of the strength and hate that I could. I've always been a kind and caring person; he made me most angry and that is why he has treated me in so mean a way. I refused him and he sought vengeance on me."

Barney could see a strong measure of fright in her face and noticeable caution in her voice. Trying to soothe any additional fright, he asked her if she was having more pain. "No," was the response; "I am most impolite, because of all the trouble, I have forgotten the manners and respect that my family taught me. My name is Myoko and I would like to sit up if you don't object." Barney hesitated for a moment, placed his hand under her back to help her rise. He immediately felt all her muscles tighten as he touched her back. It was certain that she was not sure of this person who had rescued her from drowning in her own wet paddy. As she became comfortable, Barney stated his name in return and added that his home was in a most beautiful place somewhat like hers. It was called California and if they could sail a boat from here to there, they would not run into any other islands or land until they reached his home state.

Both of them sat quietly, almost afraid to venture more conversation until she finally said that she had been aware that someone was in the bamboo. She had caught glimpses of a person several times and had wondered why someone would be hiding in such a strange place. She also admitted that several times at night, when she lay in her warm bed, she wondered if that person was cold, or hungry, and what they were doing there. Barney concluded that talking to this attractive person was going to be fun.

Before either of them realized it, the day had passed and late evening was setting in. Barney asked Myoko if she was O.K. and if she was feeling well enough to take care of herself so that he could leave. First he had to explain the meaning of his term "OK", and then also answer her question of "why?" He stated that it would be bad for both of them if they should be seen by anyone and that for now, it would be best if he went back to his cave, think about what had happened to each of them and to try to make some sense of his joy in finally seeing the old farmer face-to-face. They both smiled at the last comment.

Tomorrow he would make up his mind about how he could visit once in awhile to make sure that her wound was healing properly, and most important of all, that she trusted him. He would seek out her friendship in a way that could not draw anyone's attention. For now he had to get back to his hiding place. He stood up to go and felt the first tinges of not wanting to leave. He departed, and carefully made his way down and away from the real direction where the trail to his cave was hidden. (Even though Myoko seemed very honest and trustworthy, he could not take any kind of chance.) He slid into a cluster of bushes and walked to the edge of the cliff, turned back, almost crawling along the edge, and returned to his cave.

Barney was so caught up in the events of the day that his desire for food was completely gone. The "what if" that now crept into his thinking was, would she find someone and report his presence? He just wasn't sure. To make sure no surprises would befall him during the night, Barney decided to sleep somewhere else. When he had gone down to the surf to fish, he had seen another trail going along the beach, around some big boulders next to the high tide marks. He decided to look over this trail and take shelter anywhere that he would seem safe. He took only the ground cloth and a package of C-rations with him. He knew that if anyone found his cave, it would be all over for him anyway because it would not take them long to find him regardless of where he slept.

He did find a recess in the cliff that gave him enough protection from the wind and dampness, spread the cloth out and began the process of filtering out what he, maybe they, should do next, if there should be a next. Regardless of how hard he tried, he could not find sleep. He was not sure if the problem was finally finding such a pleasant person to talk to, or the insecurity of possibly being turned in. It had been so good to talk to someone, anyone, that it was impossible to keep his mind on the real problem.

He was awake as daylight came and he had not resolved anything as yet. *My mind is sure doing funny things,* he thought, *but it is time to get serious.* The first decision he made was that he would not attempt to venture out of his new hiding place until afternoon, and then it would be up the new trail, find another way to get to the top, then see if a search was on for a crazy American. The second decision was very simple: if no one was looking for him because a certain woman hadn't squealed, he would go back through the bamboo and see if Myoko was in sight. That was as far as he could think, for he was already on his feet moving toward the upward trail.

Rain began to fall shortly after he reached the top of the cliff, making travel a very slippery affair. He found no one at the top nor as he reached the trail leading back to his original hiding place. It seemed as though all would be well with Barney's new friend. He needed to return to the storage of his meager supplies and sort out the items used in his intelligence-gathering effort, especially the radio, maps, and all the notes that he had gathered. It did not take him long to pile everything together and decide where he could hide the stuff. He had to hide it a distance from his present hiding place. Should he be caught, that would be bad enough — but if the radio was found, there would be no telling what the captors would do. It would be extreme torture and then a firing squad.

Barney decided to carry out that night all the gear that he needed to dispose of, hike south to the edge of the valley that overlooked the fishing village, and bury it there. In the meantime he had to think of useful conversation with Myoko. The desire to learn about the people of Japan would be a good place to start. If they could leave out the issues of war, he was sure the two of them could build a strong trust and be friends.

January 13, 1945

The only item that he could take to her would be the small fish that he had caught the evening before her episode with the soldier. He made sure that they were fresh enough, put them on a small limb of bamboo and climbed the trail to Myoko's house.

She was sitting under the porch affair where he had left her. About the only difference that he could see, she had somewhere taken a bath, washed out her same cloths and displayed an attitude of expecting someone. Barney came from the back of the house and that was the direction from which she evidently knew he would come.

As he approached the open room Myoko rose, gave him a slight bow and in a melodious tone of voice, offered him her best greeting. She then asked how his night had been, did he sleep well and had he eaten this day? He responded and held out the half-dozen small fish. At first, she seemed very surprised by the fish, then asked if he had been fishing so early in the day. Barney had to confess that they were a little old and might not meet her approval for fresh fish. After looking them over she simply stated, "We will have them for our dinner this day." It was the phrase "this day" that rang a loud bell in Barney's head. If they were to share a friendship, some careful planning would have to be done in order to keep from being seen and caught. He said, "From now on, we must always consider that it's the two of us we must protect."

Myoko asked Barney if he would like some hot Japanese-style tea. She had the tea ready and poured two dainty cups full. She was right; besides being good, it was very hot and made the beginning of a serious conversation much easier.

Barney started by asking her about the growing of tea; he had heard that Japanese teas were some of the best in the world. "Do you grow your own tea?" Myoko gave a slight laugh and explained that good tea was grown in the mountains and in special climates. "No" she said, "I have not even seen tea growing." Barney next asked her how she managed to do all the farming by herself, reminding her that he had watched her for over a month and commented about how hard the work looked to him.

Myoko began by telling about her husband. They had both lived in Kobe and did not care for the lifestyle of a large city. "My husband loved the quiet of the countryside, being close to nature, and the freedom to plant things, and to watch them grow. Things we grew ourselves just tasted better and were much more healthy. He graduated from a good university and studied horticulture as his main subject, but he also wanted very much to write. We looked for many months before we found this isolated and beautiful place." Going on, Myoko explained how the two of them had worked day and night clearing all the brush and weeds from the area where the fields and paddies were now. "My father and uncle came many times and helped to build the terraces, then changed the flow of the spring that's just above the field so that we could water the crops that we planted."

Barney knew but asked anyway, "And the four of you did it all by hand and with much back-bending? Wasn't it hard and didn't it take a long time?"

"We worked for two years before plants of any kind could be set in the ground. Together we gathered bags of leaves and much decayed old vegetation for composting the soil during the construction part and as we were able to get the first level ready (that was the top soil), we mixed the rich compost with the heavier soil that was already there. In time we were able to make a good garden."

She spoke further of her husband, that he was a very gentle and most kind person, he would help anyone anytime, and "we loved each other very much."

For the first time, she called him by his first name: "Barney, we were not like most Japanese, our marriage was of our choosing, not the customary chosen-by-parents union. We wanted so much to be left alone, to grow old slowly and as gently as life would let us. We didn't even know that Japan was at war for four months." A very faint tear slowly melted into her cheek as she sat quietly, as though the horror of the war had put a wall between them.

Barney then asked her, "Didn't the military at the time require all men of a certain age to belong to some part of the army?"

"No," she answered, "only later." She spoke of how one day soldiers came and told her husband that he had to go with them at once and that he could not take anything with him. That was the last time she had seen him. He wrote such sad letters about the treatment he was receiving and that all the men like himself, the ones that were forcibly taken away, were kicked and beaten daily because they did not go to the war by their own choice. He said he could not kill another person, even in war, and should they send him to a place where he would have to kill someone, he would shoot himself first. Her closing comment was, "That is how gentle and kind my husband was." Barney noticed that the few tears he had seen before had now become a steady stream down both sides of her beautiful face and many of them were running into her wounded cheek. He felt some of her pain and anguish.

Then Myoko threw Barney a curve. In a serious, questioning tone, she asked, "You said that you are an American sailor didn't you? If so how and where did you learn to speak our language so well? You are puzzling to me; I have never seen or talked to an American and yet I feel great trust and friendship towards you. Maybe it is because you befriended me when that Japanese soldier struck me with his gun."

Barney took her back to his high school days and his splendid friendship with Koji and his family. Myoko only smiled at the many explanations of Barney's relationship with his Japanese-American family.

Barney felt that he needed to change the subject, so he asked her about her house. Had she built it? "It is so small."

She was amused by this comment, however, she said, "Here in Japan we do not stay in the house very much except when it rains or is very cold. Here we do not have the bitterness of winter that many other parts of the country do, so we do not need a larger house and, as you can see, there are no children. One room for sleeping, and another for guests, and storage of our most important things. Most houses here in the southern part of Japan have some kind of general outside room such as the one we are sitting in. My husband and I made all the flooring from flat stone that we dug up when we made the lower field and paddy. This is where we spent all of our non-working time. We cooked here, now I cook here, and do most everything under this one roof. We even took our baths here. The large stone basin in the corner" — pointing to the far corner — "is our resting bath."

Myoko hesitated for a moment, then went on. "The resting tub is filled with water and a small, but very hot, fire is made under the far corner. After an hour the water will be almost too hot to sit in. If it is too hot, we add only a little cold water until it is comfortable enough. This is not a bath, it is for warming the tired body after hard work or sometimes we share it with special persons. Besides, it makes for a very gentle place to have meaningful and sincere conversations. Many problems of the people are settled in such relaxing places. No home in Japan would be without such a tub if there is enough room. We have only one problem with it and that is enough wood to make the water hot. Wood is very scarce in Japan." Then to Barney's surprise, she asked how he was able to bathe, for he looked fresh and clean.

"There is a seldom-used trail leading down to the beach from the cave where I found shelter and when I go fishing, I often take advantage of the ocean and wash as best as I can. This is always late in the day and sometimes it's very cold, but it really makes me feel much better about myself. Without the use of soap it's difficult to really get clean." He hoped that she would not ask about the smooth shaven face. He had brought a double-edged razor with him and had used it very sparingly until finding Myoko.

He was not sure if she would understand a comparison of houses or if she might feel that he was boasting, however he had to say something further in order to get to a discussion about how they could continue to meet each other and share their friendship. *What the heck?* he thought. *I'll do it anyway.*

He began by telling her that his home in California was a simple, or very modest, house by American standards and the bath was inside. It had hot water from inside pipes and of course, it also had cold water. "And in

America one does not share one's bath as you do here in Japan. Almost all houses have inside hot water heaters where water is kept hot at all times. In most cases the heating is done by natural gas piped into the house from long pipes that go everywhere. This same gas is used for cooking and heating the house, and it is not too expensive."

This did not seem to faze Myoko. She softly replied that she had seen a magazine a long time ago that had pictures of such houses and they looked nice but she was not sure that she could live in one. The many spaces for storing things would be nice.

At this point Barney felt that they could begin talking about themselves, since bathing had been discussed, and to him bathing was a personal subject. He asked her if she was thinking about how they could share each other's day and not

put Barney in a position where both could be seen and turned over to the police or military. He tried to assure Myoko that he was greatly concerned about her safety too, and that at least for the time being, if they could sit and talk like they were doing now, late in the evening, that would be best. Barney also said that he had noticed that people did not travel along the path late in the evening and the chances of being seen would be far less than at any other time. In fact he reminded her that it was getting late now and he should go back to his hiding place.

"Yes," she answered, "I am tired and would like to sleep for I must work in the field again tomorrow. The season for planting will be here soon and the soil must be ready before then. It is best to let the cultivated field set for a week or so before planting if there is to be a good harvest."

It then occurred to Barney that he had wished the old farmer would plant corn. He began to explain to Myoko what corn was and how it grew. Again she smiled and told a long story of why the Japanese did not grow corn and it came down to one reason — they liked rice much better.

Barney returned to his lair and made preparations to hide the radio, maps and other materials, items that would surely get him killed if he should be caught with them. As soon as it was very dark, he loaded all the items and made his way down the path toward the fishing village. He had no trouble along the way — in fact, he met no one. As he approached the beginning of the paddy area above the village, he wanted to find a place where the soil wasn't too hard to dig a hole big enough for all the stuff that he had to bury. At the upper end of the first paddy he found a large space in the side of a hill where the local people used for digging for slate-type stone, like a stone quarry. Where they had dumped piles of the smaller stones and unwanted residue, he found a somewhat ready-made hole. All it needed was deepening. Barney set about removing the easier material and in a short amount of time, he had a space deep enough to hold everything that he had brought.

The one thing that he hated to do more than anything else was to wrap the items in his only waterproof ground cloth. Why he felt that he had to protect the useless material, he could not explain. Maybe it was because it was U.S. Navy property and he was responsible for it. He covered the hole over and, in the darkness, he scattered some of the larger waste material over the ground the best he could to hide any disturbance of the area that would indicate a burial place. His return was as uneventful as his going.

Back safe in his cave, he tried to sleep. Failing in this effort, he tried to rationalize the growing friendship between himself and Myoko in a way that would not cause them any misunderstanding and, above all, not expose either of them to arrest.

As he sorted through many different ideas, he opened one of the last three cans of C-rations, lit a small fire to warm it by, and tried to recall all that they had talked about this fine day. He concluded that it was all small talk and did not give him any clues that would help him with planning anything. The C-rations were bubbling and he turned his attention to this food.

Cleaning up the mess from eating, he wondered if there was some way that he could help Myoko with her farming. Because of the beating she had received, several days had been lost and she would want to catch up with the turning of the soil. He made a mental note to talk this over with her the next time they met. If he was able to work in the field it would have to be done during the day and that posed another problem. He already had the Japanese-style black clothing and the traditional woven bamboo hat to cover his face, but the hat would not be enough should anyone look at him up close.

Some really crazy ideas crossed his mind, but looking old was the only thought that held any promise of being useful. If he, or they, could find the right make-up for him, it would seem natural in the surroundings to appear as another old person going about chores relating to farming. He still had a little of the ashes and peanut butter oil mixture. That was O.K. for short periods of time but they would have to come up with something more lasting, something that would give a much better impression should he be stopped and looked at closely. This would require much more thought and he would need Myoko's help. He also knew that the time would come when she would ask him about his hiding place and would want to see how he was living. Any further thought would have to wait for tomorrow. Sleep was finally knocking at his door. For him the day, and night, were ended.

January 20

It had been a week before Barney made any effort to see Myoko. On the seventh day he spent an hour watching her work in the paddy turning the heavy soil. She was going so very slowly and Barney surmised the slowness was due to a measure of pain and discomfort from her run-in with the nasty Jap bastard who had hit her, and anguish again welled up inside him.

Today was going to be the day he sat down with her and shared his thoughts and ideas of becoming her uncle who had been bombed out of his home, had come to her for shelter, and would repay her by working and helping with the farming.

He had hidden in the bamboo just as he had done many times, and watched for Myoko to begin her afternoon work habit. She came out at the usual time, went directly to the field, and as the day before, worked slowly. It took Barney awhile to notice that she was always working so that she faced in his direction. He was not sure, but felt that she was looking for him to show himself and at least wave or give some indication that he was there watching her. For the two hours that she was working he did not let her know he was there. After she turned to make her way back to her house and had left the main path, he moved out into the light dressed in all of his "old man" clothes, slumped over and shuffled toward her. He could see the shock on her face as he came into view. First she stopped, letting her arms fall to her side, then dropping her head, she hurried to her house.

Barney continued his shuffle around to the back and into her open living space just as she opened the sliding door. Her knees gave a slight buckle as Barney called out, "Don't be frightened, its me — and I want to tell you what I've been planning. The clothes are a very important part, and if you were fooled by my disguised appearance, I hope that all others will be also."

Myoko sat down on the bench like a rag doll, her face flushed and her hands trembling. She started to say something to him when a river of tears began to stream down her ashen face.

"Please don't ever do anything like that again," she cried out. "I had not seen you for many days and had imagined all sorts of bad things, then you scare me like this. I am not sure I want to be a friend to someone who does such things."

As hard as Barney tried to restore their friendship, she would not speak or smile for a long while. The fright that he had caused had seemingly shaken all friendly feelings from her.

Darkness had settled into night before Barney could begin to explain to Myoko his idea of becoming an old man, working in her fields, being of some use and not having to hide in a cave until caught or the war's end. Myoko kept a very cautious eye on Barney for a long time before she made an effort to respond.

Her response was full of anger and doubt. She began by asking how he thought a man as tall as he was could pass as Japanese. Further, she said that the habits of an old Japanese man were set in the culture of Japan and would be impossible for Barney to learn or copy. Even though the clothes that he was now wearing looked very Japanese, they would not fool anyone into believing he was an old man doing work in the country. She was not sure about such clothes in the city, but in the country, they would look most foolish — no, they would not do.

The doubt that Myoko had just expressed told Barney that she did not want him to work in the fields with her. As she reasoned, being a friend to an American sailor would mean she would be shot where she stood if found out.

There was no way Barney would be able to overcome her objections unless he told her of his travels into Fukuoka' using the explanation of trying to find a way to escape from Japan. He assured her that he had traveled all through the countryside around that city, sometimes during the day, and had not been stopped or spoken to. He had even uttered what he considered an old man's response to greetings on several occasions late at night.

Finally he pleaded, "this idea is just that, an idea. Please help me to find a good and safe way for us to share a part of each day, or even several days each week, whatever. There has to be a way so that I don't have to hide in a cave all the time."

As he related only the facts that he felt were necessary to support what he wanted to do — to have her share with him his travels through the countryside and Fukuoka — he could see in Myoko's face greater questions and serious concern. Not knowing where else to turn, or what else to say, he asked her what she might do if found in a strange country under the same conditions. Her bitter-sounding response was, "I wouldn't be so damned foolish as to get on a submarine." It was obvious that she was not about to bend to Barney's way of thinking.

His next statement really caught her off balance, "Myoko, if I am going to cause you any problems or grief at all, if you are frightened by my being here talking to you and trying to be a true friend, you must make a report of my presence."

All was very quiet then for some time. Barney did not dare to look her in the face for fear of seeing an answer that would mean death to him.

Myoko got up from the wooden bench very slowly and was almost stumbling as she moved over near the bathing tub. Looking out across the cliff and out to sea, she said, "Day after day I watched for you and you did not come out where I could at least see that you were alright, and it hurt me to think that something might have happened to you and maybe I would never know. I am not sure, but isn't this the kind of concern and feeling that one should have for a good friend?

"Then there was the way you took care of my cut face, carried me to my house, sewed the wound and put your healing medicine on it. See, the cut is healing nicely already. You cared for me and made sure that I would be, as you say, O.K. There cannot be any greater concern than that which you gave to me when I had no friend and needed one very badly.

"And now you dress up like a crazy old man and try to make me think you are an old Japanese farmer who wants to help me work my land. You do not understand how the Japanese mind works. All your dressing up and the plan that would let you be in the open during daylight causes me real fear, not for myself, but for that of my new, foreign friend." She then turned toward Barney and again he saw nothing but tears on her pretty face.

"Barney, you have stressed the need to be part of people; you said that you could not just hide out and not have the presence of others. You have to be able to talk and enjoy being with someone. I too have that same need. I did not know how much I missed being a part of others until now. You have awakened that need."

Myoko then said, "I have some of my husband's old clothes from which we might be able to make you some work clothes. It will be most difficult to have enough cloth from them to make a proper fit, but we will try. We will begin tomorrow. For now, will you show me how you walked when you went through the city, and then how you imagined an old man, an old farmer, would move if he was walking in the country. There is a great difference you know."

Barney moved to one side of the open room and bent over as he had done walking through Fukuoka. All he achieved was to make Myoko burst out laughing. She howled with delight. Then he was most serious as he tried to copy the stooped-down pose of the tired old man that he once thought the lovely young lady standing before him was.

They began to practice what Myoko considered the typical motion and stance of an old man working in the field, and also one who had been working all day long and was so tired that he felt like falling over. Myoko had agreed to Barney's plan: that she had to be convinced that he would be taken for the real

thing by any passerby, before she would allow him to work in the fields during daylight. So the practice went on late into the evening every other day, for two weeks. After each day's workout, they would sit on the open house bench talking about families, and some of the most important likes and dislikes of each other's lives.

February 10

It was through this pattern of evening discussion that Barney was able to get Myoko to slowly relate in words, an anger that he had sensed but could not find a way to get her to express.

She began by sharing bits and pieces of her husband's early life in Kobe. When they were in their mid-teens, the army became very strong within Japan. High military leaders began to recruit, if that's what it could be called. It was more like forced induction by bribery. If a student would become part of the young army, the military would make sure that the selected students were sent to the finest colleges and universities and all they had to do was be of service to Japan. Many of their friends believed this story and were sent to the best schools to learn how to be officer soldiers. The very best students became pilots in the army and navy.

"My husband not only did not believe them but he spoke out among his friends, telling them that the offer was not good for the future of Japan. And in the end, they would suffer because the lessons that they would be learning would be to kill other people and support the army's ambitions to expand Japan's boundaries."

Myoko then spat out the cause of her bitterness: "Because my husband would not bend to the dictates of the local army, he was often beaten and verbally abused in front of his classmates and other friends. This was the main reason for leaving Kobe and finding this quiet place." In very spiteful words she said that she hated the army and except for the great loss of face for Japan, she was not unhappy that the army was losing most of the territory that they had captured over the many years. "It is not just because they killed my husband; they have caused Japan to lose all her dignity that has taken hundreds of years to earn.

Again, there was a quiet that lasted for a long time. Then Myoko said, "The anger within this damned fifth cousin of my husband's is from this brutal training that the army forces upon everyone. Now Barney felt that he had most of the reasons for the actions of the mean soldier. He made a vow that the S.O.B. would not touch Myoko again.

Barney did not attempt to work with Myoko for yet another week. During this time he fished late in the evening and practiced the art of being an old man. He shared the fish with Myoko each evening at dinner. She had dozens of ways to cook them, which gave Barney an opportunity to learn some of the simple tricks of using the small cook pot, the hibachi. Myoko did all her cooking on this one fire. She also made her own noodles from a rice and flour mixture, allowing them to dry in warm air.

The evening that training was completed, Myoko announced at their evening dinner, "Tomorrow we will try your ability to look and act like a Japanese farmer. We will go to work in the morning and work until the noon meal. If no one comes by on the path, we can work also during the afternoon. We will not know for sure if the plan will work until several people pass by and pay no attention."

They worked three days before anyone came by and all that was exchanged between them was the usual courtesy, "good day."

February 21

The feeling of success allowed them to celebrate. At the end of the working day, Myoko announced that they would have a hot bath in the traditional Japanese way and then she would make a special dinner that she had been planning for several days. Barney had been taking his bath in the surf and sleeping in his cave, as he had since coming ashore. A hot bath would give him a more relaxed attitude and lessen the concern for their safety. It would make for more friendly relations, which he wanted very much. There always seemed to be a guard or wall between them. There wasn't the free and easy conversation that he felt should be there. Maybe this evening would help remove some of this concern.

Myoko left the fields about one-half hour before Barney and as he entered the outside room, Myoko told him to remove his dirty clothes and sit on the short stool that she indicated. This he was not prepared for. He had never undressed in front of a female and he felt that this was not the time to start. Sensing Barney's reluctance to begin undressing, Myoko explained that it was the custom in Japan to have the woman of the house wash the man as she was going to do.

"We use very warm water and soap the body gently, then rinse off the soap. The best part comes next," she said as she pointed to the large soaking tub. Barney had not noticed the fire burning under the tub and was not prepared for this either.

Turning his back toward Myoko, he undressed very slowly until she stated that the water would not stay hot forever and he might have to wash in cold water. The thought of the cold water caused him to undress faster. Sitting down on the stool, Myoko said for him to relax and that she would do all of the washing. Barney corrected her by saying, "That will be O.K. to a certain point, then I will finish the bath." This brought a chuckle from Myoko.

When she had completed washing him she told him to slip into the tub very slowly for the water was very hot. Further instructions were to sit on the bottom of the tub with only his head above the water. As he got into the tub, Myoko began to undress for her bath.

Myoko had changed her dirty clothes when she came from the field and was dressed in a wrap-around style robe. As she undressed, she turned just enough so that her full front was

away from Barney's view. Slipping out of her wrap, she sat on the same stool that Barney had used and with an artful motion, began her bath.

As she washed, she further explained the importance of bathing in this manner; one relaxes in the hot bath to drive away the pains in the limbs and body. Since one was in hot water, and usually with a friend or family member, it would be natural to have good friendly conversations. Myoko finished the washing part of her bath, placed a small cloth over her lower front and joined Barney in the tub.

Barney had not said one word during Myoko's undressing and bath but he had not taken his eyes off of her. His first thoughts were, *How could a lady, undress as she has done, sit and carry on a meaningful conversation about taking a bath and treat it so casually?* The great beauty of her young body did not escape him either.

As she settled into the hot water, she began to tell Barney that the bath was not a place to be thought of as an invitation for coupling. Coupling was for the very private moments in bed with one's husband. To this point Barney had said nothing and now his only words were," I'm glad that you explained this." The closeness in the tub caused them to touch knees and sometimes toes and feet as they moved about in the hot water. This caused a slight smile on both of their faces and eased their conversation. Most of the talk centered around what they had accomplished so far in the fields and that they were not too far from being ready to plant some seeds. Barney asked about the irrigation of the crops and how often they must be watered — just words to keep him from becoming flustered.

As the fire died down and the water cooled, Myoko, without saying a word, replaced the cloth in front of her lower body and stepped out of the tub. Besides leaving Barney spellbound, it left him unsure of what he should do next. He had no cloth to cover his most personal part so he just sat there. Myoko informed him that his modesty was that of a little boy, adding, "You should not be ashamed of your body if it is not marred by scars or deformity. You should be pleased with a healthy body such as yours."

He reluctantly stood up and stepped out of the bath and began to dry the excess water from his body. The towel Myoko had handed him was the softest one he had ever touched. He finished drying himself and dressed in a kimono that she handed him. His whole body felt better than he had ever known. His skin tingled with the increased blood flow due to the hot water and he felt cleaner than he ever had before.

Myoko sat next to the hibachi and explained, "Yesterday I purchased a young chicken from a passerby and tonight we will have a very fine traditional Japanese dinner, one that is for special friendship, you will see."

The chicken had been cut into bite-sized pieces. She placed them on a cutting board and covered them with spices that Barney had never heard of. A shallow pot was then placed over the top of the cooking fire, a small amount of sesame oil was added to the pot, and the chicken placed in the oil. She cooked this for a short time and then began adding sliced vegetables. When the entire dish was steaming hot, she added soy sauce and another liquid seasoning. By now, the delicious odor was filling the open room and making the thought of eating very inviting. Myoko removed the hot, steaming pot and in the same motion placed another covered pot on the fire. This she explained was the steamed rice that she had cooked earlier that morning. She wanted to remove a small amount of cold from the rice before it was dished. Myoko placed a deep plate in front of Barney and one for herself, then placed a large portion of the rice in the center of the plate, covered the rice with the cooked chicken and vegetables, and then lowered her head as though to say grace.

As they ate, Myoko said to Barney very softly, "Before you came into my life, I had nothing but hate and loneliness in my heart. I wanted all men of the army to die as my husband had died. I really wanted to be left completely alone, no one to bother me with useless conversation, no one to offer any kind of sympathy, just no one to interfere with my lost feelings. I wanted to be alone and never see anyone. Then you came. I have given much thought about you and your country that you have told me about. I have tasted your gentleness and shared your concern for living and most of all, your deep concern for all peoples everywhere. Maybe because you are from a different part of the world, or it could be that all these good things are of your choosing, I don't know, but I am now sure that I can be your true friend."

For the rest of the evening, not much was said; nothing needed to be said. They finished their dinner, washed and put away all the cooking utensils, cleaned the hibachi and took care of the soaking tub. Barney exclaimed to Myoko how much the days working in her company, turning the soil and making the fields ready to plant, had pleased him. This evening was very special. It established the friendship needs of both of them. "I feel that being here in Japan, as I am, will not be as fearful, nor as lonely, just knowing that you are near enough to see and talk to. All this gives me a great measure of peace. We are, we will be, best friends."

Then Barney thanked her for the nicest evening that he had ever had and walked off into the night to his hiding place. His thoughts as he made his way down the path were of the unusual bathing and hot tub soaking experience were that he enjoyed the care that Myoko gave his body as she soaped and washed him. He could not help wonder if she would let him wash her body in the same manner... Oh well!

Late in the afternoon of the next day, Myoko asked Barney if he was secure in his disguise enough to consider sleeping on the wide-open bench that was in the open room. "I would feel much better for your safety if I knew you were not far away." After thinking about the suggestion for a few minutes, he thought it would be wise if the bench was moved to the opposite side of the room so it would be nearer to the outside should anyone arrive unexpectedly. This would give him a chance to slip into the bamboo and not cause Myoko trouble. This they agreed to. Barney would sleep close to another person for the first time since leaving the submarine.

PART III

Love and Danger

March–August, 1945

Late March

All went well for weeks, with field work followed by peaceful meals and occasional refreshing hot baths in Myoko's great tub. Then early one morning the noise of many airplanes filled the air. This time the noise was low and different from that of the B-29s. As Myoko and Barney looked up to see where the rumbling was coming from, a U.S. Navy dive-bomber careened over the edge of the cliffs and sped away to the south. This was the first time U.S. carrier planes had been seen and it told Barney a great deal. The attack had to be against all the area of Fukuoka, the airfield, docks, shipyard and the army facilities. It seemed that the attack went on for an hour with an occasional aircraft passing near Myoko's house. When the attack ended and it became quiet again, Barney looked at Myoko and saw tears welling in her eyes. Barney could say nothing to her, for he had feelings of anxiety and the hope that war's end was not too far away. Both of them knew that many people had just died and it caused great pain to them.

As had happened before just after a bombing, straggling groups of old men, women and a few children drifted past them moving south. No one spoke from either side and within a few hours, all the foot traffic stopped along the path. It was quiet again. Barney did not attempt to speak to Myoko for a good half-hour. Then he asked her if they could lay their tools down, sit at the edge of the cliffs and look out across the sea so that he could discuss something with her. The look in her eyes was very sad but she dropped her hoe and without saying anything, began to walk toward the area where Barney had his hiding place. Finding a cluster of rocks that overhung the very edge of the sheer cliff, he took her hand and began to try and explain his feelings about the war that was tearing both of their countries apart. He did not attempt to place blame on either side, he simply wanted to say that he was sorry, that the killing on both sides was horrible and even though they were from different sides, it should not cause them to dislike each other.

"Our friendship is as one, one you and one me," Barney-said. "With the planes that you saw today, the war is coming closer to an end, and soon all this destruction of life will end and maybe a new kind of caring for people will come from this whole horrible, stupid mess. Right now, you and I must not lose sight of caring for each other. We have no say in what's happening and the best we can do is support each other, keep our friendship safe and pray that all tomorrows will be better."

For a long time Myoko gave no response. She just sat on the rock and stared out into the far-reaching seascape. This lasted for some 20 minutes before she made any sound and then she spoke very softly with great pain in her voice, saying that the whole world must be like the ocean — no not the ocean, like the tide, always changing, going back and forth, rising and falling. "I hope that the tide of the end of the war will treat Japan as it does the sea, bringing new nourishment and rebuilding life for the Japanese people. We are really good people, it is the military that is bad." To which Barney responded, "I also hope that the end of this awful war will be kind to your country. It will take much healing for all the Japanese people, because nothing will ever be the same. A new Japan must not be run by the military. The people must have the right to choose their way through life."

They sat on the edge of the cliff for a few moments more, then Myoko stood up and reminded Barney that they still had several hours of daylight to work in the fields, and as nice as it was to sit and watch the ocean, the seeds would not plant themselves.

For the next month, the U.S. Navy planes were over the city area almost every day. Noisy explosions could be heard in the distance and often the planes would fly over Myoko's small farm. Barney wanted to wave, flash a message or do something to attract attention. He also knew that others might see his attempt to signal and so he suppressed the desire to do so. He wondered what the men flying those devices of destruction would think if they knew that the person looking up at them was a stranded friend, a caring countryman....

Neither of them had any idea of the war's progress. Without any comment, they both realized that the war would end when it ended and there was nothing they could do about it.

April 15, 1945

The new field had been planted half in sweet potatoes and the other half was to be planted in onions. Months earlier, he and Myoko had placed millions of very small seeds in soft mulch beds. When the onion sets were big enough to replant, they would dig them up and plant them in nice orderly rows. The time to do so was drawing near. That evening she and Barney examined the onion sets and she decided that tomorrow would be a good day to start the replanting.

Early, they took several baskets woven from bamboo and dug the onion sets, crossed the path to the readied field and began planting. To Barney this was back-breaking work. He was not used to bending over for hours. They poked small holes in the dirt, placed a sliver of green-looking grass part way into the hole, and pressed the soil around it. By the hundreds, by the thousands — Barney didn't count, but there were many. By the end of the first day, he was sure his back would never straighten out and the soaking tub that evening would be especially comforting to their tired muscles.

The bent-over labor seemed not to bother Myoko; she just kept on planting. As the sun began to dip close to the horizon, Myoko asked Barney if he was in need of a rest, that it was time to end the day's work. He was more than willing so they walked quietly to the house.

April 20

This day was much like the day before, bending over and setting the plants into the ground over and over. By noon all the planting was done. Only a few places needed to be cultivated and the watering ditch cleaned out so that the new plants could be watered. Myoko was some ten feet from Barney, smoothing out the small piles of dirt as Barney finished the ditch cleaning. Without any warning, the S.O.B. of a soldier came out of nowhere. It was good that Barney was bent over, and in his almost normal old man's position, for the soldier paid no attention to him.

Barney was using the long-tined cultivator to do the cleaning. As the soldier approached Myoko, she tried to move toward Barney but was only able to get halfway when she was stopped by the damned soldier. He grabbed Myoko by the shoulder and began to yell cuss words at her and demand that she change her mind about his demands. Barney, at this point, had no thoughts of getting involved, but the hatred that had grown out of the earlier mistreatment began to well up inside his throat. That bitter taste that comes from acrimony and fear filled Barney's mouth but he dared not move. However, when the damned fool hit her, he came unglued. The soldier had not paid one bit of attention to the old man and was not ready for what happened next. As the anger overtook him, Barney swung the cultivator much as one would a baseball bat, and caught the soldier square in the chest with the tines pointed straight at the soldier's heart. The next half-second was like many minutes. All of the look and shock of dying was slowed in time forever in both their minds as they realized the impact of the tool buried deep in the chest of the dying soldier He was knocked flat on his back in the newly turned dirt. The last gasp of breath hissed from his ashen face in disbelief and he was forever dead.

Barney placed his foot on the dead soldier's chest to extract the cultivator, and as he did so Myoko gave a sharp cry, a cry of absolute fear.

Barney turned to Myoko and told her that he had promised himself that the damned soldier would never hurt her again, "And now, Myoko, he won't ever."

Without saying anything more, he began to dig a hole beside the body in the soft field. He had dug about one foot deep when Myoko came apart. She began crying in a deep and body-shaking, uncontrollable way. Regagless of Barney's gentle assurance, she could not stop. Myoko seemed to melt into the ground, as she no longer could support herself. During all of the few minutes' happenings, Barney had not thought to see if any other persons were around and now with Myoko making such a loud crying sound, he did so. As far as he could tell it was just the two of them — and the body of one mean, ornery soldier who deserved to be dead.

Barney, bending down, put his arm around Myoko's shoulder and tried to quiet the sobbing. She still continued at the same loud pitch. Picking her up from the ground, he asked her if she would be more calm if she was at her house, and the suggestion reduced the loudness to a soft murmur. After several deep breaths the shaking of her body stopped and without any further sounds, she picked up the other cultivator and began to help Barney dig a grave. It took the two hours to reach a satisfactory depth of four feet. Without any words, Barney just kicked the limp body into the grave and stated forcefully, "You son-of-a-bitch, if you were a human being, we would say some kind of prayer over your no-good ass. But you got what you deserved and here is the fist full of dirt that you are supposed to have come from. Goodbye." He began to fill up the hole. By the time all was done and the soil made to look like the rest of the field, with onions replanted over the gravesite. Barney again put his arm around Myoko and calmly said, "Let's go home."

Neither of them wanted to eat that evening. Myoko made her special tea without any comment. The total silence that abounded carried far into the night. What could either of them say after taking a life? In the conflict of war, killing was a matter of killing or be killed, and was totally expected, if not demanded. To single out one person, even though it was a matter of defense, weighed very heavy on both their minds. When would someone come looking for the dead soldier? How intense would the search be? All of these questions now bore down heavily on Barney's shoulders.

He had no idea how much time had passed when he asked Myoko if she would like to be alone, or if there was something he could do to help rid her of the guilt feeling that she obviously had ... silence again.

Barney started to get up from the bench and walk to the opposite side of the open room. Myoko must have taken this move as an indication that he was going to leave, and spoke for the first time since the incident in the field. This time her words were short and somewhat clipped as though she had bitten her tongue. "We, you and I, this day have done something very bad with respect to nature — killing another person. Regardless of all his hate and anger that he took out on other people, especially me, all of our teachings tell us not to kill.

"... It is not the person that we killed that bothers me, and I think even you feel that way, it is just the act of killing that I am having deep trouble resolving. Yet, I am glad that I will never have to see him or be beaten by him again. I feel deeply grateful that you defended my life as you did, and I will always be obligated to you for that protection. But Barney, even though I am glad he is dead, I wish somehow that it had been unnecessary. From this day to forever, you and I are bound together by what happened. Forever we will remember digging a grave in the field, placing the body in the grave and covering it with the damp soil. Each time we go to the field to work or just pass by, we will remember. We will never forget, never."

Barney moved back to the bench and knelt in front of Myoko, took both of her hands in his and told her he was having some of the same feelings; "However," he stated, "we did not make the bastard mean and brutal, we did nothing to cause him to hate as he did. You rejected his demands to let him take over your life and your property. Even in Japan, I do not think that his demands were justified. He got what he deserved, and I just happened to be the one that did it to him. You and I have no cause to blame ourselves and we cannot go through the rest of our lives feeling guilt. You might be right about carrying some kind of regret the rest of our lives, but guilt — I don't think so."

Myoko put her arms around Barney's shoulders, touching his cheek so softly with her lips that he was barely able to feel it. "Regardless of our different countries, after this day you and I are one," she said. She then took Barney's hand, opened the sliding door to her sleeping room and led him to her bed.

There was no rush to passion. Myoko sensed that Barney had had some experience in bedrooms, however he displayed uncertainty about what he should do. Myoko slowly removed his wrap-around clothes as she explained to him that she had never shared a bed with anyone other than her husband. "Most often," she said, "we would take hours undressing, touching, and feeling more than the touch of each other's skin. When you have great respect for each other, the act of making love should be just that, all parts of the act should be played out before coupling can be fully enjoyed.

"I will teach you, should you desire it; you must have great patience and control with yourself and also help the other person. Come, I will show you how to begin."

Barney took his place on Myoko's bed. She began to slip out of her own dress. From the light of the night Barney was privileged to see a most beautiful silhouette of the loveliest form of a woman that he had ever seen, real or in any magazine. She moved with the grace and languor of a drifting leaf on its way to earth's floor. Instead of moving alongside Barney, she sat at his feet and began to touch the calves of his legs. She had the softest touch, her fingers glided over the smooth texture of Barney's skin, causing a grand array of goose flesh. The tips of her fingers caressed along his side muscles and over his chest. Then she instructed Barney to do the same, starting along her hips, then very slowly moving up her back to the shoulders. Just the touch of her flawless skin made Barney's hands shake. He tried to be as gentle and soft with his touch as Myoko had been, but he just didn't have the same control. She began to coach him as his hand moved up her spine.

"Only your finger tips," she said. "Allow them to touch as though they are going to break something that shouldn't be broken. Now bring your hand up my side to the softness of my neck." The farther he moved, the closer he came to losing control of the soft touching. Again, Myoko sensed his eagerness and simply stopped herself. She left her hands flat on Barney's chest just below his breast.

The warmth and gentleness of her hands made him shudder with pleasure. After some 10 or more minutes, she began to move her hand in a small circular motion, moving just under his chin, across the front of his shoulders then down to his mid-section. Myoko could not help but notice how tense all of Barney's muscles were. "Barney you must relax, let your body tell me what pleases you most. All your body is telling me now is that you are about to explode. If you are to learn physical loving, and make it an experience of great satisfaction and joy for both persons, telling the other person how much the want is, and the beauty of being close, this must be done through messages from the body. When one is as tense as you now are, no messages can be felt."

She began the chest-touching again, this time telling him to feel the softness of her hand and let his desire say more, more. Barney began to understand what Myoko was trying to say. The urgency of the physical need did not diminish, but became secondary to Myoko's soft touch and words. This was a pleasure that he had never dreamed of and he did want more, much more. The touching was transferred to the more sensitive parts of the body and for many minutes, there was pure joy in being so close and having the sensation last so long. It became apparent that Barney could not hold back much longer. Myoko raised herself over Barney's body and a new measure of deep pleasure began.... and after, they lay as one for many moments dwelling upon the bonding of more than their rich friendship.

April 21

Dawn seemed to come so swiftly. They were still holding each other closely as daylight filled the small sleeping room.

Barney had not completed his thinking about changes they would now have to make in their routine. Myoko lay sleepily on his chest. He asked her if she had thought about other soldiers coming to look for the dead soldier. What should they do with Barney until they could be sure that others were no longer concerned about the missing man?

Myoko had not had time to dwell on any changes and had not given any thought to a search for the dead man. She was not about to think of such things now. Instead, she began her delightful sexual touching and playing over again. Barney did not resist and joined in the gratifying pursuit. By mid-morning there was no energy left and they had to address the problem of discovery. Myoko rested on Barney's chest with one hand under his chin and her elbow punching very sharply into the center of his sternum — uncomfortable, but it kept Barney's attention on their discussion.

After a long series of varying suggestions, they decided to let Barney return to his hiding-place cave where he would stay during the daylight hours. He would look for Myoko only late at night, or if she came to the edge of the cliff above Barney's hiding place and tossed rocks down toward his cave.

In the late afternoon Barney took Myoko down the trail to his cave. He had not shown her exactly where it was but had given her the general direction. Several times they had visited the cliffs, and she asked where he slept and he had pointed in the direction. When they came to the big rocks that guarded the entrance to the cave, Myoko stopped and asked Barney how he was able to find a quiet and remote spot that allowed such a beautiful view of the shore and the sea. "You must have a special sense in finding good thing — like me," she smiled.

Barney helped Myoko around the rocks and into the cave entrance as he began to tell her about his search for a hiding place. He told her that he was sure he would be caught and killed but until he was caught, he would fight to stay alive. For him, it meant that he had to be near the sea because that was where the most food would come from. Commenting further, "I had no idea of the type of country, or if I could find gardens or farms to steal food from. My only thought was to survive and so far this is what I, now we, have done. I owe so much to you, not just for the food and your friendship; it's the deep, kind and caring person that you are. Not just caring about me, but everything about you — you have made being here almost total pleasure. Before I came, if anyone had tried to tell me that I would find someone like you, and I am sure there are many others that are like you, I would not have believed them. The only real problem that I have is the feeling that I should be back on my ship, doing my best to help my country end this crazy war. What I do on my ship is not all that great, but when everyone does his part, the whole ship is able to do an outstanding job. I hope you understand.

"Now that I am here, and have learned a very small amount about the Japanese people, and how some of the people hate this war and killing, I feel that some day soon both countries will begin to rebuild all that has been destroyed and maybe in time become friends. I think that America could learn some new and good things from Japan, but I am just one stranded man and you are just one lady, a farmer lady, and a gentle and caring one. But let me tell you something, you are a very beautiful lady and I want to keep you near me always."

This was the first time that Barney had come close to saying anything about his feelings toward Myoko, and it made him feel good. He also realized that somewhere in time, after the two countries stopped fighting, and assuming that he would still be alive, they would have to face the fact that he would be reunited with the U.S. Navy and would not be able to continue their much desired relationship. That did not make him fee so good.

There was a quietness to the evening and what promised to be a most unusual sunset. Barney drew Myoko close and asked her if she had given any thought about the future, the ending of hostilities and how she would begin rebuilding her life. It was the wrong thing at the wrong time. Myoko turned around very sharply and buried herself in Barney's arms. The pain she now was feeling was transferred to her fingers as she dug her fingernails deep into his flesh. Great volumes of tears welled down her stricken face as she sobbed, that this had been a consideration, she refused to think about. Through her sobbing she said that the crazy war could continue if they could be left alone just where they were now. "You to fish and help with the farming, and me, to teach you how to grow the best vegetables and other things, and let the rest of the whole world just pass us by."

Emotionally Barney could not disagree with her; still, they had to face the real facts of what could happen when peace came to all of her Japan and his America. To break the unpleasant conversation, Barney asked her if she would like to share fishing for a few minutes and maybe catch fresh fish for a special dinner. He led her down to the surf and the hidden poles that he had borrowed from the fishing village.

It took Barney 20 minutes to gather some rock mussels for bait. He showed Myoko the best place he had found for catching the most fish, placed part of a piece of bait on the hook and cast it into the deep surf. As he was fixing his own pole, Myoko let out a small scream of excitement and asked Barney if this was what he meant by "catching a fish." She had caught a larger surfperch than Barney had caught so far. "This is the first fish that I have ever caught," she screamed. Myoko was overwhelmed by her catch and it took her mind off the earlier comments that had caused so much strain on both of them. Dinner would be the beginning of another most enjoyable evening.

Barney thought that he had planted the seeds of their needs concerning what they must do for the next few weeks and speculating what might happen when the war ended. He surmised that after she had had time to think about all that was happening, she might suggest some answers on her own. It was during one of their simple but very tasty dinners that Myoko asked him, "what do you think will happen to Japan when all is peaceful again?" Barney had never been forced to dig down so deep in his mind to find the best way to explain much of what he felt would be the outcome after the war had ended. In answering Myoko, he was very careful not to state anything that might cause indifference in their present caring for each other. He began by explaining that the people of America really have great control of their government, and how people are treated at all times. As an example, he explained, "When Japan had the bad earthquake a long time ago, it was the people of America who decided to send assistance to Japan, and it was because they really cared for the people in your country that were hurt and needed help. I know that when this fighting is over, the people of my country will be very concerned about the people of Japan having help in rebuilding all that was destroyed. More importantly, they will allow the average Japanese person to find dignity and self-determination as they go about making a new Japan. The American government will select the best leaders to help in getting your economy back into production and to begin some sort of self-rule. They will not allow the Japanese military to be involved in the rebuilding process. As you have said yourself, it was the military leaders that caused all the trouble to begin with. That will not happen again. You will see, if the new Japan follows our leaders' advice and direction, Japan will become a much better country than it has ever been.

"I am also sure that you will keep your own property and maybe, if you choose, you can buy additional land and make your farm larger and more profitable. You said that now you have to give about 75% of all that you grow to the military in the name of the government. In the new future, you will sell all your produce on the open market and receive what it's worth. It will take some time to make all the changes required to have it this way, but it will happen.

"Now, you cultivate your land by hand with a very time-consuming hand tool. After many of the changes have taken place and your country is making things again, you might have a small tractor that will do all the tilling in one day. I would like to see you have one, for watching how hard you have to work and how many days it takes just to turn over the soil in your garden makes me sad. No one as young and beautiful as you are should have to work so hard to make a living. I know that you like working the soil and seeing that which you plant grow, but there are much easier and better ways to do these things and you will find and enjoy them."

Myoko looked at Barney for some time before she had a response. "What you say about rebuilding Japan sounds nice, but you do not understand the Japanese men. They will not let these things happen. Yes, I would like to have a machine that would let me do my soil turning. That is the only part of farming that displeases me."

Then Barney changed the subject by asking her if she had any plans for talking to anyone who might come looking for the dead soldier. "We must be prepared because whoever comes looking might search for several weeks, or until they are satisfied that he has gone elsewhere or might have been killed in one of the bombing raids. We will have to be very careful until we find out what is going on with them."

Myoko suggested, "during the day I will work in the fields as usual, and should anyone come asking for the dead soldier, and seem to want to inspect everywhere, and if they seem to be doubtful about me, I will walk the most direct way, straight across the path to my house. Now the most important part, if I am sure everything is, as you say, O.K., I will walk to the north end of my fields, down the path past the clump of bamboo that you used to hide in (looking happy of course) then back to my house. Later, near darkness, you can join me for the night. Before the sun comes up you must be out of sight in case anyone comes by. Will this be agreeable to you?"

Barney had the widest grin on his face as he responded, "and I will have fresh fish each day for us to share for our evening meal. We will try your plan and if no one causes problems, maybe in a few weeks I will be able to help you in the fields again." Barney held Myoko for several long moments then patted her on the cheek of her fanny and departed to his cave.

For the next few weeks, Barney had kept tabs on Myoko by watching for her near noon as she took her break and then again at the close of the day. Each time she took the long way home, passing in front of the bamboo-hiding place where Barney was standing far back in the tall canes. They could see each other as she went by and in her own way, Myoko would give a slight wave as she passed. In mid-afternoon of the third day, five soldiers came up the path and stopped to talk to Myoko. Barney could not hear any of what was said and it bothered him greatly. There was some 30 minutes of talking, hand-waving and other body language before they went on their way toward Fukuoka. Barney was in a boil the rest of the afternoon as he waited for Myoko to indicate which way she would walk back to her house. The relief that overtook him as she started to walk up the field to the north and then down the path toward him was immeasurable. As she passed, instead of the slight wave, she swung her hips in a very provocative manner like a showgirl might do, and gave him a "come over to my house" look. Barney could have pulled all the bamboo up by the roots as she passed by.

He had not been fishing for several days and thought that they should have fresh fish for dinner, so he hurried down to the surf where he kept the poles, and set about trying his luck. He had been fishing for a short time when a noise caused him to all but jump out of his skin. Myoko had slipped up behind him with a basket covered with a cloth and a most exciting smile on her face. Without giving Barney a chance to say anything, she said, "we are going to have a beach dinner tonight and really have fresh fish, that is if you can catch them." She sat down on the clean sand and watched as Barney began to catch one fish after the other. It took him just a few minutes to catch enough for dinner, which he cleaned and gave to Myoko to cook. They made a small fire from driftwood and waited until the fire had burned to a hot bed of coals. Myoko placed a cleaned fish directly on the coals and in just a little while the fish was succulently done. In her basket, she had brought two special rice balls the size of oranges and several pieces of fruit. This was truly the finest dinner anyone could have imagined.

After dinner, they sat close to each other and she repeated the conversation that had taken place with the five soldiers. First she said they wanted to know if she had seen a soldier of so-and-so height and about 120 pounds. "I told them yes, about three months ago. He was a mean and very abusive person and if all soldiers were that way, they should all be in prison or shot. They then became more specific about him. Another soldier had stated that the missing soldier had been seen talking to an old farmer in this neighborhood and was seen to strike the old man, knocking him to the earth. The old man did not get up and the two of them just went on their way. I then almost told them about being struck and that I was the old man, and had the scar to prove it. That could have raised more unwanted questions and I did not want to say any more than I had to. They seemed to think that maybe the missing soldier had deserted the army and that if so, was sure to be shot when caught. They then thanked me and went on their way. Barney, I don't think we have anything to worry about, however, it is best that we keep you out of sight for several more days. They might be back."

There was still some light on the horizon and Myoko asked Barney if they could swim in the ocean; it might be more fun than the soaking tub. Again, Barney felt a little too bashful to take off all of his clothes in front of Myoko, yet she casually undressed and walked to the edge of the surf before he could move. The greater freedom of the ocean and the salt water was pure delight and they splashed the foaming water over each other, gently pushed and shoved like two young children at play. After awhile they moved to the dry warm sand high on the beach and loved each other far into the night.

For the next week no one came by to ask about the missing soldier. Once or twice, someone from the fishing village walked by on their way to the big city, bowed in a general greeting without saying any words, and went on their way. Myoko and Barney began to feel all was well and decided to try working during the daylight hours. Most of the work was removing unwanted weeds and turning over the topsoil— troublesome, but very necessary if one wanted a quality garden. They would hoe a row at a time side-by-side, talking as they went.

May 26

One evening, Myoko commented to Barney that he was starting to stand up too straight and had lost his look of an old Japanese man, and that she was also getting nervous about another visit from more soldiers looking for the missing one. She suggested that they take a better look at what they could do to make Barney look more like an old man should anyone decide to have a closer look. Saying to him, "I have some old wigs that I have been keeping for a long time. They are from some of the plays that my husband and I were part of when we were in Kobe attending college. Let me clean them and see if we can make you a good-looking old man's beard and long braided hair. Maybe if it makes you look older, like a real old farmer, we could try out the new look by going to the fishing village to do some shopping. And — fish, we're eating too much fish. Another good chicken and some eggs would be nice. Seldom do people of such small places pay any attention to normal visitors as long as they look like the local people. We shall try anyway."

For many nights they spent hours doing and redoing the hair from the wig, trying to make Barney a typical hairstyle. If he wore a sloppy old farmer's hat that covered all his face, he should pass as Japanese. Barney laughed and commented that the hat looked like an oversized upside-down ice cream cone with the sharp peak rounded off. To see any features one would have to all but remove his hat and look directly into his face. The beard was another matter; the hair that Myoko had was very black and in order to have the old look, the hair needed to be gray or white. Barney did not know how or what Myoko used to change the color but he now had long strands of scraggly white hair for his beard.

Myoko remembered that her husband had used some kind of glue material when he had made some furniture long ago. It took her a whole night to sort through all the little boxes that she had tucked away and to find the sticky stuff. Barney had never seen glue like that which Myoko found. It was a heavy clear liquid and had to be slightly heated in order to obtain a good bond. Myoko carefully selected the thinnest strands of the wig hair and formed what she thought was a good goatee. Taking one strand of hair at a time, she began to glue Barney a most impressive-looking set of chin whiskers. This completed, she laid out the design of each side of a complimentary mustache. First the right side, then the left. The left side took longer because it had to match the right side in the number of strands, and the drooping look of being natural and old. Cleaning his face, she attached each strand of the mustache until it was all completed.

When all was done, Myoko began to brush the glued strands very carefully so as not to pull them loose, and yet allow her to form the hair into a long drooping old, but cared-for, look. The fashioning and brushing done, Myoko tested the firmness of the gluing then stood back to admire her handiwork. Her comment was, "Barney, you look just like a young-complexioned, older Japanese man. If you will remember to bend over and step like an old man does, maybe staggering just a little, having your hat pulled low to cover your face, you will pass for one who is so old that he is about to meet his spirits at the end of the rising sun. Maybe you should practice speaking in a very old feeble way, because the older you are the more respect you are given and that is a great honor." Barney looked in the small mirror and was totally surprised at the transformation. The look was so good that it made him feel old, older, and even older. Myoko had a most pleased smile on her face and softly bent down and gave Barney a soft kiss.

For many days they tried out his new look working in the field, and on one special occasion, Myoko stopped two passing friends and did not hesitate to point Barney out as her aged uncle who had been bombed out of his home and had come to work and help her with the lighter chores around the farm. They both bowed very low to show the elder respect, mumbled the Japanese greeting and gave no indication that Barney was anyone other than an old uncle digging in the dirt.

June 19

One evening shortly afterward, as Myoko unwrapped a small package, she explained to Barney that she had been able to trade some of her sweet potatoes for a piece of fresh lean pork meat, and that would become this evening's dinner; cooked in a very special way, together with choice vegetables, then served over fresh steamed rice, a most tasty meal. She began to clean the vegetables and cut the meat and she explained each step as she went. "The cutting of the individual vegetables is very important. When cooking, the taste of the vegetables depends on how they were cut," she said. "This one, the green onion, must always be cut at an angle like this and as it cooks, it's flavor will not become lost with all of the other vegetables and their separate flavors. Of course you must place the slower cooking ones in the pan first and then add the next slower ones in the correct order, so that when the dish is ready to eat, they are all cooked the right amount. You must never overcook them; they should have just the right amount of fresh crunch as you eat them, just like the ones I am giving you now." And again, he was amazed at how simple the food was to prepare and how absolutely delicious the dinner turned out to be.

Cleaning up took a few minutes and they walked slowly toward the strands of giant bamboo, sat down at the very edge of the cliff so that they could watch the soon-to-come evening color change as the day passed into darkness. From their vantage point, looking out to sea, the only blockage of their view was the vertical sides of the cliff. Out at sea, that was all there was — the beauty of the deep water turning from sky-reflected blue to almost black as the close of the evening folded around them. The reflection of thousands of colors bouncing off the tops of the gentle waves completed a panoramic picture not even a camera could have captured.

This was just one of the many sunsets that they had shared and not one of them had been close to looking like any of the others. This evening promised to be another great splendor of nature's creations. Beautiful horse-tailed clouds relinquished whiffs and thin strands in many colors of the evening's last lights. Against the ever-darkening blue of the sky, there were so many colors of red, purple, orange and yellow all mixed together that it was impossible to pick out any one of the basic colors; they were all just magnificent blends into the close of the evening. It was the right time to find the trail down to their beach and Myoko's promise of a very exciting evening.

This time Barney decided to take Myoko to the beach where he had first set foot on Japanese soil. It was a larger beach than the one where they had fished and made love some time ago. It also had a deeper inlet away from the edge of the surf for more privacy and the sand was much warmer and softer. Barney held onto Myoko's hand as they moved down the steep cliff side. It always made him feel less lost in this strange land when he could hold onto her hand this way. Besides he told himself, she really likes it. She had commented long ago that it was not one of Japanese men's, nor for that matter, the women's, customs to hold one another's hands at any time, but that he should not stop, because it was a good feeling. Reaching the bottom of the cliff, and without stopping to compare his statements with the previous story he had told her, Barney explained, "This is where I first set foot in your country. I was more frightened, a lone sailor, than anyone could ever have imagined. I lay against the rocks just back there and shivered in fright until I could catch my breath, gather some courage and find the path that we just came down.

"Tonight I feel that this is the right place for us to be together. To me it makes for a new beginning — of a bond that will be part of my life forever — just you and me. No one, and nothing else, in this whole torn-up world makes any difference. We... you and I... are at peace without a word being said, and we are very much committed to each other. I have a deep personal feeling about us. I guess the only words that say what I am trying to say are, Myoko, I love you so very much. Not just for now, but forever. I don't know how all this and the war will turn out for us, but I want to keep you with me forever and ever."

"I feel the same way," cried Myoko softly, "but how will it be possible? There will have to be many changes within the structure of Japanese thinking for us even to be seen together. It would be almost the same as now, hiding behind makeup, trying to be Japanese. There will be much anger on both sides for a long time; it may never heal the wounds that have been created by this terrible war. I just don't know. If everything could stay the way it is now for us, I would be most happy. Even if I were to go to your country, I would be looked down upon and neither of us could live with such strong feelings against us. Why can't we not think of anything but what is now, just live and care for each other until we are sure what changes the future might bring? Then we can think more clearly and have greater hope of being together for always."

Taking Barney's hand, Myoko said, "Let us walk down the sand as far as we can and let us not say any more of long tomorrows. Then we'll swim in the gentle foaming surf and then it will be my turn to be nice to you."

This they did, kicking loose shells that sat on top of the sand, picking up a polished stick, smoothed by the constant washing of sand and tide, and making small talk about the day and what they might do tomorrow.

Coming back to their original spot, Myoko quickly dropped her wrap-around dress and as graceful as a floating new blossom, entered the surf. Barney watched for many minutes, taking in the exquisite naked beauty of this very lovely person whom he knew he could not do without. Then, he too, dismissed his clothes and joined Myoko as she splashed about in the lazy breaking waves. They played among the small tide-changing breakers for a long time, flipping hands full of salt water on each other's bodies, as though to caress the skin with jeweled wetness. If anyone else had seen them playing this way, there would have been much trouble; a young beautiful lady in the tide with a very spry old man would have been unthinkable.

Dripping wet, with small shiny crystals of salt forming on their skin as the night air evaporated the wetness, they both walked away from the changing water and found their place in the sand just under the mountainous of the cliffs. Lying down on the sand, Barney held up his hand to the still standing Myoko; he was caught, and left totally without words, by the silhouette of her most exquisite nude body. Myoko began, "When you love another person, truly love them, it is very important that every move in love-making be wordless communication. You must touch the other softly with total expectation of a message coming from the place being touched; let me show you." She knelt down beside his outstretched form. "See, as I slowly move my hand over your chest, I can sense your body saying how nice it feels; then as I move to your side, the muscles tell me that this too is nice, but please use both hands and move one on each side like this." She began to stroke each side of Barney's ribs. "Just this small amount of touching and you are beginning to tell me that you are now losing control of the management of your body and it is far too early to begin our physical adventure. Barney, move your hands from my sides and I want you to begin to touch me just under the chin so that your finger tips are the only part that is against my skin, like this." She moved her fingertips ever so lightly under his homemade beard. "Ever so softly," she said gently. "Now move your fingertips down along my neck and to my throat, yes like that; don't you feel me telling you how nice it is to have you touching me this way? If you were more forceful, the body would not have a chance to respond. That would be more like a massage and that is not what we are doing."

Again, she directed Barney to move: "Sit up so that you are at my feet, like this, and now begin the soft touching on the backs of my legs." As he did so, she again reminded him to do it softly and gently, "so that I can talk back to you through the touching. Yes, that is the way," she murmured. He could tell that Myoko was experiencing great pleasure and satisfaction from his newly learned way of conversation.

Barney was having a difficult time keeping his mind on what Myoko had asked him to do and she noticed it immediately. Myoko directed him to move his one hand down to her ankle, then to begin touching the shin part of her leg. This may not have been as exciting as the back of her leg, but it did cause Barney to slow his breathing and pay more attention to her instructions.

This game went on for a long time and with each change of the body's touch, Myoko explained the reason and the response that each should feel as they became more aggressive and personal in selecting the next place to put one's hand. Even though Barney was having a real problem keeping his mind on the directions she was giving him, he could sense that Myoko was experiencing some loss of her own control. Barney, feeling that he wanted to prolong this new exercise of love making as long as he could, sat up, curled Myoko's nude body back against his chest and then wrapped her tightly in his arms. Sitting that way for a few long silent moments he squeezed her tightly against his body and said, "I've got you where I want you and I'm never going to let you go." She only snuggled closer and gave a slight moan of great joy.

Neither one decided to make the next move. They both laid down on the sand and began the same soft touching. After what seemed like hours and the final coupling, they lingered that way until the chill of the early morning told them that they must go.

June 20

They worked the fields for another day and all the caring for the fields was done. Myoko asked Barney if he felt brave. He looked puzzled, so she asked him again, "Do you feel brave?" He nodded. "Good," she said, "tomorrow, we will make our first attempt to go shopping. We will leave early tomorrow morning and get to the village before all of the best choices of chicken, and anything else that might be for sale, is gone. We will use some of the money that I have saved from my garden and sell several baskets of new vegetables. With these, we can barter for most of the items that we need; you know, a chicken, some eggs and maybe a different kind of fish, we shall see. Would you like to do such a thing?"

And as planned, the next morning early, they made their way down the path to the fishing village for a day of nervous mingling with other people. As they entered the small town, Myoko began to talk to him much as a younger person would talk to a much older almost-deaf person, saying to him, "Uncle remember, we must do this" and, "Uncle don't forget we must buy that," as though reviewing a shopping list.

The local people seemed only to recognize that new people were in their tiny village and paid no further attention to them. Barney made doubly sure that his braided bamboo hat stayed pulled down tight over his face. They spent the whole morning moving from one part of the small market place to another. If they had been in any kind of hurry, they could have visited all the stalls in the village and bought all their needs within one hour, but Myoko wanted to test Barney's nerves and makeup completely, and this they did.

As they walked about the rickety fishing piers and the waterfront, Barney saw where he had borrowed the two fishing poles and buckets. It gave him an almost sad feeling, seeing the faces of the poor-looking fishermen and their dilapidated fishing boats. He whispered softly to Myoko that this was the place where he had borrowed the poles and he further explained the sorrowful feeling that he had had after seeing the state of the people he had taken them from. She put her fingers to her lips and gave Barney a slight "Shhhh, be quiet"...

Gathering up all that they had wanted plus several extra items, they made their way with relief up the path for the one-hour trek home, going back the way they had come. Their confidence in Barney's disguise grew with each step they took. Walking to the crest of the small hill that overlooked the little valley where Myoko's farm was situated, Barney was overcome by the feeling that this was home. The late afternoon sun was cutting across the rice paddy and the other fields in such a way that everything was backlit, making the whole scene one of great tranquility and at peace. Myoko's house, small and nondescript as it was, gave the impression of being well cared for and loved. They both set down their packages and enjoyed all that they surveyed: the farm, the narrow stands of bamboo that masked parts of the view of the sea, and the low mountains that gave a nice backdrop to the entire picture.

Entering the house from the open room, Myoko commented that they should have dinner (the chicken) early and since the weather was so nice, go to the beach again as they had done the night before. This time she would take a metal tea pot so that if they became chilled, a cup of hot tea could warm them and they could stay longer.

Barney watched as Myoko meticulously cleaned the chicken, cut it into bite-sized pieces and placed the chosen pieces in a marinade sauce that she mixed from her secret store of spices. As the chicken sat, she made the fire in the fire pot, then selected the vegetables for cooking. When all the parts for the dinner were ready, she began to explain each step in the making of the dinner. She told how to treat the chicken as it soaked in the special sauce, turning it gently so that each piece received its share of the mix, then how important it was to select the right vegetables so that the flavor would complement the main ingredient, the chicken. "For instance, if you used a cabbage-tasting vegetable, you would destroy the delicate taste of the chicken. If you substituted pork for the chicken, then you might choose cabbage or broccoli as part of the dish. With fish, as you have seen me do before, you can choose other greens and vegetables. You want the flavor of each separate ingredient to come together so that you can taste each delicious part."

Myoko served the food all on one plate with a dish of cold rice in another small, deep bowl. Barney savored every morsel as he ate slowly and reflected on the care and neatness that Myoko had displayed as she went through each step of making the dinner.

After the meal was over and they had shared cleaning the dishes, Barney asked Myoko if she would like to go for a long walk up the path in the direction of Fukuoka, not to go all the way — maybe just an hour or so. He explained that he just wanted to walk with her for a while and take in some of the very beautiful countryside that he had not seen in daylight. He had in mind the farmhouse that he had almost walked into the first night that he went gathering information, and then maybe to the top of the hill that gave a long-range look into the wide valley that made up all of the countryside around the city of Fukuoka.

He had a crazy desire to see what damage the latest bombings had done to the area. If they started to walk now, they would be above the city just before sundown and have a good look with out too much trouble.

As they walked, each talked about the nice visit to the fishing village and the different types of people that made up the village. The fishermen, of course, and most important, the children and women. The women were all busy doing their chores with much visiting going on at the same time. It was a happy-looking place and they made plans to visit again soon.

The distance to the farm seemed much shorter to Barney than he had thought or remembered it being. Just as he had done the first time, after turning a sharp corner in the path they came to the place that had caused him his first real fright some months ago. As they moved past the front of the main house, an equally old man addressed them in the late-day greeting. Myoko responded without any hesitation and further stated what a nice day it had been, continuing on to say that she was taking her aged uncle for a walk to see the countryside, that he was from a small village near Kobe and his home was destroyed by airplanes. With no place to go and no one to look after him, she was glad to have him as company to help with her very small farm. There seemed to be a measure of sympathy in the old farmer and he asked them to have tea and dessert cookies with him. Barney stiffened at the thought of sitting with such an old man; really old men had a tendency to make serious observations as they talked and he was sure that he could not pass that kind of inspection. But Myoko bowed and said that they would be pleased and honored to share his house and refreshments, the good hot tea would make the ending of their day near perfect.

Barney could not crawl deep enough into his pulled down hat to satisfy himself, but he tried. As soon as the old man had set the tea to steeping, he and Myoko began a farmer's friendly conversation about how the weather was making this year's harvest one of the best that they could remember, and the different types of planting they had done and planned to do.

Then out of the blue, the farmer began to address his conversation toward Barney. He was somewhat puzzled by the answers that Barney gave but Myoko volunteered that her uncle was still suffering from the loss of his home and the effects of the big explosions. She further said that he had problems sorting out responses and questions, and found it difficult to have a meaningful conversation, even with her. "He understands, he just doesn't respond as easily as he would like."

They finished their tea and cookies, thanked the farmer for his special kindness and were about to take their leave when the old farmer said that he had something to share with them and went into his house. It took only a few moments and when he returned, he had a medium-sized package wrapped up in paper, which he handed to Barney. And as Barney had expected, the old man made every attempt to look up into Barney's face. Barney bowed even deeper than was the custom, thanking the farmer for his gift. The farmer then explained that he had become very hungry for fresh pork and had slaughtered one of his older pigs and had no way to keep all the meat and could not think of a better friend with whom to share it than another farmer, especially one with such beauty and who was so young. The farmer closed his comments by saying, "Myoko, you are like a new blossom in a beautiful flower garden, you refresh old memories of when I was also young."

As they walked toward the path in front of the farm, the farmer began to tell of the loss of all his children to the war and that his wife and only daughter had been visiting her sister and mother when a bombing took place, killing all of both families. He had been alone now for two years and was feeling the loneliness more in the past several months than at any other time. He further asked, "if your house isn't too far for me to walk, would I be welcome to visit with you and your uncle sometime and pass the day sharing our past history, and maybe give an extra hand with your farming?" Myoko looked deep into the old man's eyes and saw his pain and loneliness.

"My uncle and I would be very honored to have you visit us whenever you feel you can spare time away from your own farming. Our small farm is not as large or as grand as yours and my house is very small and not so nice, but it is ours. We hope to see you soon." Myoko, taking Barney's arm as if he needed to be led up to the path, thanked the old man again for the refreshments and especially the generous sharing of his meat.

Barney was about to come out of his skin with the invitation to the old man. How could they keep Barney's identity from the old man and would he, if he learned the secret, not tell others? After they had walked some distance from the farm, and before Barney could say a word, Myoko began to explain to Barney that as she looked into the old man's eyes and measured his wrinkled face, she had no way to say no to his request. "I saw deep down into the soul of that person and found the same pain that I was having with the loss of my husband. I only lost one person and that poor man now has no one. He lost sons and a daughter, his children, which in Japan is the whole future, and the most important reason for being. Barney, I couldn't say no because he needs you and me as much as we need each other. It will work out— for some good reason, I don't think we will have any trouble, we shall see." From the farmhouse to the top of the hill where they could see down into the valley and into Fukuoka was some thirty minutes walk. As they came to the top of the hill, the sight that lay before them made them gasp in awe. Stretched out below them was nothing but the burned destruction of a city that once had been homes and work places for thousands of people! Now there was nothing but rubble and blackness. The dock area, where Barney had so carefully photographed and counted the people, was no longer. Very few timbers and pilings could be seen and far to the north, the airbase could not be identified. The area to the south was out of their view but Barney was sure that the ship repair facility and the army base were equally devastated.

He tried to say something to Myoko but the tightness in his throat would not allow a word. Barney sensed the trembling through Myoko's body as he held her close. Finally, he said, "This is what happens when men stop talking to each other and feel that the only way anything can be accomplished is to go to war. I do not choose to blame the people of your country, but this same kind of destruction happened when Japan's military leaders decided to have war with my country and without any warning, bombed the Islands of Hawaii. I do not know if the leaders of Japan told all the people the truth about Pearl Harbor, but the Japanese Navy chose a Sunday morning to make their air strike against Hawaii and many military personnel and civilians were killed, just as the people down there were killed. It isn't fair to attempt to blame the average people of your country. But, the way Japan began this war made every person in America very angry and wanting a strong measure of revenge ...

"Let's not think or feel angry toward each other, but hope that out of all the carnage and destruction, a greater understanding and caring for each other will emerge. If each country honestly knew about the other and how much alike all the people are, the thought of killing each other would never happen again. At least let's hope so. Myoko, that is the one and only speech that you will ever hear me make about who's who and this terrible damned war." Taking her in his arms he said, "We have had a most interesting day, now let us go to the sand and the cooling waters of our private beach, make a small fire and think only of each other."

They turned back in the direction of their coming and walked hand in hand without thinking what it would look like to any one who might pass their way. The world was not all crazy or bad— at least their small private part of it wasn't. They found their beach as Barney had suggested, made a small fire in a protected cove of rocks, curled into each other's bodies and said nothing about the day's travel. What was there to say? Long after darkness, shedding their clothes, the two slipped into the frothy shallow breakers, sat down in the cool wetness and just held each other.

PART IV

Duty & Separation

June–October 1945

For a while, the whole world seemed to be just the two of them; no one passed by and they did not wander away from the immediate area. They worked as they chose and often went to the edge of the cliffs to watch the end of the day as it changed into darkness, and loved each other. Seldom did they see any American planes passing over.

The only disturbance was on a late evening after the work had been done. A group of twelve soldiers came marching down the path still looking for the missing soldier, at least that was their excuse for the visit. The leader, in a brisk and very demanding tone, told Myoko that the army had followed the travels of the soldier from his lookout station to as far as her farm. "No one has seen him past the fishing village. You told the other soldier who stopped by that you or your uncle had not seen anyone of his description passing on that specific day."

Again, Myoko said that they did not always pay attention to the people who might pass by. "We are always busy at our work trying to help grow food, because of the needs brought on by the war. My small farm isn't much but we try and help as much as we can. The person that you are asking about could have passed by our house and we did not notice his passing."

The tone of the leader became more demanding and he started to turn toward Barney for further conversation. As he did so, Myoko stepped in front of him and began to explain, "My uncle does not hear very well and because of being near bombings where he lived, he is much disoriented. I have a very difficult time trying to tell him what to do when he is helping me with the work. Please don't confuse him too much, for it will take many days for me to get him back to where I can help him."

The soldier leader looked at Barney's downward-turned, hat-covered face and gave a gruff retort that maybe her uncle would be better off if he had been killed, then he would not be a bother to anyone. The leader made a few more derogatory remarks and voiced more suspicions about the missing soldier, finally dismissing the effort to find him with the comment, "The no-good bastard must have deserted and is hiding in some big city, locked up with a whore, and maybe will get killed by a Yankee bomb." Then all twelve soldiers went on down the path.

It took Myoko and Barney the rest of the day to settle their nerves and attend to the necessary chores.

June 25

It was another few days before a visitor came their way, bringing what he thought was bad news when he told of the Americans invading an island that neither of them had heard of. The excitement was that the mainland of Japan had been invaded for the very first time in all of Japan's history and everyone would have to help defend their homeland. "In a few days," he said, "soldiers will come by and give you instructions as to how you should make preparations for the defense of our beloved country. Okinawa is only a few hundred miles from the Japanese mainland," he added; "the closest main island is this island. Kyushu will be the next most likely place for the Yankee dogs to defile our sacred land. You must be prepared," he yelled as he hurried down the path toward the fishing village.

For Barney the news was very sobering, for it meant that soon he could be among the people that meant so much to him, his people, American sailors. To Myoko the news was the sharpest pain that she had known since she learned of the death of her husband. Her first thought was about losing Barney, for he would surely return to his own country and family. The thought of foreign military taking over Japan did not matter to her much. She felt so far removed from the larger cities and villages, she imagined that no one would bother to deal with one little person on such a small farm. She was well aware of the present food shortages in the city and most other places, even the smaller villages were without the basic staples such as rice and, of course, cooking oil. It was only because her place was so small and the fishing village so remote that she was able to keep more than was permitted. If they had inspected her farm and learned of how much she was growing, and compared it to how much she reported, she would have been shot — and what would have happened to Barney? He would have the only loving friend he had found. *I care for him so much.*

June 28

No one came for several more days to tell them how and where they should help in the defense of her country. When two older men did arrive, their interest was in how much they could frighten them and what food they could take. Myoko and Barney pretended to be uninformed, and said that they were not aware of any armies coming to their part of the country. How were an old man and a widow supposed to chase away many armed soldiers, and with what? "All we have is a few old farm tools such as this almost worn-out cultivator," she said. "Do not try to frighten us; other soldiers have already done that when they came looking for one you lost, who most likely deserted anyway."

One of the soldiers said, "Within a few days some armed citizen-soldiers will come and have a meeting in the fishing village," pointing toward the small village that Myoko and Barney had visited. "They will give all the people instruction in the use of firearms and all other weapons such as grenades and high explosives. It may become necessary for people to turn themselves into human bombs, tying high explosives to their bodies and charging into the invading army — anything to kill the enemy. We must get to the village and inform the people there about their duty to the Emperor."

After they had gone and Barney next looked at Myoko, she was shaking her head in an uncontrolled fashion from side to side. Grasping her shoulder, he had to shake her very hard in order to bring her back to her senses; even then she was near hysterics. Barney sat her down and began to rub the back of her neck and talk to her very softly: "They cannot make you do those things if you are not here. If we must, when the time to really fight comes, we will disappear into the hills, or better yet, hide in my cave. You must go to the meeting and say that I am far too old to even hold a stick, let alone shoot a gun or throw a bomb. This way you will be able to keep track of the real danger and also, maybe learn the current news. We will wait until the home guard comes to tell us when to go to the meeting and then make final plans. I will not fight my own country's soldiers, nor will I kill any of your countrymen. And I don't think that you can kill anyone, regardless of what country they're from."

Myoko was able to give a small nod at the last comment that Barney made and then she said, "Barney, how can civilized human beings even think that way, just kill, kill, and more killing? Life comes very hard to all peoples, and to some harder than others. Why in all that is good on this earth, must some of us kill others? Surely, the world has not gotten that bad. Is it a matter of not caring?"

Barney helped Myoko to the open room where they both sat and stared into open space saying nothing. This was going to be a long and quiet night for both of them.

June 30

Two days later, just as the home guard soldiers had said, militia men in half-uniforms stopped to tell Myoko and Barney that a meeting was to be held the next day at 8:00 AM in the fishing village, and both of them must be there. Myoko took the opportunity to voice an objection for Barney, saying, "Can't you see this old man is so old and weak that he cannot walk to the top of that hill, let alone the mile or so to the village?" Barney was bending over and struggling with every movement as though it would be his last, and Myoko added, "He would die before we could walk 20 paces."

The senior soldier walked over to Barney and took him by the arm as though to turn him around. Barney took a quick, deep breath and fell sideways away from the soldier, and down on to the ground. As he hit the solid earth, Myoko let out a loud scream and yelled, "What do you expect from and old man who can't even stand up!"

One of the other members of the home guard let out a laugh and told the leader, "You must really be afraid of the Yankee dogs if you are going to send such a warrior to save Japan." The ribbing was all that was needed to let Barney lay where he had fallen and as they turned to depart, the leader yelled at Myoko, "If you are not at the meeting, we will send someone after you and it will not be pleasant, do you understand?"

After the men were out of sight, Barney rolled over in the dirt and laughed so hard that Myoko first thought he was having a breakdown or had gone completely crazy. As she bent down to help him up, Barney grabbed her around the waist and pulled her to the ground beside him. For a few brief seconds, they both enjoyed the deception that they had played on the soldiers. After getting up from the ground, Myoko commented, "Since we have been wallowing like swine, we should slip down to the beach and enjoy swimming and lying on the warm sand,"

The gleam in her eyes told Barney that just lying in the sand was not all that she had in mind, and off they went — an old, old man and a farm lady holding hands, appearing not as lovers, but demonstrating the aid one might give in helping an old, old man. Again they laughed together.

July 1

Early the next morning Myoko left for the village to attend the call-to-arms meeting and left Barney to his own tasks. He had mentioned that should they find the need to hide out, the cave would have to be enlarged and plans made for food, water and sleeping requirements. Myoko had some misgivings about living in the ground, but if that was Barney's choice, she would follow him. In her mind, she admitted that regardless of what

Barney did or wanted to do, she just wanted to be close to him and share each day as it came.

The trip to the fishing village took an hour, and as she entered the outskirts of the little serene place. She was again struck by its simple and quiet beauty. Set in a deep cove and protected from high seas and strong winds by the same steep cliffs that protected her own house, it painted one of the prettiest pictures that Myoko had ever seen.

Near the dock area, she found a large group of men, women and children all gathered around a dozen militarily-dressed older men who looked too old to do much of anything. Myoko only nodded the quiet respectful greeting typical of the Japanese and blended into the crowd.

After some minutes of milling around and trying to look important, one of the soldiers climbed up on an over-turned fishing boat and began shouting, in a most insecure voice, about the reason they had been ordered to the meeting. Then to everyone's surprise, the leader told them that all was not going well with the war and that the Americans were at this very moment, knocking at the door of Japan.

The Ryukyu Islands, he said, just a few hundred miles south of the island they were now standing on, had been invaded by thousands of Yankee murderers and this island — all of the home islands — would undoubtedly be next. "Our soldiers are fighting valiantly; many have paid the supreme sacrifice, and that is why we are here now," he went on.

Clearing his voice, and trying to sound more sure of himself, the soldier told them what the Emperor expected from each person. He said that men, women, and if necessary, the children must be ready to make the final sacrifice, just as the heroic soldiers of Okinawa. "This morning we are going to tell you about some examples of actions that can be used to defend our country.

"At the present time, we do not have enough guns to give to every small village such as yours. We will have a few sent to you and the men will be given instructions on how to use them. The main item for all your people will be to plant a device called a land mine in the suspected areas where the Yankee dogs might land. These cause a big explosion when run over or stepped on. This has proven to kill many of the invaders when used on some of the islands that were once Japan's.

"The last resort will be to tie grenades and high explosives on your body, as we are about to show you — killing as many of the enemy as you can. This will mean great glory for you in the hereafter world. It will also bring much honor to you family. Now all of the men will go with this man," pointing to one of the other soldiers. "Women and children, come close to me so that I can show you how to attach the grenade and also wrap the explosives on your bodies so that you will have the best success."

The instructions were simple and when the women's instructions were completed, they were told that they must register their names and where they lived so should an alarm come, they could be found without any delay. Then they were dismissed.

All the way back to her house, Myoko cried streams of tears and felt mountains of pain. How could they ask small children to tie bombs around their little bodies, run into an army of soldiers who were shooting many bullets, throwing explosives all around... How could they? she asked herself. For the very first time she also asked, Isn't there a real God, one who cares about all people, especially the children?

When she returned to her house, Barney was not to be found. Myoko moved about the house as if drugged, mumbling to herself, "Why should I work in the fields if it's all going to be destroyed? Why should I try to find peace? Why should I love and care for Barney if we are all going to be made into human bombs and be foolishly killed, and for what? Japan cannot defend a small island like whatever that island was called."

She felt she was at the lowest point of her life, lower than when she learned of her husband's death, and could not find a way to regain her joyful spirits, when Barney walked up the path from the beach toward her and the house. Myoko could not move from the wooden bench; she just sat there numb and totally confused with all that had happened to her this day.

Even as Barney knelt before her and took her hands, she still could not move. It took her an hour to explain the events of the meeting that morning and what they had asked all the people to do, and she closed with a deep hurting sob, "Barney I just cannot do it. All I can see is little children being blown apart

and the children are all that Japan has left to carry on all that is meaningful to the people of Japan. If we are to sacrifice the young, even the very young, there is no need to survive and there is no hope for any future, any future at all."

Barney was at a complete loss to try and find an answer for her distraught emotions. All he could say was, "They can't kill all of us. Some must be left to bury those that are killed and I want to be part of those who survive." Then Barney remembered the clan history of the Hatfields and the McCoys who lived in the back country of a mountainous region in America. Barney then related to Myoko that the two families almost killed each other off: "However, two of the living changed the history of both clans. A McCoy fell in love with a Hatfield, I do not remember which one was which, but in the end their love for each other and their families was so strong that they were able to show all the remaining families how foolish their fighting had been, and how terrible the waste of lives. The fighting and killing stopped and a reasonable peace settled over the mountains. This is what I think will happen with our countries. The war will end soon and we will help each other to insure a long and true peace for everyone. We must believe this or, as you have said, what's the use of living?"

They talked long into the night and finally decided exactly what they would do should the plans of the militia become real.

July 2

All the next day, the two of them began to gather the items that they would need if they were to hide out in the cave. The day before, while Myoko was attending the village meeting, Barney had dug deep into the cliff side and enlarged the cave considerably, making sort of a sleeping place for both of them. To one side, out of sight of the opening of the cave so no one could see if a fire was burning, he created a small cooking area and a place to store all their survival items: cooking pot, cooking pans and the buckets that he had stolen from the fishermen.

He had also made a special place for the fire pot that Myoko cooked on. Dry firewood was plentiful on the beach and if they fished late in the evening and gathered wood at the same time, all they had to worry about was the other foods that they would need to stay alive. When he told Myoko what he had done during her absence, she only shrugged and said that it seemed like a nice place to be buried in.

When all the items were gathered together, they waited until it was almost dark before taking the first items to the cave. When Myoko saw the improvements that Barney had made and how much more room they would have, she commented that maybe they could just live there forever and to hell with the rest of the world. It took them just a few minutes to put the items in the places where they would be used, and then Barney led her down the path to the beach. *This,* he thought, *is where we seem to be completely removed from all the troubles of the world and maybe Myoko will rekindle some of her good feelings, or be able to sort out the good from the bad, and hopefully feel better.* They made a small fire near the base of the cliff and held tightly to each other until the chill of the late night brought on the shivers to both of them. Putting out the last remaining coals from the fire, they returned to the house and slept exactly the same way, held close to each other.

The next day, Barney realized he had not paid much attention to the calendar, the only reason for concern having been the harvesting of the crops he and Myoko had planted and which they would need if they chose to hide out. As he asked Myoko about food that would be available and the spoilage, he noted that the fourth of July would occur on the following day. He sat crunched up on the beach and began to reflect on all that the great day of independence stood for in America. Many other parts of the free world are aware of the value and meaning of real independence. *All Americans are reminded of the value of that freedom and what it had cost before Pearl Harbor and the many lives it was costing now,* he thought. Now, here, removed from being a part of the onslaught for final victory caused him to reweigh why he had been sent to this part of the enemy's home ground. He felt so useless, that what he had tried to accomplish for the war effort was a total loss and most likely had been a crazy plan from the beginning.

Myoko noticed the far away look in Barney's eyes and asked if he was still with her. In reply, he said, I've been thinking about a very special holiday that belongs only to America. It's the day that America won and declared its total independence from England. Americans cherish this day above all others because it is the day of the foundation of all our freedoms, liberties and rights, and as the American Constitution says, 'justice for all.' Some Americans argue that there are people in America who do not have equal rights and justice under this system and, in some cases, they may be right ...

"The freedom that you have spoken about not having here in Japan will be very affected by the outcome of this war. I do not know how Japan will be governed when it's over, but if America wins you can be assured that the people of Japan will have much more freedom and many more rights than they have ever had before. One of these days when we are hiding in the cave I will tell you about some of the history that brought about the Constitution and how it was fought for, just as it is being done again now."

Barney told Myoko that they must make a list of all the foodstuffs, where they were to come from and when, such as the time of ripening of the rice, so it could be harvested and stored in a safe dry place, also the sweet potatoes and cabbage. "We must be prepared to hide for at least two months to make sure that all the conflict has passed us by and it's safe to contact the American soldiers. All will be safe for everyone then. The Americans will treat everyone with equal concern and care." But there was an absolute blank expression on Myoko's face in response to all Barney had said would happen in Japan.

Myoko, following Barney's suggestion to make a list of their food needs, went inside the house and returned with several pieces of thin paper and an ink brush. Then almost in defiance of Barney's comment to list the needed foods, began drawing pictures of the foods. Barney could understand the language very well but he could not read all their written symbols. But as he watched, a slow smile crossed his face. Myoko was regaining her humorous and subtle expression. When the list was finished, Barney asked which should be served first, this drawing or that one? This broke the tense mood that had overshadowed them as Barney was telling her about liberty and justice.

July 4, 1945

Early that day, Barney asked Myoko if she would please help him to celebrate the true meaning of freedom and liberty. He said that all he wanted to do was stand on the edge of the cliffs, look reverently out to sea and be thankful for all that they had, even under their present circumstances. This they did, walking to the northernmost stands of bamboo. Barney held Myoko's hands and quietly gave thanks for the closeness of this person standing beside him, and that so far he had been able to stay free from capture. Most of all he was thankful that the horrible conflict that had been going on for years was about to end. His ending comment was, "We just want to live in peace." Myoko then lead Barney away from the cliff and up the main path that took them back to her house. Her only words were, "I think that I could really enjoy your kind of world, especially the freedoms and liberties that you have talked about. It would be nice to have even a small part of what you said, here in Japan."

Over the next four weeks, they went about the business of making woven baskets for the storage of the vegetables they would harvest. No one came to tell them of any preparations for an invasion, and the anger in Myoko's heart slowly diminished. But they were greatly puzzled that no one had called Myoko to the village for further instructions in the defense of the Japanese homeland. They had decided that when the call came, Myoko would place a large sign on her house saying that she was taking her dead uncle's body back to his home for the customary Japanese funeral, and then they would disappear to Barney's cave until everything was over or they were dead.

August 4

That morning, Myoko arose early and informed Barney that she could not stand not knowing what was happening. She was going to the village to learn all she could and to try to find out if the home guard was doing anything about plans to make all the people into living bombs. Barney wanted to go with her but Myoko said that he would be out of place, as everyone considered him too old and not able to be part of any serious planning. She hoped to be back by noon and would try to buy some needed staples such as flour, if any was available, and maybe some local shrimp for their dinner.

Barney knew that the thought of children being laced to a grenade or other explosives and made into living bombs was eating at her heart. He had, in the short time that he had been in Japan, learned that all children in the Japanese culture were considered the most valued asset in the family and as such, the children looked at the adults with great respect and obedience. He knew that to Myoko, to throw the children into the wind where they would be gone forever would kill all the deep family ties, and that all that was important to those who remained would be gone forever... Nothing that was truly Japanese would exist. Because of his love for Myoko, Barney had an almost equally pained feeling for the children, should such a drastic event take place. All he could do was express his deepest sympathy and comment that in no place on earth should any child be made to pay the ultimate penalty for the sake of a few more days of a lost war, and, that God would surly punish those who made such demands.

Myoko dressed in her best peasant-like clothes, carried a basket of woven bamboo on each arm, walked to the top of the small hill and disappeared beyond. Barney sulked about the small house trying to choose some effort that would keep his mind off Myoko's absence and still be useful while she was gone. There were always many items to be done in the fields; the rice was soon to be harvested and the weeding in the sweet potatoes was a little behind, but Barney wanted something that would give him a measure of pleasure while still making a needed contribution. The only real item left that would allow him a desirable choice was the surf and a fishing pole. He knew that he had become sloppy in his effort to look like an old man. One could never tell when someone might be watching. So, he reviewed the steps that he and Myoko had gone through so many times and departed to the cliff on the trail that led down to the beach. It was the farthest away from his cave, which was going to be their hiding place should the home guard decide to make soldiers of everyone.

This spot was the quietest of all the cliff beaches and offered the best opportunity to catch larger fish. At the moment, he could not define the need to have a conference with himself but there was a gnawing notion that he had to think seriously about the near future and what he could do to keep Myoko. At the bottom of the cliff, he found the cluster of rocks beside which he and Myoko had built small fires and spent several special evenings talking and being close to each other. Placing bait on his hook and coiling the line in large loops, he hand-cast the line out into the surf as far as he could, then set the pole against the rocks so that even the largest fish could not drag the pole into the water. He sat down in the warm sand to take in the view and absorb the tranquility of all that he surveyed. To his right, and about halfway to the horizon, was a group of small fishing boats. He wondered if the boats could be from the village that Myoko was now visiting and if they were catching any quantity of fish. To his left, the southern direction and toward the village, as far as he could see, was a placid and blue ocean. This was special all right, a place that would let him think about the situation he was in, better than any other that he knew. He watched his fishing line sway back and forth as the slight waves caught the line and moved it with the changing flow of the tide.

Regardless of the lack of information about the ending of the fighting and an obvious end to the war, the thought that was bothering Barney the most was how to hold on to Myoko when everything was peaceful again. His thoughts led him back to the reason that he had come to be here in the first place and what had happened to the submarine that was to pick him up. All of a sudden, Barney had more what ifs than he had had when he first landed in this part of the world. The one what ifthat he had not thought of was how he would get out of his present state of hiding and explain to whomever his rescuers were what had happened to him in the past ten months. Most of all, how would he explain his involvement with a Japanese woman — one whom, in a sense, he had helped to grow food that had helped to feed the Japanese military, or at least Japanese people — those who built weapons.... made bullets... and killed his own countrymen...? It had been too many days, weeks and even months since he had given any thought to "his country."

Now for the first time a great feeling of longing and a whole wave of new loneliness came over him. It was partly due to missing his own people, and partly to feeling that he had not done all that he should have done to fulfill his responsibility to his shipmates and country. He had been sitting in this isolated place thinking only of not being caught, feeding himself and in a strong sense of the word, living a much dreamed-about existence — with a most loving and caring enemy anyone could hope for, or be captured by... but an enemy of his country.

At least an hour had gone by as all these thoughts passed through his mind, and only because the fishing line suddenly gave a strong surge did his attention turn back to the fishing. His first catch for the day was a nice surf perch of about four pounds, one of the largest fish that he had caught. He placed the fish on a stringer and rebaited his hook. Barney repeated the cast and sat down to wait for another fish.

The next reflection that caused him concern was their meeting, and why Myoko had been so kind to him instead of turning him over to the soldiers or the police. Just what kind of a person was she? What was the hurt, and even the hate, that dwelled deep inside her? A hate that would in a sense cause her not to obey the laws of her deeply wounded country? The little that Barney knew about the total dedication of all the Japanese people was death before dishonor. Did that apply to women also? Myoko had had no children. She was too young to have children who could have served in the war and been killed, but she had lost her husband. Did this lady for whom he felt so much have a deeper anger than he was aware of — one which caused her to choose as she had? Regardless of whatever it was, Barney was most grateful — because without her, he surely would not be alive. Within the next hour Barney caught three smaller fish, cleaned them in the surf, then just leaned back against the big rocks and enjoyed the sun.

It was near noon when from the south, and far out on the horizon, a dot appeared that caused Barney to pay extra attention. Even at that extreme distance, he could make out the silhouette of a fighting ship with its tall pagoda superstructure and a great volume of smoke streaming from it. The ship was obviously on fire. It had to be a survivor from some close battle or it would not still be burning, and where was it headed for? The shipyard south of Fukuoka, no doubt. When the ship was close enough to identify Barney concluded that it had been a medium-sized cruiser, and from what he could see it had been blown to pieces on the topside, and was listing 30 degrees to starboard. As it struggled past his position, Barney could see small numbers of men scurrying about the ship still fighting the fires.

It took about 45 minutes for the ship to pass out of Barney's sight and the event only added to his sad feelings. Even though the ship was Japanese, it was still men killing other men, and there had to be a large number of dead human beings blown apart on what was left of the ship. Again, why did he feel that way? He should feel some measure of victory in that another enemy ship had been beaten in battle, that more of the enemy were dead and could not kill again, and that the war was just that much closer to being over. Barney did feel glad about the event, but he also felt hurt that men did such devastating things to each other. Then of course, whoever had done the destruction to this ship surely could have been hurt just as badly... and these people were his people. Some of them had to have been killed, and the ship possibly rendered as helpless as the one he had just seen. This only deepened the remorse that Barney felt.

The noon hour was at hand and Barney wanted to be near the house when Myoko returned. Then he could learn what was new with the plans to mobilize all the local people and maybe some news of the progress of the war as well. And he wanted to tell Myoko of seeing the Japanese cruiser that had passed by. He just wanted to have her close and safe at his side when so many unknowns were going on. Barney smiled at himself. He wanted to be with Myoko regardless of the reason.

There is a saying among the men who go to sea in ships that concerns weather: Red sun in the morning, sailor take warning. Red sun at night, sailors delight. That early evening was another one of God's masterworks of many colors. Barney and Myoko had sat on the beach and enjoyed many very beautiful evenings and some of the most glorious sunsets that either of them had ever seen. For whatever reason, the master painter felt that He would outdo all His past efforts and paint a new, a very special composition with colors that He had never used before.

Barney paced from one side of the cliff to the house wondering what had happened to Myoko. She said that she would be back no later than one o'clock and it was now evening. He had considered all the worst things that could have happened to her and now he was in a complete frenzy within himself. He had become so engrossed in her absence that he no longer thought about his own safety or exposure to any passersby. He was not thinking about anything but Myoko, so sailors delight was not the frame of mind he was in presently. He remembered a rock pile that was at the northern end of Myoko's upper paddy. He could see over the hill to the south farther if he sat atop the pile and looked in that direction.

Another hour passed and as the last details of the landscape were fading into darkness, he saw a shadowed outline of someone coming up the path. The figure was very close to him before he knew that it was Myoko. He almost fell from his sitting position as he hurried to meet her. His fear and concern, plus a great measure of self-anger, must have shown on Barney's face and in his actions, for Myoko took several steps backward as though to ward off the onrushing man. Without any hesitation he folded her into his arms and held her hard against his body, saying "I thought that you were gone from me forever and that I would never see you again. You were gone so long and you said that you would be back near noon. What happened to you?"

The onrush of questions and Barney's explosion of concern overwhelmed Myoko and she asked him if she could please sit down before she tried to respond to all his questions. Slowly she said that she was most happy that he had missed her and that nothing bad had happened to her in the village.

Myoko said that shortly after she arrived there, a home guard person came and began an open discussion about the state of the war and the effects that it was bound to have on all peoples of Japan. He said that the Island of Okinawa was now in the hands of the Americans and that most of the Japanese soldiers had fought to the last man and had given great honor to the Emperor and Japan, but that now was the time to start thinking about what each of them must do to save their country from imminent capture. He talked about the meetings by the home guard and that in fact everyone from a small village such as theirs would be taken to one of the likely invasion places, armed or shown how to turn themselves into human bombs, much like their glorious kamikaze pilots. He stressed that all Japanese people must be prepared to sacrifice themselves when the time came. "One thing that this guard person said that caused me great fear was that the invaders would rape and kill all the women and children, showing no mercy to anyone.

"Barney, in your own words, you said that if any American was known to do such things, he would be charged for his crimes and possibly put to death. You also said looting or taking of private property, or causing any kind of harm to the civilians would be punishable, and that the person caught doing such things was sure to be put in prison. Say it again to me. I need to hear you make me sure that this is so, because the man in the village gave such a strong and sure picture of what we could expect. He said that the Americans would rape, kill and eat the children. It frightened everyone so much that they are ready to do as the authorities ask."

Barney repeated, with all the feelings that he could muster, his assurance that no one would even scratch the skin of any civilian as long as they were not involved in any part of the fighting. All civilians would be removed far away from any part of the danger and taken good care of. All would be given medical attention, hot food if available, and a temporary place to rest and sleep. The children would receive special attention and be kept with their respective families. When their home areas had been made safe, all of the people would be allowed to return and begin to start rebuilding their own normal lives — if one could call anything normal after such a horrible war experience. "I promise you and everyone else that no harm will come to anyone who is not involved in the fighting."

Then Myoko continued to explain to him about the rest of her day. When the home guard man left, most of the women gathered at the fishing pier and began to discuss all that they had heard.

"Barney, I feel that maybe I did a bad thing at this meeting. I could not just be quiet and say nothing. Long into the meeting, I stood up and slowly explained about my husband and that he had died on a small island fighting for the Japan that he loved so much. I further said that I had read about other wars that the Americans had fought in and in no instance had any American been known to do the things that the home guard soldier had said. I also said that I could not believe anyone could do to the children the things he said. Some of the other women became very angry with me and even shoved me with great anger. When most of the shouting had diminished, I again began to ask one lady at a time, if she really felt that any human being could shoot, cut in half or bash with a club, her small child.

"I asked each one to please look inside of herself and ask if she could imagine such a thing. Americans are known throughout the world for their love and kindness, especially toward children. This I have read in many noted books and lectures at school. We cannot believe all that the home guard person told us. Barney in the end, I feel that I made a good impression on most of the women, but there were several that may report me to the police. It is good for us that the village has no police and anyone who wants to make such a report must go to the city or write a letter. Anyway, it was most frightening.

"After the meeting, several of the younger women asked me about what I had learned at the university and was it hard for women to get into such a school? When most of the women who had objected to my statement about the Americans, had left so that they could not hear any further discussions, the remaining women wanted to know what I intended to do about my own children. Some felt sorry for me because I had no children, but asked if things became so bad as to turning children into living bombs, would I help hide the smallest of their children in some safe place. It seemed that they were willing to sacrifice their own lives for Japan but not the lives of their children. The only thing that I could say, Barney, was that when the time came, we could make such a decision. All of these things, plus a small amount of shopping for a few remaining bits of food, are the reasons why it took me so long. I am sorry that you became so upset with me. Now can we go to the house and make dinner? I am so hungry."

As Myoko prepared dinner, she seemed far removed from the task. She was slow in the cleaning of the vegetables and as she began to place them in the steaming basket, it seemed to Barney that she was not sure that was what she wanted to do. There was a constant wash of tears slowly flooding her beautiful, but very hurt face. Barney thought that perhaps, added to the cause of her sadness, might be distress at having caused him concern because of the long time she had been in the village. He was sure that later would be a better time to ask her.

As she began to serve the meal, she spilled the soup on the small table and began to cry with uncontrollable, deep shaking. Taking her hand and pulling her close he said, "Something different and frightening happened to you today while you were in the village didn't it? In the very short time that we have been close to each other, we have always been open and shared our feelings and thoughts. Now it is more important than ever. Myoko, we must work harder to survive and try, if it's possible, to make a future for ourselves. If we can hold ourselves together then we can surely have a very strong and long future. Right now, holding you close to me, I can sense a hurt and pain in you that I have never felt before."

It took some time for Myoko to settle down enough for her to even begin to speak. When she did, all that she could say was, "the children, the children, they are going to waste, no, throw away all the children and for no reason at all. Barney, if you could have seen the anger and fear on the faces of the mothers in that small village and known that something was going to happen to all the mothers in Japan. It hurts so much knowing what will happen to them, it's the children. If there is truly a God such as you have told me, he cannot let such a thing happen to these small, unknowing children." As she finished, Barney had tears running down each cheek and onto his shirt. For the first time in all his life he felt completely helpless, and all he could do was hold onto Myoko and share her grief. Warm, late night darkness closed around them as they sat, saying nothing.

From August 4nd thru August 10th, it seemed that everything around them stood still. No one came by on the path and even the small fishing boats that could usually be seen close to the shore were missing. It was as if Myoko and Barney were the only two people on the planet.

August 12,1945

Several days later, a lone home guard soldier came riding a most worn-out horse. He stopped next to Myoko and in deep sobs, told them that a great firebomb had been dropped on each of the cities of Hiroshima and Nagasaki, completely wiping them from the whole of the earth. Many people had been killed, if not all of them. Hundreds of them simply disappeared as though they had never been there. No buildings stood for miles around, and on the outskirts of the towns, every building had much damage. It seemed that the end of Japan was near. "No one can fight against such a vast and horrible weapon, no one. I was sent to tell all that the world as we have known it for hundreds of years is coming to an end and everyone must be prepared to bow to the American Yankee dogs, who will undoubtedly be here soon." Off he went toward the fishing village to inform them of the sad news that Japan was doomed.

For the remainder of the day Myoko and Barney said very little about the statement made by the soldier. Both seemed to have feelings that they wanted to share with each othe and yet, there was something in the changes of events that caused them to hold their thoughts within themselves.

As late afternoon began to drape long dark shadows across the landscape, Myoko asked if they could once again go down to their special beach, catch fresh fish and have their dinner on the sand. At this time of the year the weather was slightly humid and warm late into the night and most comfortable for swimming or just splashing around in the surf. Myoko took one of the baskets that they had woven from thin strips of green bamboo and placed several vegetables in it, along with a large bowl of fresh steamed rice, then handed Barney the metal teapot. It seemed to Barney that almost like magic, Myoko always had a pot of fresh cooked rice available.

This day had become perplexing ever since the soldier had come by. As they gathered the items for the beach, things that they had done before seemed hazy and almost unplanned.

Barney gathered his share of their needs for the evening; he rolled up one of the tatami mats and a soft handmade blanket from the outside room. Several times they had stayed late into the night, and often were chilled from unexpected weather changes.

Myoko carried the basket in her right hand while Barney carried the cooking pot and teapot in his left hand, with the mat and blanket slung over his shoulder. They walked down the path leading to the hidden beach holding onto each other with their free hands. It had been several days since they had enjoyed the outdoor experience and the feeling of being free from all the world's troubles, protected in their own small world without the intrusion of war. The enthusiasm of this freedom brought the first smiles that they had passed to each other in a while.

At the bottom of the cliff the tides of the past days had washed the sand from the rocks highest on the beach, which made for careful stepping as they made their way to the clean sand farthest down the beach. Once before, the first time they visited this beach, they found this same spot and stayed the night held close in each other's arms. Barney had a slight flush of color as he remembered swimming in the salt water and making love in the sand. How he cared for this wonderful, soft-spoken, beautiful person!

Barney pulled some mussels from the rocks for bait and placed the sticky globs on the hooks, casting them far out into the back of the boiling surf. He set the two poles into rocks so that any fish that happened to hook itself would not pull the poles into the water. Barney walked down the sandy beach picking up dry wood for a small non-smoking fire. The beach was littered with all kinds of wood but the driest hard pieces were not that easy to find. After he had his arms full he walked back toward Myoko feasting on the grandeur of the evening and the slowly setting sun. Just as he came to Myoko he was overcome with the feeling: if our world could only stay this peaceful and this beautiful, and if only we, Myoko and I, could stay with each other like this forever.

The fish seemed to share the expectations of the evening, and it took less than a half-hour to catch more than enough very delicious fish for dinner. Dinner was slow, drawn out, to make it last as long as possible.

Instead of swimming, they walked up and down the sand commenting about the strange feeling of the new peace. Then Myoko sent Barney's mind reeling as she began to tell him what she thought would now happen to them. Myoko had begun by saying that regardless of their love and caring for each other, the Japanese culture would make it impossible for them to marry and live together. "We have talked about the many differences between our two cultures, and that your own people frown upon a marriage such as ours. We would be locked out of each other's families, and living without the strong ties and strengths of family relationships would be near impossible for me. To me, family is everything — it is the bonding of all family members that allows people to survive and have meaning in their lives from one generation to another. It is a must in any relationship."

As they walked down the beach, Barney was at a loss to make a response of any kind to Myoko's statements. In his own mind he knew many of the concerns that she had stated would be true. Before he enlisted in the Navy, he had seen how most mixed marriages were treated and he knew that he would never be able to stand up to such treatment directed toward his Myoko. He thought about their living where she now lived and it did not seem unreal to him.

Everything was buzzing around in his head so fast that he was finding it impossible to concentrate on any one part of what Myoko was saying. As they reached the southern most part of the beach, where the giant bamboo clusters came down to the sand, he asked if they could sit in the darkness of the bamboo and think about the future, until there was a sure direction and some formal announcement of the end of the war.

Sitting on the sand with their backs leaning against the bottom of the cliff, he began to tell her of the parts of her statements that he thought were correct, then to explain to her what he felt would be the kind of life they would have if they lived in his country, and that he could never stand seeing her mistreated in any way. Barney further said, "People all over the world can be very cruel to each other and when it involves differences of race, it becomes very bad. People do not remember, or think, that they are just plain human beings — they are always trying to be, or make themselves into, something they are not. If we could be just that, human beings, and treat each other as such, the world would not see hatred and destruction such as this war has forced upon the whole world."

Barney admitted to Myoko that he had had biases toward many other people, and had felt very bitter toward the Japanese for the starting of the war. "But being here, the way I am now, hiding and not being able to be open — just observing the many interesting ways of the Japanese people in secret — I can see that the war was not of their doing, or of their choice."

They talked like this far into the night, and only when the night turned cool did they walk back to their cold fire and blanket. Myoko asked Barney to remake the fire. She placed the pot over the new fire and added some of her choice tea. Barney placed the mat next to a large boulder and sat leaning against it, looking out into the darkened surf and cooling night. Myoko brought the tea and Barney gently pulled her down to the mat so that she sat between his outstretched legs, with her back tightly snuggled against his chest. He placed his arms around her and they drank the hot refreshing tea without further comment.

August 15

Several days passed without any changes in their daily routine, but a deep emotional struggle was taking place within each of them. For Myoko, it was the hurt and the feeling of loneliness that she had known after her now-dead husband had been forced into the Japanese army. It also was the bitter hate she could not dispel after learning of his death. Many of the same feelings were beginning to return as she realized that once again she was about to lose a person who had come to mean so much in her life — a man out of the sea who had replaced much of her desire to live. A most unlikely person had shown her a love and tenderness like that she had read about in books. Yet she found it impossible to tell Barney of this emotion. She frowned; not speaking was the way a Japanese woman was expected to act.

Barney's sight became blurred before tears began to run down his face. He was caught between the most beautiful and demanding emotions of his young life and a deeply committed responsibility to the Navy and, more importantly, to his country. The latter, there was no way he could deny. He knew that he would have to find the U.S. military forces and make all the facts known about his presence in Japan and what he had been doing for the many months after he was supposed to have been retrieved by the submarine. Again, there was no question about what he had to do to rejoin the U.S. Navy. But ... Myoko, his Myoko! Barney knew that he could not have escaped capture without her being involved in his desire not to be caught. She had provided the hair for his beard, shown him how to walk and act like an old, old Japanese farmer, taught him to understand many of the real customs and ways of the everyday people of her country— and he hadn't even gotten to the love that this woman had shown and shared with him. Myoko was a part of his being, she was what made all the beautiful colors of the setting sun so bright and make the cool of the night so warm. There was no part of Barney's flesh that did not tingle at just the thought of her presence. There had to be a way to make sure she would be a permanent part of his life.

Early the next day, a U.S. army jeep with four soldiers came crawling up the path toward where Myoko and Barney were working in the sweet potato paddy. Barney bent over to make sure his stance was that of the oldest farmer in all of Japan and slowly moved away from the edge of the path to the opposite side of the paddy. He was not ready to make his presence known to anyone yet.

One of the soldiers spoke good Japanese and asked all the questions — mostly who and how many lived there, and where the path led to. Myoko answered all the questions and at no time did any of the soldiers make reference to the old man working in the field. To Myoko's surprise, they asked if she needed anything like food or medicine. After they had departed down the path toward the fishing village, Barney asked Myoko about the questions and her answers. Myoko's response was that they seemed very pleasant and did not in any way seem angry or belligerent toward her. She seemed very surprised and wanted to know if all Americans were that respectful. Barney almost laughed and assured her that the vast majority were and besides, he assured her, "They had strict orders to represent the United States of America in the very best way — but still, as hard as most of them try, there are always a few bad ones, just as the soldier that lies buried in the paddy at our feet." It was the first time that either of them had mentioned the dead Japanese soldier and it caused a ripple of fear in both of them.

Late that night, Barney explained that he had made up his mind about how and when he would seek out the proper authorities to explain his presence and how he came to be in Japan. He said that he could not tell just anyone, for he was sure that the U.S. Army would not be concerned about his story as much as the U.S. Navy would be. Besides, he was a sailor and wanted to tell it to the right people. "I will leave early in the morning and be in Fukuoka by late evening. That's the easy part," he stated. "The hard part is what will happen and how I will be able to return to you and let you know what they will do with me. At this time, I cannot make any real promises to you, Myoko. But as long as I have a breath of air in me, somehow, sometime, I will be back to get you to be with you."

With her head bowed very low, Myoko said softly, "Something inside of me tells me that it will not be as you say it's going to be. I feel that we will never see each other again. I will simply stay here and do as I have been doing since my husband was taken away and killed. If you really mean your promise, and want to be with me, I will be here working just as you found me, looking like the old farmer tending the small farm, longing for the person who touched deep inside of me and allowed me to feel like living again. You must keep your word to me Barney; it is all that I will have to hold onto. It will be my prayer every day."

The next day, as planned, as the sun began to show its first glow, Barney and Myoko stood in the short path that led from her house to the wider path that would take him north to an unknown reception. They held onto each other briefly. Then Barney, because he no longer cared who might see them, very gently kissed each cheek to wipe away her small tears. He then gave Myoko a long lingering kiss on the lips saying, "That was long because it was two kisses in one; one for saying a short goodbye, and the other for the soon hello. I will not be gone any longer than I have to." He turned and began his walk to the north.

As he guessed, it took Barney all day to arrive at the outskirts of Fukuoka. He stood on the same hill overlooking the far city, just as he had many months ago as he had begun the survey. This time there was a new anxiety to his heartbeat. The war was over and below him, he could see many military vehicles moving about. There were several dozen war ships anchored in the inner harbor. The only ship that he could see at dockside was a well-marked hospital ship with its giant red cross painted on the top deck and the sides. The scene was so different from the earlier one, on his first visit.

Barney's presence on the streets seemed not to attract anyone. The streets had a surprising number of Japanese men and women moving about in the all-but-destroyed city. Scattered along random corners and in the more open spaces were small groups of armed U.S. soldiers. Most of the soldiers had a patch on their shoulder with a gold shield, a slash diagonally across the shield, and a black horse's head in the lower right half of the shield. All of them seemed relaxed and unconcerned about any aspect of the people or the town's happenings.

Barney had come to the conclusion that he had to find a U.S. Navy group to try and explain his situation to, and the most logical place would be near the harbor. As he moved toward his destination, he observed that several of the few remaining buildings that hadn't been blown to smithereens had American flags flying from makeshift poles. Other poles were attached to buildings at an angle so that, hanging downward, they displayed all their colors. As Barney stood looking at the American flags flying, the most overwhelming emotions that he had felt in a long time caused giant tears to form. *This is my country's flag. I have missed seeing it for far too long.*

Near the dock area the activity picked up. Many Japanese men were busy carrying boxes, and in some cases, sacks of material. The material turned out to be large quantities of food supplies coming out of several cargo ships moored to the dock. As each Japanese lifted a sack or box, an American soldier would indicate the truck he should take it to. Where the truck went to when loaded was only a guess but Barney could not help but think that much of the supplies were being shipped in to feed the near-starving population of all Japan. Regardless of the food destination, the thought that America cared for the people of Japan enough to make sure hunger would no longer be a major problem made Barney swell with renewed pride in his country.

At the far northern end of the dock was a new prefabricated building, the kind that the Navy Seabees were noted for. *This has to be some sort of Navy responsibility,* thought Barney, and he headed in that direction. Still sporting all the trappings of his Japanese disguise — clothes, woven bamboo hat that covered almost all of his face, and long thin stringy beard — he walked up to the door of the new building. Inside, sitting at desks with a half-full coffee pot near at hand, were two Navy enlisted men. Barney had not spoken English in so many months that for a few moments he had to rethink just how to say the words that he had rehearsed in his mind all morning: I am an American sailor, I was sent here to Japan many months ago to gather information and was stranded. Will you please help me?

As he stated the words, the two very surprised men looked at each other, both showing doubt and an expression of don't bother me with your problems. Then Barney asked if they could direct him to the Navy Intelligence person or the Shore Patrol.

His direct mention of Navy Intelligence caused a closer look by the two men and they asked Barney enough questions to satisfy them that her was an American. One of them started to give him directions to another Navy office, then hesitated and said that it might be best if they called the officer in charge of the dock operations to obtain some better instructions. After several attempts to make a call, a conversation took place over the phone and Barney was informed that a jeep would come and take him to the correct place. Barney could not avoid the feeling that all was not good with the instructions the enlisted man had been given over the phone.

The offer of a cup of coffee distracted his thoughts and even though he had often dreamed of the taste of coffee, the first swallow was almost bitter, after having had nothing but tea for so many months. It took the total amount of the cup to bring back the most cherished flavor enjoyed by all who sailed the seas. The second cup tasted even better.

It was at least half an hour before a jeep with three burly-looking men wearing SP badges came sliding up to the building. The one in the passenger seat jumped out first and in a belligerent tone of voice asked, "Where's the bastard who thinks he's an American sailor?" The look on his face was one of intolerance and disbelief.

Looking down at Barney still holding the now empty coffee cup, he asked, "Where did you get the stupid idea that you could be a sailor, let alone an American? All you dumb gooks think that you can con special privileges out of the easy-going Americans and that you had nothing to do with starting the war." Without slowing down, the shore patrolmen raved on as to how many of his friends and buddies had been killed and wounded by such assholes as he (Barney) was, and that the best place for such as him would be a firing squad. Barney's only thought was that this jerk was one of the few bad Americans that he had compared the Jap soldier to, and he had the same feeling now that he had then.

Barney asked in his calmest tone to be directed to the nearest Navy officer of the highest rank so that he could report the shore patrolman's behavior.

The other two shore patrolmen began laughing at Barney's response and, calling the offensive sailor by name, said, "You had better do as he says, he just might be one of the people that CID and Navy Intelligence is looking for. They dumped a few special information-gathering guys in here a long time ago and so far none of them have shown up. He could be one of them and usually they're officers, so your ass will be in one big jam."

After being all but shoved into the jeep, Barney was driven for what seemed like an hour before they stopped in the area of the air base that Barney had so carefully mapped and recorded. The gruff and unhappy sailor grabbed Barney by the sleeve and collar, shoved him through two broken glass doors and into a room filled with Navy men of just about every rate and rank up to commander. True to the best traditions of the Navy, every one looked polished and starched, ready for inspection.

After the weird stares with the flavor of what the devil, and just who are you? Barney introduced himself exactly as he would have if he had been called before an officer — name, rate, and serial number. Several minutes passed before a chief petty officer asked, "Where the hell did you come from and where did you get a serial number, especially one that is in the Navy sequence?"

By now, Barney had become somewhat weary of the attitude of everyone who had spoken to him so far, and he did not feel that he should be subjected to any more abuse.

"Just who is the most responsible officer in this group, and may I sit down with that person and try to explain how I came to this point in my life? I would prefer to have an officer from Navy Intelligence, for my being here is a result of their orders." The word "orders" almost stuck in Barney's throat for he had not been ordered to the task; he had been given an opportunity to do something special and, as he had been told, the Navy was in dire need of the information he was to gather. The word "orders" drew the hoped-for attention and soon another officer led him into one of the side rooms and asked him to relax. The officer was a full lieutenant, sporting a U.S.N.R. badge and a set of what Barney had always cherished, the golden wings of a Navy pilot The wings reassured Barney that at least he was going to share his crazy experience with someone of above-average perception and his story would be given an honest evaluation.

First, the officer stated that he was not a regular intelligence person that most of the trained people were in the major cities and his duty was to gather all the information that came his way. He had been flying from one of the new carriers and was volunteered to do some shore duty. This area seemed most interesting, at least more interesting than sorting out such persons as war criminals and prisoners of war, or worse yet, trying to find out how to feed and support the basic needs of the Japanese population. "Now that's one for you! Blow each other to hell, and then turn around and feed the dammed losers better food than some of the service people who fought them have. Barney, you would have thought that there would be something special for the winners wouldn't you? Good old U.S.A., we do it every time!"

The lieutenant then sat down in one of the flimsy chairs and directed Barney to use the other one. "Now," he said, "just what kind of bullshit are you going to feed me?"

Barney was flushed with sudden anger and it showed strongly in his reply. "Sir, I've been insulted by everyone since I came here, I have only one objective in being here. If you feel that what I have to tell you, or explain to you, is, as you say, 'bullshit,' I see no need to go any further. Can you get me to a regular intelligence person and let me do what I feel is important, and my duty?"

The lieutenant was not drawn back by Barney's response to his statement. Instead he smiled a faint smile, raised his voice to a sterner note of authority and explained that within the past month, since he had been in this nothing place, he had personally heard more weird tales of woe and sad stories than the whole U.S. Navy could dream up. "In fact" he said, "just look at you, dressed in the clothes of a back lands coolie or farmer, longer hair than any G.I. would be caught dead with, and what's with the funny-looking hair hanging down from your upper lip? I don't care who you say you might be, you do not ring true to me, so don't blame any of us if we think you look a little strange." Then, pursuing further, "now let's hear about your Navy assignment and how you became involved with Naval Intelligence."

Barney was about to tell the lieutenant to shove it. He stood up in anger, wanting out of this very unfamiliar and unfriendly place. He caught himself before angry words were spoken, and sat down again. He began by identifying the ship he came from and the sub that had stranded him. If this did not bring a more friendly attitude, then he would tell all of them to "shove it."

Barney asked if the lieutenant had a U.S. capital ships' registry and if he would look up the destroyer that Barney was serving on when all this nonsense started. "Now, look up the Seawolf and you will find that these ships are important ships in our Navy." The lieutenant had to admit that he did not have a registry close at hand but stated that he would phone to confirm Barney's information.

"Now let's get on with what you were supposed to do once you were on Japanese soil and what crazy group of men sent you here in the first place."

First Barney told him where he had been hiding, leaving out Myoko and her farmhouse. He told of the caves and how, after not being picked up at the time and date indicated in his verbal orders, he had hidden all the records, the radio and the remainder of support materials by burying them near the fishing village, how he had stolen most of his food from the small farms that lay along the path leading to the fishing village. He explained how he had crept into the fishing village and stolen some fishing equipment, fish being the mainstay of his diet. Then at the conclusion of all this, he said that he had found some very unusual help — help that in fact, as far as he was concerned, had saved his life and kept him from being detected and caught.

Then Barney made his strongest statement. "I choose not to go into that part of my stay here until I am positive that all measures will be taken to see that the other person will not suffer in any way and will be treated with the utmost respect and security. For me, this one item is mandatory. Then, and only then, will I go into exact details from the moment I left the sub until right now."

Barney had not given a great deal of the detailed step-by-step information that he was prepared to give, but it must have been enough to make the lieutenant call for the chief that Barney had encountered when he first came into the building. He gave him instructions to confirm the two ships that Barney had named and asked the chief to contact a commander, and see if the commander could come down to their facility. "Tell him we think that we may have one of the lost Navy men that some people have been asking us to keep a lookout for."

As the lieutenant's attention came back to Barney, he had the same short smile on his face that Barney had noted earlier and before the lieutenant could explain or say anything further, Barney asked if there was any way they could find him some clean Navy clothes, help him remove the glued-on facial hair from under his nose, a haircut, and most important, some food and a place to sleep for awhile. The lieutenant assured him that he would be well taken care of and that new clothes would be provided. He would even make sure that Barney's ratings would be added to the sleeves of the shirts. "You did say that you were a petty officer first class didn't you?" he asked. Barney had just had his first checking question, the first of many that he would experience in days to come.

Answering the officer, Barney calmly stated, "You know darned well that I said that when I left the sub, I was a fire controlman second class, and so I still am, unless you have the authority to promote me here and now."

The grin on the lieutenant's face became a little more friendly and he said that guest quarters were at a premium, in fact any sleeping space was all but non-existent, but something that was dry and comfortable would be provided.

Again, the chief was called and the clothes, razor and other items Barney had mentioned were sent for. "As to food, we all are eating out of one mess place provided by the few Sea Bees down near the docks. Food's good and the cook has a sense of humor about his cooking. The chief will find you a decent place to sleep.

"There is only one thing that I'm sure you understand. We will keep close tabs on you until all the questions about your presence are cleared up to our satisfaction. You really can't blame us can you?" he asked.

Barney shook his head no, and with that, both men stood up and rejoined the men in the outer room.

The first night away from Myoko was earth-shattering for Barney. He did not sleep all night. The chief had supplied him with a standard military folding cot, a somewhat thin mattress and two G.I. blankets for warmth. The only cold that crept into his bones was the thought of Myoko alone. Throughout the night he kept going over all that they had shared and done together, planting and keeping the small paddies growing with loving care, harvesting the fruits of their efforts and, most of all, the evenings on the beach fishing and Myoko's making the delicious dinners out of almost nothing. She could really make fish taste different each time she cooked them.

August 18

It was two days before the requested officer came down to see just who this guy Barney really was. The first morning of questions centered around the meeting that he claimed he had had in Pearl Harbor that started him on this so-called journey. Barney could only remember one of the three men's names and could not remember the exact department or branch that they said they were from. "After all," Barney said, "it has been almost a year, and at that time I didn't think that I would be abandoned like I was."

Late in the afternoon of the first day of questions, the lieutenant who first talked to Barney, a Lieutenant Rich Tracy, joined them and a more serious tone of questions began. Lt. Tracy wanted to center his questioning on the two ships that Barney had asked him to check on. After many targeted questions, he admitted that the two ships had existed, but so far, he had been unable to learn if Barney had been part of the crew. The word "had" upset Barney and after some moments had passed, he asked what Lt. Tracy meant by saying had existed. It was then that he learned of the fate of both ships. His first real home in the Navy was the destroyer. Emotions and tears welled deep as Tracy told of its sinking, with all but a small handful of men surviving. The ship had been blown out of the ocean off the Straits of Samar, along with several other destroyers and several small aircraft carriers. As for the submarine, it had not reported back to Pearl from the patrol on which Barney was supposed to have been dropped off. No word of how or where, and it was presumed sunk. Even though Barney had been on the sub but a short time, he felt very close to all of the crew. Anyone who went down into the sea in such a machine had to be very special, and Barney's heart seemed to all but stop as he reflected on the young and brave men who seemed to enjoy the duty that took them in harm's way and to the end of their lives.

Then another shocker was dropped on him. Lt. Tracy commented that he might or might not be one of the men that certain people were looking for, and there was a different strain of doubt about Barney in the tone of the lieutenant's questions. For the rest of the day a lot was said to him, and many questions that seemed to have no relevance were directed toward him. After all that he had learned about his ship and shipmates, Barney was so numb that most of the questions, and the answers he gave, seemed very far away.

It was noon the second day of answering the officer's questions. The tone of the questions had not changed from the day before — surly and accusing — making Barney feel like a criminal who had committed a major offense. For several hours Barney listened and tried to make some sense out of their abusive attitude. Then he had had enough. In the strongest tone and with self-assurance, he stated that he regretted having made his presence known. "I could have stayed where I was and no one would have thought anything of it. I had visited the fishing village dressed as an old

Japanese man, walking like an old man, and no one even bothered to ask me about the weather or anything else."

It was at this point in his speech that he remembered a way to prove at least part of his story and maybe establish some credibility for his being in Japan. Regaining his composure, Barney addressed the two interrogators, "I have a means of proving most of what I have been trying to explain. Near the fishing village, I buried all the information that I collected: the radio, maps, camera, film and the few items given to me for sleeping and warmth. All are U.S. Navy issue, and if you will have one or more of your men drive me to the place, I am sure that the stuff will help you to better understand my situation. It will take all day to make the round trip." In Barney's mind, he could see Myoko standing in her field working the vegetables as they passed by. This made his heart jump back to where he felt that it should be, feeling great!

Lt. Tracy immediately said that it sounded like a reasonable suggestion and that he would like to be one of the persons making the day's outing. Barney felt that Tracy would have jumped at anything to keep from sitting in a stuffy room asking ridiculous questions. A day in the country would be a special treat. Then Tracy made a suggestion that Barney was not prepared for. "You can also show us the cave area and the places that you claim you fished, even some of the farms that you, let's say, 'borrowed' food from." The two officers agreed and arrangements for the trip were made for the next day.

That evening while Barney was having his G.I. dinner, Lt. Tracy came into the Seabees dining area, selected his tray of food, then like a homing pigeon, sat with Barney. As the two of them finished the evening meal, not a great deal was said about the next day, just conversation about how the occupying forces were trying to help the Japanese people with food and the basic needs for survival. Tracy said that he was sure that much more would be done later on but the important problem now was health, food, clothing, etc. As he finished his last bite of food, the lieutenant really hit Barney between the eyes when he asked if it would be possible to meet the person that had helped Barney for the many past months. He stated that he had met some really pleasant and helpful Japanese people since he had been doing this crazy job. He felt that meeting such a person would help him better understand more of the troubles that Barney said he had gone through.

Barney sat frozen for a long time before he responded. "Lieutenant, the first day you asked me questions I stated that I would not tell anyone the name of, or show anyone, the person to whom I credit the saving of this poor soul's life. I insist on making sure of this person's security. I do not know if the Japanese people would seek some kind of revenge if they learned that this person had helped an enemy of their country. I cannot take a chance on this person's life."

Tracy was not one to be set aside by such a short answer to his question, besides he had a very strange feeling that there was much more to the protector of Barney than was being stated. It was not a negative feeling, but one that put a smile on his face and made him sure that there were strong and binding ties between the rescued and the rescuer. For some unknown reason, this made the lieutenant feel good, and anxious for tomorrow's journey.

August 20

Breakfast was early and fast. A new jeep and two soldiers with horse head patches on their shoulders, carbines at the ready, met them as they stepped out of the eating area. Barney noticed that shovels and a pick had been strapped to the spare tire bracket. The box, the lieutenant stated, contained some rations to tide them over, for he was sure that they would not find any eating-places along the way.

Barney was not sure how they found the right road that would take them to their destination.

Some six to eight miles after leaving the city area, they came to the farm where the farmer had invited Barney and Myoko in for tea and, upon their leaving, had shared some fresh pork with them. It was also one of the first places from which Barney had "borrowed" food when he realized that he was stranded. He just pointed out that it was one of the paddies from which he had taken some sweet potatoes, and made no additional comment.

A great hard lump formed in Barney's stomach as the jeep and its passengers started up the slight rise from which, when the top was reached, he would be able to see the place that he had spent the past months — Myoko's home and her small farm. There was nothing he could do about anything now. If she was working in the paddies, he hoped that she would not notice who was riding by. As the jeep came to the top of the rise, the lieutenant asked the driver to stop. As the vehicle came to a full stop, he commented that he had never seen such a beautiful little valley, "And look at that little old man treating his land like a piece of art. HI bet that he doesn't allow a single weed in his paddies. Gosh, what a peaceful looking piece of earth, the war surely never touched this place," was his final comment before he asked the driver to move on.

The swelling of joy and pride that Barney now felt replaced the concern and anxiety that had enveloped him just a few moments earlier, because this place that the lieutenant spoke of was a part of him and would be so forever. As the jeep passed the field Barney had a difficult time trying not to look too long and hard at the small, bent-over little old farmer working away in the soon-to-be harvested cabbage paddy; the patch that he and the little old farmer had so enjoyably tilled, and the warm soil in which they had placed the plants. Myoko did not look up as they made their way toward the fishing village.

Ten minutes passed before they came to the first paddies that were the outskirts of the fishing village. Barney asked the driver to slow down, as the site where he had buried the equipment was a short distance from the first paddy, at the bottom of a mound of dirt and rocks. The jeep was stopped and Barney pointed out the place where he had hidden the gear. Each man took turns with the shovels and just as Barney had stated, a large waterproof canvas package was unearthed. Barney carefully unwrapped the outer covering; the radio, which showed no damage, was the first item on his list. Next was the makeshift bedroll, then all the maps, the camera and several canisters of film, just as Barney had left them.

Barney took out the handwritten sheets containing all the records that he had made clearly showing his observations, the reason he had been sent here in the first place. He handed these to Lt. Tracy and exclaimed, "These maps and my notes, along with the film and radio, should establish some positive credibility in what I have been trying to tell you. I hope that you will stop treating me like some spy or enemy."

The lieutenant made no comment and asked the driver to drive on down to the village that they could see below them. "We'll have our lunch there and enjoy as much of the day as we can before we have to go back to that stuffy office."

In the village, Barney pointed out where he had stolen the fishing poles and gear, addressing some of the local people in his most accurate Japanese. It was the first time Tracy had heard Barney use the language and he was somewhat surprised at how natural it sounded. "How long did you say you've been stranded here?" he asked. Barney responded, "Let's sit down by the boats that are pulled up on the sand, and I'll tell you how and where I learned about good Japanese people." As they walked, Barney reflected back to his high school days and told of the great friend he had then, and how they would play word games in Japanese with him and the parents "That's where I really developed a respect for the language and the Japanese people, at least the Japanese that lived in our country. I feel I've learned much more of their culture and desire for a peaceful life since I've been stuck here. The person who helped me has great insight about the average Japanese people." Then Barney made his first slip: "She's well educated and has read many books about many different places." Barney caught his error and looked at Lt. Tracy as though he had been shot.

Tracy, looking sternly at Barney, said, "Let's sit on one of these boats and you can better explain your last comment. I had a very different feeling about the help you claimed to have had and I knew that something special had happened to you, if what you were saying was true."

At first Barney did not know how to explain all that he had experienced, that he had omitted some information when questioned by the intelligence officers. He simply did not want to admit that he had not told all that he knew. Then Barney stiffened his back and told Lt. Tracy that he would not at this time tell just who the person was that had helped him but that he would later explain all the important details. The details that he did not reveal were the close, loving and intimate feelings that he had developed between himself and Myoko.

As Barney completed narrating most of the most important events of his being in Japan, he stated, "Lieutenant, this conversation is between just you and me at this point and all I can ask is that you pay me the same respect that you yourself would want under the same circumstances. When I am sure that she will be respected and security provided, then I will tell you and anyone else her name and where she lives."

Lt. Tracy sat very quiet for some long moments before he spoke, then he admitted that he did not know what he would do if he was caught in the same exciting fix. "The most important thing right now, though, is to satisfy intelligence that you are who you say you are and get all the pieces put together. The equipment and all your detailed notes will go a long way in helping to back up your story." They both smiled and walked to the jeep and began the ride back to Fukuoka along the same trail by which they had come.

The "little old farmer" was not in the paddies as they came past Myoko's farm and this was a great relief to Barney. He was not sure that he could hide any longing emotions should he see her working in the fields. At the last paddy, Lt Tracy asked just where Barney had found his hiding place, "can you show me where it is?" Stopping next to the farthest stand of giant bamboo that hid them from view of Myoko's house, Barney led Tracy down the path that went to his cave.

Inside the small enclosure, Barney pointed out some of the digging that he had to do in order to have room for the radio and a reasonable space to sleep. He explained, "I stored my rations in the side holes, and the fishing poles I left down on the beach," pointing down the path that led to the hidden sandy cove. My friend and I would go down to the beach after we worked in the garden all day and swim first, then we'd catch our fish and cook them right on the beach. It was during these times that we talked about all that was wrong with the war and the killing. She would explain that the people of her country knew very little of the war until the bombs started falling. She said that there was nothing that the people could have done about stopping the war. If anyone had tried, or said anything against the war, they would have been killed as traitors. It's real frightening that such strong fear can be forced upon people when they are so uninformed."

Tracy was not satisfied with looking at Barney's hiding place and without saying anything, he carefully made his way down the narrow path to the bottom of the cliff. For a while Barney was almost angry at the lieutenant for invading the place where he and Myoko had spent most of their leisure and gentle times. This was their beach, their sanctuary and most of all, a place where the outside conflict did not touch any part of their relationship.

Barney went to the fishing poles and asked the lieutenant if he would like to try his luck and have some fresh fish for his dinner. The lieutenant declined, but asked Barney how he was able to get bait and fish in the foaming surf. Barney pointed out the rudiments of the tide changes and how the fish at high tide swam just in back of the white water. For bait: "Look at all the mussels growing on the rocks; they're one of the best sources for all surf-type fishing that one can use. You just pull them from the rocks, pry them open and use the inside meat for your bait. Mussels are also very delicious, just select the ones about three inches long and place them on hot coals, they pop open when done and make a very tasty seafood treat."

They walked down the beach as far as they could and then walked up the beach to the very end where the steep cliffs prevented any further passage. Tracy turned on Barney very swiftly and all but yelled: "Barney, you don't know how lucky you've been to find a place like this, not to hide from the war, but to find safety and security with so many of the needs to survive so close at hand! You were able to find all the right food — vegetables, the freshest of seafood, and even to have one of the local, so-called enemy share his fresh-killed pork with you. I can't help but envy all that you say you've done and your great fortune in having a person who came out of nowhere to help you stay free and un-captured for so long a time.

"Maybe you should look at it this way," he continued, "If you had stayed on the destroyer and been a part of the reported battle at Samar, you would most likely be one of the missing, you would be dead... But here you are, standing on one of the prettiest, quietest beaches that I've ever seen, and you have some of the most exciting tales and remembrances that anyone could ever dream of. Barney, I do not disbelieve any part of what you have said and shown me. Everything you shared with me on this trip will be in my report, and I will ask that you be shipped to Pearl. Every effort will be made to locate the men who volunteered you for this crazy responsibility."

Driving back along the narrow path, Barney was very quiet and it wasn't until the outskirts of the city came into view that he asked again of Lt. Tracy, "Please, whatever you put in your report, do not make any reference to the person that helped me as being a woman. Can you just say 'person' at this time and let it go at that? When I am sure that all will be taken into consideration, and her security assured, I will be most pleased to introduce her to the proper authorities." After a long pause, Tracy acknowledged he could not help but keep Barney's secret until the correct time to make it known was forced upon him.

It was late in the evening before Barney first felt pangs of hunger and he made his way along the waterfront to the Sea-bee's eating place. Taking one of the stainless steel trays, he noticed that the main fare for the evening was something that he had not even thought of in at least a year or more: steak. The cook that was serving the food commented that he was sorry that the meat was on the tough side but all the good old flavor of American raised steer still remained.

As the cook served Barney, he asked if Barney was the guy that had been stranded on this godforsaken Island and how had he managed to survive. Barney's answer kind of threw the cook off balance as he said, "I had to do all my own cooking and also all my own scrounging of food and shelter. This allowed me to be very selective in what I had to eat." It was obvious that the cook felt somewhat insulted and was about to give a negative retort when Lt. Tracy and the main officer from intelligence came up behind Barney and asked what the evening meal was going to consist of on such a fine evening. After all three had received their food, Tracy asked Barney if the three of them could sit in the corner so that Barney might add to his verbal report before he put anything into a written report. As they sat down, Tracy began telling the other officer about the most unusual trip and how Barney had pointed out so many aspects of his stay on the island. He thought it would be great if Barney could help him describe the most important places and points.

Then Tracy jumped right into the details describing the remote fishing village and told the officer that if he had a choice, he would find some old clothes and join the fishing village for the rest of his life. "That little village is the only totally peaceful place that I have seen in the three years that I've been in this part of the world. Other than some damned Jap soldier coming to the village to scare hell out of the local people, the ones who work, fish and live there, I doubt that any of them were touched by the past four years of war. Maybe a son was taken off to fight and die in some unheard of place, but that would have been all. Major, it was a place where dreams are made and long lives enjoyed."

The major then took over the conversation by asking Lt. Tracy if he was satisfied with all that Barney had told them and would he write up a formal report, have it ready for his review by the next day at noon so that he could get the proper authorization to have Barney shipped back to Pearl. It was at this time that Barney apologized for not remembering the major's name and asked him if he could repeat it. The major looked somewhat displeased for just a moment, then in a strong tone, "It's Major Rickards, class of '41." No everyone understood his stiffness and direct attitude: he was West Point, a man of distinctive military education and training.

Rickards asked Barney if he would mind helping out with the local people as an interpreter, since he seemed to have a knack for understanding their ways and attitudes. "It will be for just a short time until I can get your paperwork squared away and get people in Hawaii to meet you and get all of your story put together and confirmed." He went on to explain some of what was going on and his, and Lt. Tracy's, responsibilities, closing with, "I'm sure you can be of great help."

Barney sat very quiet for some time until Lt. Tracy asked him if he understood the major's suggestion. It was then that Barney simply said that he was just going back over some of the thoughts and fears that he had had over the past months, and he was wondering exactly how he could help with some of the problems that the U.S. occupation military had to be having with the Japanese population. As they walked out of the eating area, Barney informed the two officers that he would be glad to help in any way he could and was ready to begin whenever needed.

Throughout the rest of the evening, Barney went over the many items of concern that he and Myoko had talked about, covering the exact question, what about the change in Japan after the war? Now it was after the war — and he was not sure that what he had told Myoko would happen was going to happen. As sleep confused his thoughts, he felt sure that Lt. Tracy would let him in on some of the future requirements for the Japanese people. He would seek him out at breakfast and ask for some direction and understanding, for he had a lot at stake to make sure his Myoko would be understood and protected. He missed being with her so much...

PART V

Going Home

August 1945–January 1946

August 21, 1945

Lt. Tracy was not at breakfast and this caused Barney to fret about his thoughts the night before. Late afternoon as Barney was about to leave for the Navy pier to obtain some new and proper clothes, Lt. Tracy drove up alongside and asked where he was off to. Barney explained, and Lt. Tracy offered to drive him to the pier and volunteer to vouch for him to the supply people for Barney's status and need for clothing. Then he said, "We're going for a drive around the city to try to find a place that still has four walls and some good Japanese food." The comment about "Japanese food" sent a cold chill down Barney's back. Instantly he thought about all the great meals that Myoko had cooked and shared with him, but he was not about to explain to Tracy how he became so familiar with this country's food. He smiled and asked Tracy where he learned to like raw fish and rice.

As they drove around after getting Barney's new clothes, Barney began to ask simple questions about how he was supposed to help the intelligence people and who he was to work with. To his surprise, Tracy said that to use Barney in their efforts was his idea and that Major Rickards was glad to

157

assign Barney to him. Tracy went on to explain that he found it hard to put any real trust in what the local people told him, which was very little.

"We just don't have the knowledge and feelings about these people to make any kind of good impression on them. We are very much the conquerors and they the conquered. We've been in their country for such a short time we don't know how to act, and how to treat them — as a long-time enemy, or as respected human beings. I find their culture, what little I know about it, to be very fascinating and one to be respected. Have you noticed how the children treat the older people? And, I have so far not heard a parent raise his voice in talking to his children. In my house when I was growing up, there was a loud roar going on most of the time. Of course, we had five kids, brothers and sisters, to share parents with... Barney, I guess what I'm saying is, I really like these people, and that fishing village you took me to... I could stay there forever."

It was some two hours of slow driving and Barney asking the street people, in his most polite Japanese, about where they might find good Japanese food, before they found an eating place that seemed to understand what Barney was asking for. It was very narrow, almost a hole, in the center of a block of buildings that had somehow escaped any war damage. What drew Barney's attention were large buckets of clean water filled with some of the largest shrimp that he had seen. Barney asked the wrinkle-faced, bent-over older woman if they could have some cooked with ginger and vegetables. The old woman gave a guarded slight smile and told them that it would be an honor to serve her fresh food with one who spoke Japanese so well. First Barney wanted to assure her that they would pay extra if the food was cooked in the traditional Japanese way, with all the special flavors that made the food so tasty. "We will discuss that after you have made up your minds about my ability to be a good cook," she said as she shuffled toward the back of her very crowded four walls.

As Barney knew it would be, the food was better than either of them had expected. The vegetables were cooked just as Myoko had shown Barney and their freshness made him wonder just what farmer she had gotten them from, and if she had perhaps "borrowed" them as he had when he was first stranded. No, he said to himself, she looks too honest and besides, the farms are too far from here.

Lt. Tracy insisted on paying the little old lady three times what she thought it was worth. This seemed to cause her some measure of embarrassment but she did not argue with the unexpected money, even though it was in the standard occupation scrip.

As they sat on what could almost have been a sidewalk, a pushcart with several cases of what looked like beer, piled as high as one could reach, passed by. The poor driver, or pusher, was all but hidden by the heavy load. First the lieutenant looked at Barney and then at the beer, and turning to Barney he asked, "Do you know where we can get some ice to chill several bottles of that stuff?"

Barney remembered that the supply ship at the dock had ice-making capacity and since the lieutenant was from intelligence, he should be able to scrounge enough to cool at least four bottles. It took very little effort to convince the man with the beer to part with six of the big one-and-one-half quart bottles of the liquid. As Tracy paid for the bottles he said, "The ice man might want to know what we are up to, but if we trade him two bottles for the ice, he can't be too inquisitive, I hope!"

They drank the cool beverage with nothing but smiles on their faces and as the last of the brew was drained from their bottles, Barney again began the questioning of how he was supposed to help Tracy with the Japanese. His only comment was, "Just as we did this afternoon, only don't tell anyone, especially the major!"

Several weeks had passed with Lt. Tracy and Barney driving throughout the main industrial areas trying to find facilities, and local people willing to begin some kind of reconstruction. Most of the large manufacturing establishments were destroyed or non-functioning, and the machinery used in those plants blown apart. Each day they would drive a little farther away from the main part of the industrial area in search of some kind of starting place. They felt that if they could get one or two small production projects underway, showing that the Americans wanted to help them regain important parts of their lives, others would be encouraged to become involved and start their own businesses.

September 7, 1945

The first real opportunity came when Barney was trying to find a new eating place, one that might have a different source of hard-to-get meat other than fish. He and the lieutenant had driven south toward the destroyed shipyard area and found a small foundry that had made aluminum cylinder heads for aircraft engines. Only the back portion of the structure had been damaged by the bombings.

It took them all day to find a person willing to talk to Barney and to be responsible for a foundry. At first the Japanese man gave the impression that he wanted nothing to do with rebuilding the small smelter, convinced that the Japanese government would take it away from him. When the man finally was assured that it would be his own plant and that all he produced from his efforts would be his to sell or trade as he saw fit, he became very talkative and began to ask questions about help in getting started.

Through Barney, Lt. Tracy began to explain there were tons of destroyed aircraft that scattered all across Japan — mostly Japanese, some American — and that it could be arranged for the smelter to receive the aluminum material and turn it into the many badly needed household products for all Japan. Cooking pots and pans, forks and knives, things like that to get them started.

The Japanese man started in amazement at the statement about forks and knives, then burst out laughing. He explained, "Even though you have conquered our country, you will never get the people of Japan to use those dreadful contraptions; we will always use chopsticks!" and the friendly smiles on Barney's and Tracy's faces assured the Japanese, now a businessman, that he could trust these two men to do what they were promising.

Promises made and promises kept are often different things when dealing with a higher authority. This Barney and Lt. Tracy found out as they attempted to secure all the salvageable aluminum that could be found.

The Tokyo high command demanded to first know, why and secondly, what would be the intended use of the material, and, the most asinine question of all, what are the everyday people of Japan going to use the pots and pans for? Then to add a real insult to their efforts, all answers had to be written out and ten copies approved by all major commands in the area. To Lt. Tracy, this was all beyond the call of duty and he wanted no part of such a useless waste of time.

Lt. Tracy asked Barney and the foundry person to join him for a ride. They went directly to the Japanese air base that had been one of Barney's objectives when he first came to this land. Tracy had obtained one of the largest U.S. military trucks that he could find from the motor pool. With a U.S. Navy enlisted man as driver of the big truck and the three men in the lieutenant's jeep, they drove to their destination.

Most of the destroyed aircraft had been bulldozed into several large piles away from the main building site of the complex. Lt. Tracy, with his intelligence identification, had no problem in gaining possession of the unwanted metal. The base military police even rounded up a dozen Japanese workmen to do the sorting and loading.

As the procedure moved along, Lt. Tracy noticed that Barney's mind seemed to be somewhere else. Barney was standing far to one side and looking out across the base toward a large stand of trees and the remains of some old wooden buildings. As Tracy approached him, Barney asked if they could drive over to the piles of rubble, for he had to make sure of something that was important to him. As they entered the quiet tree-covered area, Barney went directly to what was left of one building. As he poked around the stone and cement debris, Tracy noted small tears sliding down Barney's cheeks. With a personal and respectful tone in his voice Tracy commented, "Something very significant happened to you here in all this mess and it hurts, whatever it was— still hurts, doesn't it?"

For longer than either of them realized, there was only the sound of a few creaking, broken pieces of wood and the almost quiet rustle of the wind moving through the trees. Barney sat down on the edge of a broken slab of concrete and related how, when he was trying to gather the information that he was sent here to get, he had killed an old man and placed his body upon the very pile of broken material that he was now sitting on. "I thought that I was alone and as I was concentrating on the activities at the air base, this old geezer came up behind me and demanded to know what I was doing. Without really thinking and before he could raise any alarm, I grabbed him by the throat and choked him to death.

"Only after the act was over did I realize just what I had done; I had removed from this earth the life of another person, an old man who had done nothing to hurt me or, for all I know, wouldn't have caused me any trouble. Sure, it was wartime, but the look on his face as he died will stay with me forever.

"From the moment that I learned that the war was finally over, I have been very disturbed about what happened to his body. Was he found? If so, did he receive the burial, which is so important to traditional Japanese? I cannot help but feel that maybe there could have been some other way. It was not like killing that bastard of a soldier that hurt my friend. Lieutenant, I don't think that I told you about the Japanese soldier that attacked my friend. He deserved everything that he got, he was a mean S.O.B."

When Barney looked into the face of his friend, there was a smile of pleasant surprise: "I knew that there was something special and unsaid about the person who helped you to stay free and survive during the time you were trapped in this land." Barney, with deep concern flushing over his face, stopped Tracy in the middle of his statement: "Lieutenant, if you believe in really personal confidence and trust between you and me, you will not say anything about what I just said to anyone for the time being; it is very important to me and to the other person."

For the first time since they had met, Tracy abandoned his somewhat starched military attitude and placed his hand on the shoulder of his much-disturbed Navy companion. "Barney, you have told me and Major Rickards a lot about all that has happened to you during the past months of the war and in spite of all our efforts, we cannot find one small error in what you have said to us. I am not sure if the major feels that there is something special about your savior, or whatever you prefer to call her, now that I know it is a her — but I find no reason to spill my guts to Rickards about this most exciting, and I am sure, beautiful part of your visit."

All of the emotions of missing Myoko seemed to burst within every fiber of Barney's body. It had been two months since he had last seen her, and each day brought a new torment of loneliness and an inner struggle to resist the urge to just quietly leave and return to her small farm and the closeness of her beauty — where, most of all, he felt he wanted to be and really belonged.

As Lt. Tracy sat on the same pile of debris that Barney occupied, Barney began the detailed description of first seeing an old man meticulously caring for his small paddies of rice, cabbage and sweet potatoes. Of how over about a month's time, he became so attached to the farmer that when he saw the damned soldier strike the old man he wanted to kill. Barney said, "That was the very first time in all my life that I wanted to kill, and was sure that if I had had a gun, or other means, I would have done so. That old man became my only link with people and allowed me to stay hidden and not do something foolish and get myself caught.

"Anyway, after the soldier knocked him down, disregarding my own safety, I carried the limp body of what I thought was an old man to his house and began to clean him up. That is when I learned that it was not an old man but a very frightened and badly hurt young lady!" Barney went on to detail all that had taken place and was surprised at his feelings of gratification in the killing of the soldier and, in a way, revenging the brutality that the soldier had inflicted upon Myoko.

"Lieutenant, this person came to mean so much to me that there was no way that I could not become respectfully involved with her as a best friend and, as you said, a savior. Most of all I care for and love her more than anyone or anything I have ever known. Now you know the whole story of Barney and his adventures as an almost-spy who became stranded on the enemy's home ground, fell in love with one of the enemy, and is in no way ashamed of it."

Tracy's only comment was, "What a beautiful and yet exciting adventure. If Hollywood tried to write a script on such a story, they couldn't do justice to what you have gone through. Now, we had better get back to the truck and get our first bounty to the foundry."

For the next week, all they did was collect as much aluminum as they could lay their hands on. As they collected the salvaged material, their Japanese colleague was busy cleaning the smelter equipment and getting it ready for service. Coal, and some coke for firing the smelter, was scarce but many of the blown-up factories still had leftover supplies that they simply commandeered.

September 15

On a bright sunny Monday morning, the first smoke from the foundry furnace belched, then began to curl out from the rusty tin smoke stack.

The forms and designs for the first products were the work of a friend of the smelter owner, and even though some of them were somewhat crude, the intent for their use was evident. The overly thick gauges of metal for the pots, the crude wooden handles (made for a man's hand) made them look like a blacksmith had gotten a fast idea and just started pounding.

Barney suggested that the owner get his wife involved in what pots and pans should look like and how big or small they should be. At first, the Japanese man seemed very insulted. Tracy and Barney explained the reasons: that "women will be using them, and if the pots and such do not meet their approval, they will not buy them." With gruff comments about Japanese women not having any place in a man's business, he accepted the point that the two Americans had made. Several days later the pots and pans took on an artful design and the sizes changed, as well as the weight of the pieces. Lt. Tracy and Barney were so delighted with their first solid project that they decided to have an announcement party on the coming weekend and allow all of the friends of the foundry owner to attend. The news about the foundry traveled by word-of-mouth, which was faster than any other means of communication.

When Lt. Tracy invited Major Rickards to the event, it was the first that the major had heard of his and Barney's project, and for several hours, he was very militarily upset. Tracy said that he wanted to have the major introduced as the American behind the whole idea and that he and Barney were just carrying out the details of the plan. "Major, isn't this what we were sent here to do, to help these people get back into rebuilding their country and lives without any forced military and government controls? That is exactly what this project has done and it will make this office look very good at Tokyo headquarters."

The real scrounging for the celebration began for both groups of people. The Americans wanted to show that they meant business in helping the Japanese rebuild a new and self-determined, privately owned business. The Japanese wanted to prove that they were not only very grateful, but could be trusted to do what was being asked of them.

The Japanese food and delicacies, most of which the Americans had never seen or tasted, were abundant. None of the Japanese had ever had a hot dog or hamburger with all the American trimmings. Where the Japanese obtained all the American and Japanese flags was a guess. Small and very carefully handmade flags had been attached to every post and foundry piece of equipment. Now Mister Morita, owner of the first new privately-owned business in all Fukuoka, and maybe all of Japan, wanted to make sure that the whole world knew that it was the Americans who helped him rebuild this most significant first enterprise — thus all the joined American and Japanese flags.

Several dozens of the first utensils had been set out on makeshift tables and little place cards written in Japanese telling all who could read that this pot, cup, bowl or tray, was the idea of a woman or friend, and that Mr. Morita would like to learn about any other new products that anyone could suggest. Already, the idea of free enterprise — previously outlawed in Japan — was demonstrating the right way for creating a greater understanding with both the local Japanese people and their new business opportunities. The opening of the very first postwar business and the shared grand party to announce the event was more than a huge success.

September 26

Several days after the event, Mr. Morita came to the office of Major Rickards with three different small groups of men and asked if he could talk with Lt. Tracy and Barney. At first the Major was upset, because the Japanese would not say what their concern was, and none of the American personnel could speak or understand the Japanese language. It was a mad scramble to find Lt. Tracy and Barney. Some thirty minutes passed before the two could be found and the reason for the visit determined.

It was very simple; the men with Mr. Morita had been at the celebration of the new foundry and were very impressed with how Morita had become the sole owner of such an important business, which had been impossible in Japan before the war. Morita had explained to them that he could not have done anything without the direction and personal help from the three Americans. Further, Barney spoke the Japanese language very well and, more importantly, he had a strong understanding about how the Japanese people thought and felt. Mr. Morita stressed that Major Rickards was the leader of the Americans and wanted to help other local Japanese men start or rebuild badly needed businesses.

The Major, through Barney, asked each group to write down the type of business and the products that they wanted to produce and where they could find a suitable building to begin their venture. They were to have all of this done by one o'clock the next day. They were to bring all of the asked-for information with them to a meeting that would be held in his office to discuss the possibility of each group's request. All of the Japanese men slowly exited the major's office, talking all at once in a most excited fashion. After they were out of range of hearing the major asked Barney what all the departing excitement was about. Barney explained, "They were doubtful about success because they were not asked to fill out many pages of questions and were asked to come back in only one day. To them, it was too soon for any good decisions."

Mr. Morita had assured Barney and the major that tomorrow would be needed to put each plan on paper so that all problems could be examined and a positive plan could be made by both sides, thus making real progress. Barney further stated that each of them seemed pleased to be asked back the next day and that they would do as the major asked, write down all their ideas and be ready at one o'clock.

The following day's meeting went better than any of them had hoped for. Each Japanese man had written down every last detail and had come up with many pages of Japanese writing. It took several hours, with each group having Mr. Morita read, then having Barney interpret, the pages so that the major and Lt. Tracy could understand.

The conclusion from the long meeting was that each Japanese man would select which need he thought was the most important in helping rebuild the local businesses; the two remaining ideas, as good as they were, would help the group with an operational plan to get the needed project underway. At first this idea seemed to cause a great deal of discouragement among the three groups, but Barney explained that the major's office was just a small one and that he could do only so much at one time. Also, he informed them that they needed to learn how to start a new business, from the very beginning to final success, and they could learn from each other as they went along, making adjustments for new and better ideas.

Major Rickards then asked all of them to do as they had done yesterday, to go to one of their homes, or to Mr. Morita's office, and decide which project was to be first, add any new ideas to their list, and to be back in his office the next day at eight A.M. and he would get very serious about helping them with their new businesses.

It was the major's turn to buy the beer. He was so elated with the two-day's events that he announced that he would even buy dinner if they could find a Japanese place that had good food. Barney looked at Lt. Tracy and smiled, "Shall we take the major to our little hole in the wall and let him taste some of the best there is in all Fukuoka?" Without any verbal response needed, the three men walked out to the jeep and drove slowly through the main part of town. Barney drove straight to the place where he and Lt. Tracy had first sat down at a little old Japanese lady's small eating place and begun a friendship that each of them now cherished.

The little old lady remembered them at once and commented, "You do keep your word, you came back to my most humble table." At the same time she sat down three large unlabeled bottles of cold beer, one for each of her guests, and they dined on the most delectable foods that the culture of Japan had to offer. With a serious shortage of food in the whole of Japan, Rickards asked, "I wonder who she had to bribe to find such fresh and rare items and ice to cool the beer?"

Toward the conclusion of the meal, the major began to express his gratitude for the efforts that Barney and the Lt. had made in getting the foundry project started and stated that he was sure the new projects would be just as successful. But from the somewhat apologetic tone of his voice, Barney could feel that something else was about to be stated, and it would affect him; he was right.

Major Rickards turned toward Barney and began, "You came to us, the lieutenant and me, out of nowhere, with a most unusual and hard-to-believe story of how you got here. We have gone through all that you told us and everything checks out just as you stated. You became involved with the local Japanese people in a most beneficial way for my office and I want you to hear it from me firsthand: the two of you have made me look very good with the headquarters office in Tokyo.

"Right now my problem is this, I can't keep you here too much longer. The Navy wants you back ASAP and I have orders sitting on my desk asking that you be transported to Pearl Harbor on the first available transportation. I would like to keep you here until we can get at least one of the new plans into place and have something substantial to add to your file and also for me to report to Tokyo. In addition, and I hope that you won't mind, I have asked for you to be transferred to my office on a permanent basis for the sole purpose of helping the local Japanese people better communicate with us Americans and make it easier to help them. I hope you don't mind." Further, the major went on, "I have not heard from Tokyo about keeping you here, but I will call them tomorrow and try to get an answer if that's agreeable to you. What do you say, Barney?"

Barney looked at Tracy and then let his thoughts go back to the very first time he ventured down several of the town's streets as he gathered the information that he was sent here to get. First the feelings and fear he had had when he killed the old man at the air field, and then learning he was stranded in this land, and all alone. His impressions of the soldier that had hurt his Myoko and then most of all, Myoko, the deep feelings of loving her and now being so far and so long away from her. Barney's only objective was to return to Myoko and try to build a permanent place in Japan or somewhere on this very disturbed earth.

The major's words of "What do you think of my request Barney, would you like to stay here for awhile, maybe even a year?" brought Barney back to the discussion at hand. At last Barney found a smile to respond to the major's comments and as he glanced at Tracy he noted the same smile of understanding on his face. "Major, if you can swing such a request and have me become a part of your operation and let Lt. Tracy and me work together, I will be very pleased. When would you know for sure?"

October 12

Several weeks passed and no further mention of Barney's staying in Fukuoka was made.

Several meetings had gone by regarding the new project that the men had selected, and which was a real challenge for the major's office. Clothing and the material for basic tailoring needs seemed to be the most urgent item on the new business list. It was also one that each of the Japanese men could best understand. The clothing of the total population of the city looked very threadbare, and that which was still wearable and not too worn out, looked to be cut from the same piece of cloth. They all looked the same, one color — if black is a color. The first need they had was some kind of weaving machine that would be suitable for the desired type of cloth. Almost all of the prewar weaving machines had been used for war materials during the war, and finding just one such machine looked impossible. Lt. Tracy came up with the best potential source for the much-needed machine. He remembered during a stopover in Australia that he had been lodged in a sheep rancher's home. The rancher was very proud of the quality of wool that came from his animals and had given Tracy an almost continuing lecture on the value and use of wool.

It was one hell of an argument convincing the Tokyo staff to try real hard to acquire one weaving machine. However, they reluctantly asked the Aussies for help.

Barney could not stand the pressure of waiting for some kind of word about being able to stay with Major Rickards' office any longer. After asking Lt. Tracy if he had heard any comments about the subject, Barney took the question directly to the major. It was a short request: when? Rickards told Barney that he had called Tokyo as promised and was told that everyone was going home, that he should send Barney to Pearl Harbor as directed, and that he himself had been putting Barney's transfer off until someone said something — so, "I guess Barney, you had better get all your gear in order and plan to leave for Tokyo on the next air force flight available. I'm sorry to see you leave, for you have done more to help in solving some of the local problems than anyone else, I will miss you.

"The only record that I have of you is what has happened in this office. I will make sure that the many positive things that you've done for me, and the local Japanese people will be recorded and forwarded, along with a strong recommendation for your return to this office. I know that in time, you can achieve more for us and the local people than anyone else."

At four that afternoon, Barney found Lt. Tracy and informed him of the decision and that he wanted to take the lieutenant over to their little old lady's eating place for one last good Japanese feast. This they did.

As the DC3 made its way over the deep green mountains and valleys toward Tokyo, it felt to Barney that all life-giving blood and energy had departed his body. An umbilical that even in the smallest way kept him attached to the soil where he and Myoko found each other and dwelled for such a short but beautiful time, had been cut. The aloneness that he knew when he was first stranded was nothing compared to the deeper, painful emotion that now possessed his every fiber. As the great Mount Fuji came into view out his window, he made a most determined promise: I will come back to her, I don't know how or when, but I will be back just as soon as I can.

Barney reported in to the Navy office at the Tokyo giant air base and was told that he could get out on a B29 flight leaving later the same day. The flight was stopping at Guam for fuel and then on to Hawaii. If there was no problem in flight, he could be in Pearl some 36 hours from now. The sailor that had given Barney the information was surprised at the somewhat negative response that Barney gave. If he had known how much, and why, Barney wanted to stay in Japan, he might not have been so puzzled at Barney's attitude.

Barney's stopover at Pearl was a short review of the details surrounding all the events that took him to Japan in the first place and no, any request for his return to Major Rickards was unknown. He was put up in the Royal Hawaiian Hotel, the resting place for the submariners who were fortunate enough to return from their underwater war. He thought, *Maybe they let me in because I once traveled to the very edge of war on a sub, therefore I had some kind of priority to be accepted into the submariners' inner circle.*

Barney's stay was short, yet he was in a hurry to get to wherever he was being sent. He wanted to find a way — any kind of way — that would let him return to Myoko. His final transportation was one that he knew and enjoyed most. One of the newer 2200 Sumner class destroyers was returning to San Francisco, no longer needed in pursuit of an enemy. It was a great feeling to have a strong fast, steel-decked ship to walk about on and shipmates with whom he had a strong bond.

In San Francisco he was sent to Treasure Island for a review, what they called debriefing, of the days that he had spent in Japan. The same doubtful attitude was obvious from all the questions that he was asked. Barney felt that his review was required just to fill in some blanks on an endless series of forms. Since he was still considered as part of the crew of the destroyer that had been sunk off Samar, he was able to claim some extra benefits — survivor's leave, clothing replacement and most of all, considerable back pay. The Navy could not find any record that Barney had been transferred from the destroyer and he was listed as killed in action. The difficulty of bringing him back to life was like starting the war all over again.

Barney was finally told that he would be separated from the service and that this would take place at camp Shoemaker, California, some place over the hills behind Oakland. The Camp was overflowing at the present and not too many people were concerned with who was doing what, when, or where. The chief gave Barney an open liberty card and said for him to check in each morning for any change that might happen, and then get lost, go into San Francisco or wherever. "Keep out of sight but look busy while you are doing it." Another hurry up and wait instruction that all the services were noted for.

November 9

Two weeks later, Barney checked the list of transfers for separation to Camp Shoemaker and found his name on the list. The next procedure for him seemed like a fatal blow to all the thoughts of his being able to return to Myoko. It left no space for the hoped-for, last-minute maybe to happen. Mustering out of the Navy at this point in time was a certainty. He was told by the chief yeoman when he first checked in that he had to stop by the chiefs office for a final lecture and sign some more papers.

The chief's office was on the Golden Gate bridge side of Treasure Island's vast facilities, and as he slowly walked in that direction dampness filled his eyes. He was about to lose forever the best life that he had ever known. This led to the greatest fear he had ever experienced, a loneliness he could not control, and most of all, the feeling of loss of a joy and value he had found in another person that was greater than anything and anyone else in his whole young life.

As Barney opened the door to the chief's office, the chief looked up and in a loud and most demanding voice shouted "Where the hell have you been, I have had the whole base looking for you since yesterday afternoon." For many moments, Barney was totally numb. It was the last gruff and demanding statement that he had expected to hear and he had no response. When he started to speak, the chief told Barney to trot his ass down to the first office that was near the main entrance to the building and report to a W.A.V.E., Lieutenant Still. Startled, Barney turned around and as he departed, commented to the chief, "Since I am soon to be a taxpaying civilian you could at least speak to me in a somewhat civil tone!" Then he made his way to the office to which he had been told to report.

Entering the lieutenant's office the thought entered his mind that this was the first female officer that he had ever had personal contact with. Do I say yes sir, or yes ma'am?

The lieutenant sat facing away from her office door, and when Barney started to announce his arrival she cut him off very sharply: "Damn, you had us scratching all over this base trying to find you. We have what you may consider positive news. A high priority request concerning you was received yesterday at noon, and that's the reason for all the fuss. We need to go over to the Navy Intelligence office and review the request that was sent. Do you know a Lt. Col. Rickards in Japan?"

With all that had happened to him since he became involved in Navy matters and the intelligence people, the thought that came to him first was, *What have I done now?*

"So you are Barney Walters, the lost guy that everyone is looking for. I am Commander Wilson, and I'm responsible for all that is supposed to happen in this office. Please sit down, and you, too, Lieutenant Still. First, Walters, let me ask how you got mixed up with my old classmate Rickards? Even though he is Army, we attended an intelligence school together in '43."

Barney very briefly explained. The commander then proceeded with what he stated was a most unusual request, considering that the war had been over for many months. The need for personnel to be sent back to Japan, and especially to be attached to Intelligence, was really unusual, in fact most unusual. "Barney, have you done something really wrong that they sent a most urgent request, or is this another general foul-up?"

Barney was sitting completely numb. In his mind, all kinds of good thoughts were starting to get mixed with the statement that the commander had made, and all he could say was "Not to my knowledge." The commander began to define the text of the request to have Barney sent back to Japan. First he said, "You have two options: one, you can remain in the Navy and be paid your regular pay and be under the direct authority of the Navy. Two (this is the one I would like) — you can be mustered out of the Navy and then hired as a civilian, especially assigned to the U.S. Army Intelligence Agency, Japan for duty as they prescribe. The salary and all the special allowances that are part of working for the agency will amount to a great deal more money than you are earning now as a second-class petty officer. The best part will be, you will have only Col. Rickards' office to report to and that's a big advantage. Regardless, you need to make up your mind today so that we can get you under way."

The commander then turned to the W.A.V.E. lieutenant and said that the reason he had asked her to stay was so that she would have all the information firsthand and could expedite all the required paperwork ASAP. He then directed Barney to go with the lieutenant, sit down, come to a conclusion, and be back in his office within an hour. Dismissed...

The W.A.V.E. announced that there was no way she could make Barney a civilian and do all the other required paperwork in even a week, should he choose that option. If he stayed in the Navy, it would be much easier but still take a minimum of three days to get Barney on his way. She seemed pretty upset that unwanted effort on her part would be required regardless of Barney's choice and was letting him know how she felt.

Barney had made up his mind as the commander was giving him the details. As he and the lieutenant sat down in her office, he asked her just how much time she would like to do proper justice to his paper work. With a smile on her face, she said "at least two weeks." First, she would have to get all of his records together. Some kind of record had to be made up to cover the lost time that he was supposed to have been dead. "You will have to help me get that straightened out." Next, he would have to have a complete physical examination. Then there was his pay schedule; she didn't know how much time she needed to figure out all his back pay, since he had drawn some without any pay records to show accountability. Just how that was to be handled and many other items had to be taken into consideration before she could hand him over to civilian personnel so that he could become a civilian employee of the Army. "At that point I will be through with you." Then she added, "Just what did you do that has caused so much demand that you be sent back to an enemy country?" Barney's only answer, "Nothing wrong, I hope."

As Barney sat listening to the W.A.V.E. lieutenant go over all the different paperwork procedures, he began to wonder what she would think if she knew all that had happened to him. What would be her feelings, and maybe her comments, about American servicemen becoming involved with the enemy, especially the Japanese girls?

What the hell? he thought. *It's none of her business.* The W.A.V.E. had made out the first of several discharge papers, and brought Barney out of his mental wanderings by asking him to sign all five copies of each set of papers. She stated that she would try to arrange for a physical for him the first thing the next day. By the time she had finished giving him all her directions, it was time for Barney to be back at Commander Wilson's office with the information that he could not possibly be ready to leave for Japan before two weeks. With a smile on his face Barney thanked the lady lieutenant and made his way to the Intelligence Office.

After Barney had related to the commander the problems of changing him from a sailor to a civilian, the commander just smiled and stated that he was well aware of the time frame but

he wanted to see if the lady lieutenant would become arrogant about being given what he knew would be an impossible task in such a short time. He stated, "She handled it like any sailor should, she didn't complain." Barney thought that all this fooling around was a bunch of horse shit on the commander's part, but he too, was a sailor and made no comment. Commander Wilson gave Barney a list of personal questions that seemed to relate to security matters, and Barney quickly answered all with what he felt the commander would expect him to say. He was then told to follow the procedure that the W.A.V.E. had given him — but that he should push all the people that he would be seeing as fast as he could; If there were any problems to call him and he would straighten them out.

It took only two days for Barney to become a civilian but when he was introduced to the civilian personnel office, the process became another matter. When he informed Commander Wilson of the problems with being processed for the civilian position, as promised by him, all hell broke loose. It seemed that the civilian personnel office did not like being told how and when to do their job. After a very brief, and very loud, discussion with the director of personnel, Barney was asked to return to their office and meet with the director personally. This meeting turned out to be just the opposite from the last meeting with the same office, but when they got down to the rating that Barney had been told he would receive should he accept the civilian position, the director began to back-peddle by telling him that no one was ever hired for the first time with such a high GSA rating. Barney simply picked up the director's phone and dialed the commander's number, expressing the new problem. This time Wilson replied "Just sit tight, I 'II be right over," and hung up. The commander must have run all the way, for the vibration of the phone had barely stopped when the director's door burst open and the commander's first words were, "Don't you assholes know how to take a simple directive? I signed the approval to hire this man myself and you don't need any further consideration or approval to get the job done. I want this man on the earliest and best transportation possible to the destination set forth in the orders that I sent you. Are there any more questions?"

The director did not seem too upset with the commander's outburst. He stated that he would do all the paperwork himself but it would still take several more days. Barney, with a somewhat surprised expression on his face at the conversations that had taken place, softly asked if he could have a choice of the transportation — because he had a few things he wanted to take with him and that at least one might not be acceptable on an airplane. Would it be possible to take one of the sea-going military transports that often went directly to Tokyo?

"The request said ASAP," quoted Commander Wilson. "That can mean almost anything. If that's the way you want to go, it's O.K. with me, I just want to get you out of my hair. I have more important things to do than shepherd one sailor through the civilian process." Then he belligerently stomped out.

The director, with a gruff expression said, "That's what an officer and a gentleman is supposed to act like after spending four years at Annapolis."

He then asked if Barney could come back in two days: "I will have everything done that is within my power to be done, and will have some idea when you can catch the next ship that's headed for Japan." Then he surprised Barney with the big question: "What's all the hurry to get you back where you just came from? It would seem to me, based upon your Navy records, that you would want to spend some time back in your own country." Barney gave no answer.

All the rest of the day Barney spent on the phone calling about small gasoline-powered tractors, the kind that a slight person could operate and not have too much trouble. He finally found one that sounded just right for his purpose and made arrangements for pickup the very next day. The biggest problem that he had was finding the type of clothes that he thought would be needed for all seasons in Japan and having them altered by the date he expected to be leaving. What couldn't be fitted now would be easily tailored after he had a permanent place in Japan, wherever that might be. The next most important thought was, *If only I could let Myoko know of the changes.* How much he wished he could tell her.

November 15

The return trip to Pearl Harbor was just another trip upon the ever-beautiful sea. He had no duties, and spent most of the daylight hours listening to the sea stories that always amused him. Some of the personnel were getting off at Pearl for duty but most were assigned to various duties in Japan.

Of all the different people on the same journey as Barney, several were in the intelligence branch of both the Army and Navy. Two of the Navy personnel were W.A.V.E. lieutenants who kept exclusively to themselves. After several attempts to be friendly with the two ladies, Barney gave up all effort. But on the last day before entering Pearl, one of the W.A.V.E.s sought out Barney as he was visually inhaling the last of another most colorful sunset. "Lieutenant Weston and I do not mean to be unfriendly towards you, but you have both of us somewhat puzzled. We have never encountered a civilian security person before, and all we can find out about you is that you are some kind of special person assigned to headquarters, Tokyo. We do not want to get off on the wrong foot before we're assigned to our new duty in Japan."

Barney, as briefly as he could, explained that he had been Navy just a few months ago and because of his expertise in the Japanese language and his understanding of their culture (better than most) he had had an opportunity, by working closely with the Japanese people, to restart some of the most needed industries. "They do not like, or trust, any American and in most of their minds, they have lost a great deal of face by not winning the war. Several of the key officers in intelligence feel that I can be of important help in working directly with the Japanese who wish to become capitalists like the Americans. It's a very difficult emotional problem for them to admit defeat, then turn around and accept aid from an enemy." Barney further explained that he had been successful doing that kind of work before he had been sent back to the states.

Again, he explained to the lieutenant about his Navy duty, but left out all the events that had brought him to Japan in the first place. After his somewhat short dissertation of his Navy experience and the loss of his destroyer, she held out her hand and said, "I'm Margie, and unless they change my assignment, Lieutenant Weston and I are supposed to search Japanese records to try and find out what happened to many of our unaccounted-for ships, subs, and most important, the many prisoners that the Japanese held and how they were treated. From the stories that we have heard so far, most of the men were tortured and many killed for no reason."

After a long pause, Barney commented that he would like to learn what happened to the men and ship he had served on. With all that had happened to him since leaving his destroyer, he still felt a strong bond with the ship and the submarine, along with their crews and special shipmates.

Margie asked where he would be sent and added that if they found any information about the two, she would gladly share it with him. They exchanged addresses where they hoped to be sent and said goodnight.

November 24

A slow boat to China! Barney guessed that the person that coined that phrase had never taken a boat to Japan. The number of days it took to reach Tokyo seemed like years. This slow time was well spent, however —it helped Barney to organize his thoughts and project some kind of mental agenda as to how he would like to become involved with the people of Fukuoka, and most likely other cities on the Island of Kyushu. He forced a slight smile in remembering how successful the foundry project had become once the Japanese people realized how easy it was to trust some of the Americans.

Without any effort, it seemed to Barney, his inner self was gently warmed by reflection on all that he and Myoko were to each other. Saying to himself, "Yes Myoko, here I come, back to you and all that we have talked about and promised to each other, back to where we belong."

Barney had not seen how complete the war's devastation had been all over Tokyo. The fire bombing of the inner city had completely destroyed twelve square miles, and the casualties had been far greater than was caused by both of the big bombs dropped on the cities of Nagasaki and Hiroshima. The fighting had been over for almost a year and a quarter, and still, block after block lay in piles of ruined debris. Just the thought of all those wasted people, most of them plain civilians, caused a painful throb.

The US military response to civilians was don't bug us or get in our way we have more important things to do than to find a place for an unrequested and non-military person. Barney had not thought that he would be welcomed with a band, or even basically friendly assistance in obtaining transportation to his ordered destination — however he did feel that he could be aided in finding a reasonable place to stay while he arranged his temporary needs.

It was Margie who came to his rescue. While he was traveling through the many halls and rooms trying to get some help, Margie had poked her head out of a small cubicle and asked him what he was doing in her territory.

Over a cup of her great Navy coffee, Barney told her of his immediate problem and asked her if she had any good ideas for solving it. Maybe because she was a female and part of the intelligence group, she had been treated much better. Female lieutenants, certainly attractive ones, were a novelty on most posts, especially in a foreign country. She definitely had an edge.

Margie stated that there were several good places for officers to find housing — small, but for Japan, OK. She asked if Barney could drop back in the afternoon and she would have a place for him. They set 1600 hours and Barney left to spend the remainder of the day walking through the remains of the city.

Margie was waiting for Barney when he returned to her small office. She handed him an address written in Japanese and told him to find a peddy cab that would take him to the address. Barney thanked her and was turning to leave when she asked him if he was not going to thank her by buying her a drink at the only good after-work watering hole. "You might meet some very interesting people who could help you get to where you need to go."

Barney was not much of a drinker; a good cold beer was just his speed — one good cold beer and not much else. The thought of a cold beer at this time of day was a great proposal and he would be glad to pay. The so-called watering hole was part of the occupation headquarters building and had been made over to suit the new tenants, American style.

It was four bells per the Navy time machine. Walking into the American type bar, Barney was struck by all the high-ranking brass that filled the room. There were several two- and three-star generals, many colonels and majors, with a lesser number of captains and lieutenants. Barney was the only civilian in the whole crowd. Finding a small table toward the back of the room, he sat observing all the loud conversation that was taking place. Shortly, a very attractive young Japanese waitress asked Barney what he would like to drink. "Just a beer, I'm a one-beer-a-day person," he said, and then to himself, *and that's all I intend to have.* Setting the bottle of beer and a cold glass down on Barney's table, the waitress said, "Ten cents please." Barney paid and responded "Domo arigato"; the waitress gave a small nod and gave the same response. He noticed that the beer was one of the best of many good Japanese brands. He slowly poured about half of the golden colored liquid into the glass and took his first taste. It was a great beer.

As he observed the drinking that was taking place about the room, Barney noticed that almost all the drinks being consumed were either scotch, gin or bourbon, the hard stuff.

At the fifth Navy bell, Margie and Lt. Weston came through the wide door and the whole noise level of the room changed. It seemed that every officer's head turned toward the two very attractive W.A.V.E.s. Several of the men made wolfish sounds, with a couple of whistles thrown in. The two ladies paid no attention to the unwelcome noise and catching Barney's eye, they hurried to his table.

As Margie sat down, she began to tell Barney that they were having a great deal of fun with his presence. Many of the other personnel on their floor were asking what a civilian was doing here and why attached to intelligence? "We have been telling them that you are here to investigate reports of misconduct and theft of U.S. government property, but we don't think any of them are guilty. You should have seen their eyes bulge. Well tell them the truth after you leave."

Each W.A.V.E. ordered her choice of beverage and Barney kept his promise to buy them a drink. There was some random conversation about the day, and then Lieutenant Weston introduced herself as Carol Weston, and said that she and Margie had thought about dinner at a very special Japanese restaurant and invited Barney to share it with them. She went on to say that the place was just a nice walking distance from where they were now and the restaurant was considered one of the best in what was left of downtown Tokyo.

Barney quickly agreed and said he would be honored to foot the bill, with the added comment that as a new civilian, his pay and allowances were greater than theirs.

As the three of them started to walk out the door, a hand reached out and grabbed Barney's arm and in a very authoritative voice, demanded "Where the hell have you been, I was informed that you left Treasure Island some two months ago and now I find you here in Tokyo with two darned nice looking fellow Navy persons. Just what is going on?" Barney turned to see to whom the demanding voice belonged and was astonished to see the smiling face of Rickards — now a colonel. Before Barney could respond, the colonel continued with the comment that he had informed Mr. Morita that Barney would be returning to work with him and would be continuing to help the business-minded people of Fukuoka. "Barney," the colonel said, "I know that Morita has planned a special celebration for you and is inviting many of the local people who would like to start some kind of business. You really made a great impression on all the people you helped. Besides, see the silver bird on my collar? You're responsible for that and I am very grateful. Now can you tell me just who these lovely ladies are and I will buy us all a drink."

Before anyone could say anything, Carol took the colonel's arm, turned him around and informed him that they were about to walk to a very good Japanese restaurant, and

he was about to join them. "No arguments Colonel, just come along, you can treat us to a drink there." With a somewhat amazed smile, Rickards did not object.

After being seated in the restaurant, Colonel Rickards asked Barney to do the honors and order the food, exclaiming to the ladies, "Barney found a most unlikely little hole in the bombed-out rubble of Fukuoka that was run by a little old lady. She had taken over what was left of a building and as best as she could, rebuilt her hole-in-the-wall place to eat. The food she served was of the best and freshest that I have ever had here in Japan, and Barney, I will apologize to her when I get back for not visiting and eating her really great food."

Seated toward the back of the restaurant, the colonel ordered drinks and began to relate to Carol and Margie all that Barney had done under his command while in Fukuoka some months ago. As the interest grew from the two women, the Colonel began to relate just how Barney had arrived in Japan and the most unbelievable story that he and Lt. Tracy had ever heard, which he added, turned out to be all truth and absolute facts. No fiction.

The waitress asked if they were ready to order and began to recite some of the dishes that she thought Americans might like. Barney interrupted her and, in his very best manner, asked in Japanese about dishes that he was fond of and knew that everyone would enjoy. They would most likely not be on any menu that served Americans. The waitress smiled pleasantly in response to Barney's request. His fluency in the Japanese language brought several ahs from the W.A.V.E.s. Margie made a strong response, "you do sound like a very well-spoken Japanese — where and how did you become so proficient? The Japanese language is not easy to speak as well as you just did."

Without any hesitation, the colonel answered the question. "Barney all but lived with a very special Japanese-American family in his home town. His special high school friend was part of that family. Even though the war was on, he took serious interest in the Japanese language and culture, especially, what did you say your friend's name was, Koji?

"His friend's family could not speak one word of English and Barney took it upon himself to learn and communicate with his parents. So he learned very well and it's a great benefit especially to me and, of course, the U.S. Army. In short, we all are in his debt."

Barney just sat and as the colonel concluded, he was pleased that he had not had to explain to the ladies all that had allowed him to know the Japanese and their language so well.

The many dishes were served and to the pleasure of all, the food was excellent. As the dishes were removed, Rickards began to ask Barney what had been the trouble in reporting to his office. Barney went through all the indifference of the Tokyo military people and their regulations and then explained how Margie had come to his aid and was directly responsible for his being at the watering hole, which led to this meeting.

Colonel Rickards, regaining his West Point attitude and voice, directed Barney to be at the airfield "tomorrow" at 14:00. He had a DC-3 at his disposal and expected Barney to be on board. Barney interrupted the colonel by informing him that he had several large crates that he wanted to make sure did not get lost. "It's a gift to the little old man that was of such great help when I found myself stranded here in Japan. He uses a crude hand cultivator to turn the soil in his three small paddies. The crates contain a small garden tractor and some attachments that will allow him not to have to work so hard at his plowing. It is the least I can do to repay the help he gave me."

It was the first time in a long time that he had referred to Myoko as "he" and it gave him somewhat of a guilty feeling. The last thing that he wanted them to know was his deep involvement with a Japanese lady. Barney was not sure if Colonel Rickards was aware that Barney's little old man was a very special lovely lady to whom he was totally committed.

The Colonel told Barney that the crates would easily fit on his plane and to be sure that he had them and himself on board at the stated time. "I want you in my office as soon as possible; we have hundreds of indigenous people to work with and I can't do it without your help." As an afterthought, Rickards added, "Let's all go back to the American club and let me treat each of you to a nightcap. I have some important things to attend to tomorrow and some things have to be gone over if I'm to keep my job."

November 25

Cold, dark, gray fog had moved into the Tokyo area. The stuff was so thick that Barney had to ask the airport ground personnel directions to the flight line and Colonel Rickards' waiting plane. Earlier that morning he paid several freewheeling G.I.s fifty dollars for the use of a 4 X 4 truck and some 30 minutes of their muscles, getting his crates transported to the air base. He refused to tell them what the crates contained, which helped Barney to feel as though he was having some measure of revenge for being stuck in Tokyo when it was not necessary.

The base personnel were very helpful in placing the crates on board and strapping them down securely. With nothing else left to do, he began casual conversation with several of the Japanese workmen who had really done all the work in placing the crates on the plane. Barney asked about their families and how they had come to be working on the base. Given their answers, Barney was more than pleased with what he had assured Myoko would happen to the Japanese people during their long discussions about American's helping to rebuild the Japanese economy. He had just found proof that what he had told her was already happening.

It was at about this time that a slow rumble in his stomach informed him that he had not had any breakfast. Asking about, he was given directions to the passenger waiting room where he found a small canteen-style food service. Something that he had never heard of was featured on the menu board hanging on the back wall: rice pancakes with sausage. The cooks behind the little counter were young Japanese girls who presented nothing but serious efficiency. The pancakes were about the size of flattened tennis balls and there were plenty of them. They tasted very good.

Waiting was never one of Barney's strong suits. He roamed about the hangars and office buildings until they became boring. Making his way back to the colonel's plane, he settled down on one of the long passenger bunks and began to think about all the work he had in front of him, and to enjoy the warmth he felt knowing Myoko was not too far away. His thoughts went back to the many times that they had walked along the beach below the cliffs, the fishing in the surf and the wonderful dinners Myoko had made for the two of them from almost nothing. Eventually he dozed off.

About noon, two airmen woke him from his slumber and informed him that Rickards had called to check if Barney had arrived and gotten his crates on the plane. The airmen were asked to tell Barney that the colonel would be ready at the stated time and not to wander too far away from the plane. In an hour three airmen came struggling aboard, announced that they were the pilot, co-pilot and flight engineer and asked if he was ready to go. Barney responded, "Just as soon as Colonel Rickards gets here; he sent word that he would be ready to fly at the set time, so he should be here soon."

The aircrew had not been told about Barney, so the questions began to fly. When Barney informed them that he was assigned to the colonel's staff and that he was to work on some special assignments, they suddenly became very quiet. Again, Barney felt a measure of pleasure in the fact that he had pulled something over on a few more people. He was beginning to enjoy letting everyone who chose to ask, think whatever they wanted to about his being a part of the colonel's intelligence staff. He was sure that if they knew the truth, there would be some persons who would have bitter feelings toward him and what he was going to be involved in. *Oh well, that will be their problem, not mine,* he thought, for he not only felt great about helping the not-so-long-ago enemy rebuild their country but also proud and privileged that his country had the strength and moral character to do so.

Barney knew that Rickards was arriving, for the plane crew became very active and started the preflight routine, making sure that everything was properly tied down and ready for takeoff. The colonel stepped inside and shouted, "Get this thing

out of here, let's go home." For several minutes, Barney sat buckled in his seat repeating in his mind, home — home and Myoko.

As the plane lifted off, the scene below them was one of burned-out rubble with everything destroyed. It was only after they had flown a number of miles away from the general area of Tokyo that he saw that some of the farmland and rural dwellings were still intact. Water buffalo were being used to turn the soil in some of the areas, and for mile after mile he noted farmers with their long-toothed cultivators flaying away at the soil just as he and Myoko had done so many times. He thought, *Not any more. She will have a new farm tractor to do the backbreaking work and it will take less than half of the time.*

The sound of the plane's engines being throttled back brought him back to the real world. It was time to land and get the show on the road.

Barney had no problem unloading the heavy crates. Some of the Japanese work force, now employed at the base, was well aware of the assistance that Barney had given to Mr. Morita and the foundry. They were glad that the "Yankee" was again here to help.

Barney's first objective was to find a home, and one not in the military complex or in the larger part of town. He had made up his mind a long time ago that if he was to work with the Japanese, he would have to separate his lifestyle from that of the occupying forces. Regardless of the assistance that the Americans were giving, they were still the victors and the Japanese were the losers. The feeling was just part of the Japanese philosophy of losing face. Always on his mind was to let Myoko know that he was close, very close, and would see her as soon as he could make the arrangements. Keeping her a secret was very important and he did not voice any eagerness to deliver the large crates.

Barney had been looking for a suitable living space and had had no luck. The city had been so torn by the heavy bombing during the war that there was not much left, let alone a place to live. It seemed that the whole population was doing the same. With the city lying in ruins, his chance of finding what he wanted would be impossible.

Mr. Morita had begged Barney to visit with him and meet with several other Japanese men who wanted help in becoming business owners. At the meeting, Morita let Barney know that several of the men who wanted to start a clothing business had indeed made arrangements with a Tokyo importer. And, six of the Australian sewing machines had been delivered along with some of the very best wool. A second business had begun: turning wool into fine cloth. The silk industry, now long gone, provided some of the most experienced weavers in the world, and they had begun to manufacture the cloth that was needed. All was well.

Barney had voiced his living space problems briefly with Mr. Morita, who agreed that finding such a place was near impossible, but he would try to help. Mr. Morita reminded Barney that houses like he was used to in the United States were not to be had in Japan: "Japanese houses are much smaller due to the shortage of space and the materials with which to build them. We will try."

As Barney sat mulling over the problem, he could not help but think that if Myoko was a little closer, her home would be a perfect place. He had not had much time to dwell upon his Myoko in the past few weeks yet she was always there, the center of his longing. She was his very soul.

Mr. Morita sent one of his factory workers to ask if Barney could have dinner at his home, stressing that his home was small but a very happy and humble one. Could Barney be there at six o'clock on Friday of the coming weekend? Yes, he could — just the thought of being with a family again caused Barney to smile to himself and begin to feel somewhat happier.

Barney had made arrangements with Colonel Rickards for the use of a jeep and a Japanese driver for all his business requirements and was told that he could put it to his own use when needed. Friday was the time it would be needed. Even though he had toured many of the different places in the city, he was not sure just where Mr. Morita lived. The jeep driver was more important than the jeep.

Barney was driven directly to Mr. Morita's home. He made his way up the path of a very beautiful garden setting. He was amazed at the neatness of everything that made the place so pleasing. Mr. Morita met him at the entrance of his home and as Barney removed his street shoes in the entryway, Morita greeted him with a very polite bowing of the head and "Welcome to my most humble dwelling."

The two of them entered what Barney thought was a small art gallery. The room was full of pieces of art that he had only seen in some very selected magazines: vases, ornamental flower arrangements with real flowers, brocaded silk wall panels, several old but ornately carved wood tables and a storage chest. Barney could not help but think that this was just the kind of place he would like to live in. The style and decorations were reflective of many decades of Japanese history.

As the two walked about the house, Morita began to explain his great fortune: "A friend of mine was aware that a very high Japanese official, who was provided this place by the past Japanese government, was out of a job due to the end of the war. He could no longer keep it and I was able to take legal possession with the help of your Colonel Rickards. I am now the owner. Regardless of your not being involved directly, you are the one responsible for so many things that it is hard for me to know how to thank you for."

Morita pointed out some of the features of his "humble" home and stated that many of the trees and shrubbery were almost as old as Japan. "The little trees are several hundred years old and the cuttings that they came from go back almost a thousand years. Such things are what Japan is all about. Our culture places the greatest value on things that represent many generations of love and caring, the Japanese way. I know that you have a strong feeling about much of our history and understand most of our traditions. This is very important to you and to the people who will have the pleasure of knowing and working with you. It is a deep-rooted trust and must not be taken for granted. I know that you will honor all of this in the best Japanese tradition."

Circling around the dwelling and coming back to the entrance of the house, Morita exclaimed, "It's time to meet my family and have some refreshments." Mrs. Morita was a very delicate-looking lady and at once, Barney was very impressed with her. She also bowed deeply and welcomed Barney to their home, then directed the two men to a room that was set for refreshments and dinner. Sake, poured warm and in small delicate white cups, was served. The cups had very ornate designs engraved along the sides.

Before dinner was served, two very happy and active children entered the room and were introduced to Barney. Their giggling and pleasant appearance reinforced that this was a very happy home.

The meal was in the very highest Japanese tradition. The majority of dishes were seafood based with different types of vegetables cooked in a variety of tasty sauces. As the evening meal ended, Mr. Morita directed Barney to another small room and stated, "This is my business meeting office. We can enjoy a very important conversation and not be disturbed."

Morita began by telling Barney of the great need of his important services by a group of Japanese men who wanted to build a multi-product company. "They have plans to make a number of badly-needed tools, machinery, electrical products and such. The problem is that they are not sure how to manage the process with respect to your occupation regulations and the paper forms required. To be the owners of such a big business is very strange to them and they want to do everything the right way. They are well aware of the help you gave me with the beginning of the foundry and they are much impressed. Could you meet with them and maybe help or advise them to understand how to begin?"

Barney was almost stunned. The proposal that had just been described to him was the very reason that he was in Japan. Barney did not want to be too obvious or show his eagerness, so he responded slowly: "Mr. Morita, you meet with the men you mentioned and have them set a date and time for a long meeting, and I will be pleased to try and help them. Also, I have a lot to learn, myself, about the legal requirements. First, I must find a nice place to live. I do not want to be housed in any of the American military facilities. I think that it will be very important to share and show my serious attitude toward the Japanese culture and the changing ways that are now taking over in the new Japan. I feel that I will gain greater respect from the local population if I am living as they are, and among them." Mr. Morita nodded agreement and sounded very pleased.

Morita's next statement was what Barney wanted to hear. "One of the men who is part of the business group you will meet has a very large estate on the outside of the main part of the city and has several very pleasant guest houses on the property. I recently had the pleasure to briefly visit his estate and Barney, let me tell you, it is one of the most beautiful spots in all Japan. He stated to me that he would like to offer you one of the larger houses for your own private quarters. He even has full-time gardeners and a person to maintain the house. Regardless, whether you work with the group or not, the offer is yours to decide."

Barney was ecstatic — what Mr. Morita had just said was the answer to what he had been trying to find for weeks. Now it was going to be his — for just doing what he was supposed to be doing, helping the interested local people to rebuild their economy and become members of the rest of the free world.

It took two weeks for Morita to arrange the meeting with the group of men who were asking for Barney's assistance. It had been decided to meet at the estate home of the person who had the house that might be right for Barney. The meeting was to be held at 1:00 on a Saturday afternoon so that it would not interfere with any work of the members.

Barney was as nervous as a cat all that Saturday morning. Regardless of how much he tried to lay out a proposed agenda for the procedures and paperwork required by the occupation forces he could not, because he did not know specifically what projects the men would be asking for.

He finally decided to simply tell them "I will do my very best to help all of you to meet your objectives for the ventures that you decide upon."

The jeep driver must have had some idea of the meeting for as they drove to the estate, he seemed more careful in his driving and did not try to pass too close to any people who were out walking. There were always crowded streets and walkways all over town as though no one had anything to do.

The meeting place was in the northern outskirts of the city, on a long piece of land overlooking forested slopes and the southern part of the Sea of Japan. As they drove, Barney was taken back by the grandeur of this part of the city. He had never had a reason to visit it before, so this was very new to him. The whole area was winding roads with much-cared-for gardens along each side of the narrow streets. As they drove up the estate driveway, the whole entrance was a most beautiful garden with carefully trimmed ornamental trees and blooming flowerbeds. Barney had never seen such a quiet and beautiful place, not even in books.

As they approached the front of the main dwelling, a small group of well-dressed Japanese men stood waiting for him. They bowed their traditional greeting of honor for Barney. The thought went through his mind, *I must be in the wrong place for I surely don't deserve this kind of reception. This is more like what a general or even a prime minister would expect.* Barney reveled in the reception for it might never happen again. Not too bad for just a plain sailor.

There was no foolishness in getting the meeting underway. There were a few bows and some handshakes as each person was introduced, and then Morita asked everyone to please adjourn to a large outside room where an equally large table had been set for this most important occasion. Barney was asked to sit at the head of the table and Mr. Motsushita, the host and owner of the great property, seated himself at the other end. Morita quickly established the direction of the meeting and then gave a short overview of how Barney had first asked him to open a rusted-out old foundry — one which was now a strong successful business contributing to the rebuilding of a new free economy. In addition, Morita quickly gave a description of the clothing industry and how that had led to another very important business — the weaving of wool for much needed clothing and bedding.

As each man stated their general ideas, Barney was amazed that they had already decided on just five major product areas. Throughout the rest of the afternoon, each detail of several previous meetings came to light. The seriousness of the group had already been established and the selected officers were in place. Financial considerations had been taken into account and all that was really needed was Barney's direction through the legal process, to make sure they stayed within the framework of the occupational laws and the regulations of the new Japan.

Barney carefully recorded all the men's names and addresses. He made notes of some of the more important concerns and suggestions along with each man's positions in the proposed business venture. Most important of all, just who was going to be the banker? Barney had never had any training in finance or keeping of important records, and he wanted to make sure someone who was greatly experienced would be chosen for this most important responsibility. He did know that without proper finances and solid management of funds, the new company would go nowhere. The five men had taken every item, large and small, into serious consideration and had set firm plans. The meeting was over.

Mr. Motsushita's housekeeper, stepping ever so quietly, slipped into the outside room and announced that refreshments were available and that a special dinner would be served within the hour. The refreshments were a welcome break. As each person began to stretch and move toward the refreshment table, Motsushita took Barney's arm and directed him to one side, saying that he understood from Mr. Morita that Barney was having problems in finding a suitable place to live. Barney did his best to explain all the different areas that he had sought out, with no results. Motsushita quickly informed Barney that the problem was one that he would be honored to solve. He had several guesthouses in different places on his property and all were empty at this time. "I like peace and quiet so they remain empty, even though there is a desperate need for housing.

"The one guest house that I think you will most enjoy is situated on the very edge of my property and is separate from all the others. It overlooks the shore and ocean to the west, which is the best place to humble oneself with the most beautiful of sunsets. It is most private and will allow you the serenity and quiet that Mr. Morita has informed me that you enjoy. I will direct you to it after our evening meal. You might like to spend the night in the house should you choose to do so."

Very little was said about the proposed business plan throughout dinner. Each man wanted to make sure Barney knew about his background and experience as it related to any kind of business. Several of them had past experience in some of the proposed products. Finally, Mr. Morita stood abruptly and informed the group that there was much that needed to be done. Each different project had to have a business plan. "Barney showed me just how important such a plan is if you want to keep from making large mistakes and have the best opportunity for long success. You must give serious consideration to a site for the new venture. Each man needs to set his own personal program on paper so that the most important ones can be selected and projects begun. I am most willing to place my home or business office at your convenience for our next meeting."

At that point the formal meeting was over, and Mr. Motsushita led Barney out into the closing evening, out to the edge of the gardens and down several steps to a place even Barney could not have dreamed about. The setting where the guesthouse stood was in a garden all by itself. Many different types of flowers graced the garden with some of the most magnificent colors that nature could have provided.

A path led down to a point that overlooked the beach below and the ever-churning ocean. Typical of the Japanese, everywhere one looked there was something different in the landscaping, and at the edge of the garden was a special place for quiet reflection and just being alone with oneself.

As Barney looked from one side of the vista to the other, taking in the grace and beauty of the surroundings, he could not help but think of how great this place would be if he and his Myoko could be sitting at the edge of the garden, looking out across the deep blue sea, planning their future. This would be the perfect piece of heaven for all their tomorrows.

Barney had a great deal of things to think about, and he set some of them down on paper so that it would prove he was going to keep his part of the bargain. He declined to stay the night but did accept Mr. Motsushita's occupancy offer and left thanking him for his generosity.

For the next several weeks, Barney met with a number of other men who were interested in starting a new business. All seemed eager but needed strong business plans and a great deal of assistance in just the basic planning and proper legal paperwork.

For the five who had already made the commitment, Barney found that when it came down to some final questions, it was difficult for them to understand how they could become the owners and not have to have the Japanese government telling them what and how to do it. How could they be owners and not subjected as in the past to the military government?

Barney had kept Colonel Rickards well informed and asked assistance from some of the intelligence legal minds to help draft a general agreement of partnership for each of the prospective business partners to read, approve or reject, and sign. Just the sounds of such a legal-sounding paper caused some confusion among the men. This was very new to them and they had to be reassured and have much of it explained. Barney pressed Colonel Rickards into the act and had him present the partnership document and answer all their questions. Just having a very important U.S. military man explaining it in a very friendly manner made all the difference, and they seemed very pleased. Progress was going to be just a little slow.

Later Colonel Rickards cornered Barney and gave him a bit of a third degree, asking how he had managed to get such men together in one group with such serious plans and determination. He left Barney feeling better about what he was supposed to have been doing since he first met the colonel.

All the discussions with the business group had cemented a very close relationship among them, and especially with Barney. He was beginning to feel a personal partnership with each person as they developed their programs. He gained a feeling of security, realizing that he would be able to stay in Japan for a long time.

The painful longing to see and be with Myoko was beginning to cause a distraction for him. Several times, he had had the big crates loaded on a GI truck when Colonel Rickards ordered and assigned him in another direction. For Barney, keeping his relationship with Myoko to himself was most important. Regardless of his emotions, he did not want any problems for her. In both the Japanese community and also the occupational forces, there remained a very negative attitude about American personnel having any kind of relationship with the conquered enemy. For Japanese women, it was all but criminal to have a close American friend.

Moving himself into Motsushita's compound was the first real joy that he had had in a long time. It was easy, because all he had were some civilian clothes and some working materials such as notepaper, pencils and other needed supplies. The Jeep driver carried all of his belongings to the house in one trip. When Barney was first shown the house, he did not pay much attention to the inside. Altogether there were seven rooms. The general sitting room was the largest, with plenty of room for the accommodation and entertainment of guests. There were two average-sized bedrooms of Japanese design, a cooking space, and a patio-like opening to the south and the sea. It seemed funny to Barney that there was also a space for a live-in maid. The most luxurious space was for the "soaking tub" as Myoko called it. The firebox was controlled from the outside and the heat funneled under the tub — a very safe and efficient configuration.

It took Barney several weeks to get acquainted with all the surroundings of his wonderful new home. There was so much to be grateful for that it took him many trips around the garden to make sure it was all his, even if it did not belong to him. Only his Myoko was missing.

January 12, 1946

Barney was in the Colonel's office dealing with some of the constant paperwork concerning the requirements of the occupation business, making sure that his advice to the new business group and all the details would be correct and in the right place. His mind was concentrating on the final paper process and he did not notice the colonel silently staring at him. Without any preamble Rickards simply asked Barney, "When are you going to do it?" There was only one thing Barney could relate the question to: the tractor. The crates had been the curiosity of everyone in the complex. Even the Marines had made comments about "Barney's big boxes."

Barney guessed that the time would never get any easier so he began to explain. "Colonel, I have attempted on several occasions to find time to do what you are alluding to, but each time you have had a different assignment for me. I would like to arrange to take the tractor to my friend this next Friday if there is no conflict. Can this be arranged?"

The Colonel's face lit up as he responded to the question. "Barney, I have been aware of your friend for some time. Before Lt. Tracy departed, he invited me to the little old lady's restaurant and ordered some of the same food that you first enjoyed with him, along with the cold beer of course." For several minutes, Barney could not answer. His first thought was that Lt. Tracy had reneged on his promise to keep confidential Barney's special friend's part of his survival. But Tracy was part of the intelligence group so he had been obliged to relay the information.

As Barney settled in to his new and most beautiful surroundings, he would spend the evenings sitting at the edge of the cliff, reflecting on the many times he and Myoko had done the same thing. That now seemed like years ago. Tonight, as he again sat taking in another many-colored sunset, Mr. Motsushita came whistling across the garden, shouted a cordial "good evening" greeting and quickly commented, "I have been watching you sit alone and wondered what was going on in your mind. Is something bothering you? Or are you missing something or someone who is very important to you? No person should be so selfish as to keep such a fine evening to himself."

Wanting to be with Myoko and reflecting back to all that had brought him to this place was taking up far too much of his time lately, and was distracting him from the responsibility to Colonel Rickards. As he pondered Mr. Motsushita's question, he focused on this man's very important friendship and his feeling of personal trust. Barney had to respond in some way that made sense, but he was reluctant to just blurt out his relationship with a Japanese lady.

But he had to begin somewhere and sometime, if he was ever to solve the problem of having Myoko in his life. He took a deep breath and began by asking Mr. Motsushita his thoughts about American personnel having relations with Japanese personnel, either male or female. "I do not mean just physical going to bed kind of relations, but one that bonds two people together for life — one of great respect, trust and faithfulness. I have been most fortunate to have found a lady with whom I have the deepest of personal feelings and want very much to have her share my life. I am sure that she shares the same feelings; in fact she is responsible for my being here now, wanting to make a life together here in Japan."

Barney had been watching Motsushita's expressions as he slowly explained part of his answer. So far there was no wrinkling of Motsushita's face or any adverse reaction, so Barney went on and expressed that he had great trust in Motsushita's friendship and was sure that he would understand what Barney was saying.

Barney began at the very beginning of how he first came to Japan and the part Myoko had played in keeping him alive. He expressed very strongly that he and Myoko had spent many hours discussing the differences between their cultures and some of the problems that would be caused. "I have attempted to assure her that as our two countries came together in the rebuilding of Japan, a very strong bond and a different, more positive respect for our two cultures would develop. As you have become aware, in some ways this is happening faster than anyone had ever thought, and I am most proud of the small part that I have played in bringing some of this about."

He was about to continue further but Motsushita quickly asked, "Just where is this lady now? Within the past months, I have become very fond of our business and personal relationship and learned that you are a person of great trustworthiness. Our business group would be at a great loss without your assistance in helping to establish what you like to call a free enterprise company."

The next statement from Barney's friend was somewhat of a shock. First, he commented that two of his partners were of the old school and still held great prewar attitudes about all foreigners, especially because Japan had lost the war with America. "If any one of the two learned that you are very friendly with a Japanese lady, they would be most unkind toward you. As it is, they have voiced some objections to setting aside any rewards for the many services that you are, and have been, contributing to us all. I will do my best to keep them in a good attitude about you. Let's just not mention your lady to them or anyone else for the time being.

"If I can be of assistance in helping you to resolve your dilemma..." Motsushita hesitated a moment. "Personally, I find that when two people really care each other, it makes no difference what country they are from. But they should fully understand the potential problems that those differences might make with others from either side."

So far so good, thought Barney. He needed to express to Motsushita that the American occupational orders had forbid any military personnel from cohabiting with so-called indigenous persons, but the order had turned out to be a joke. Many of even the highest-ranking officers were the first to establish meaningful relationships with Japanese women. After all, they were some of the most beautiful in all Asia. "I do not think that such an order applies to me, a lowly government employee, but I do not want to cause any hardship for Myoko."

The two of them sat enjoying the sunset and the beginning of the coolness of the evening, talking about the many changes that were taking place around the world, and always getting back to their two worlds, America and Japan. The more they shared their knowledge and the lack thereof about each other's culture, the more that a close respect and bond became obvious between the two men. Finally, Motsushita stated that he would like very much to meet Barney's Myoko and when could he bring her here?

One of the warmest feelings that he had ever experienced came over Barney. Then, "I have a great deal to do before I can be sure that she will not be subject to some problems, both with the colonel's office and possibly from some of the Japanese people. I brought her a small garden tractor with several needed attachments so she will not have to work so hard in preparing her garden. She has a strong attachment to the three remote paddies and the area and also loves the hard work. The place that she lives in is very special to both of us and we would like to keep it that way. We have not discussed marriage or anything like that. It just seemed too uncertain up until now. Maybe with your help, we can find a way to make marriage possible."

As Barney sat late into the evening overlooking his special part of the China Sea, he was allowing his emotions to take over every part of his thoughts and judgment. Somehow, it had to come to some kind of resolution. Rethinking all that he and Mr. Motsushita had talked about only several hours ago, the only conclusion that he could come to was to sit down with Colonel Rickards and explain everything, hoping to get his permission to use a truck to take his gift to Myoko.

The day was only Tuesday, but Barney had made up his mind to repeat his request for the truck for the coming Friday, hoping that he could have the weekend to have a reunion with his special friend. He wanted to tell her all of the details of his return to America, the position that was given to him and, most importantly, the friendship of Mr. Motsushita. His mind was made up — tomorrow was the day he would act, by addressing the whole issue of Myoko to the Colonel.

As Barney entered Colonel Rickards' office, the colonel looked up and smiled with his usual military bearing. Barney did not give the colonel a chance to say anything. He immediately stated that he wanted to have some of the Colonel's time to discuss the problem of taking the tractor to his friend, and he continued on with the request for the use of a truck for the coming Friday.

Barney was not prepared for Rickards' response. "I have been waiting for you to make up your mind about the tractor and your friend. Your big crates are taking up room that could be used for important military things." He gave a wink to Barney. "I have only one small but very personnel request for you. I want to go with you and meet this person and see some of your hiding places, like the cave on the edge of the cliffs, and where you did some fishing. When Lt. Tracy told me about the lady and all that came about during your stranded months, it was a story that I wanted you to share with me. I assure you that I will respect your and your relationship, but you have to understand, I am very interested in meeting her and seeing the places where you spent your last days of the war. I would really consider it a personal honor to return to the places that mean so much to you."

Barney was almost angry with himself. He had undoubtedly lost a great deal of time by trying to keep Myoko from being found out by both the Japanese and the US military. As though cold water was being drained from a barrel, the fears he had recently built up regarding Myoko slowly just drained away.

"Myoko's home is about two hours away and requires driving over some very poor roads. In fact, near her house the road is just a path that the people have been using. If you have no objections, I would like to leave so that we can arrive before noon. I will have the tractor and the extra equipment on the truck ready to leave by 09:30. Several of the Japanese workmen want to go with us and see just how the tractor works. They will handle the unloading and do whatever needs to be done when we arrive." All was said and done. Barney began to feel much better than he had in a long time.

The excitement of seeing Myoko in a few days began to cause his emotions to soar. Everything would soon be fine.

Barney was beside himself for the rest of the week. He sought out Mr. Motsushita and told him of Friday's plan. Motsushita was as pleased as Barney was happy.

January 18, 1946

Early Friday morning, Barney and his two Japanese workmen carefully un-crated the tractor and its three main tools and loaded them onto the G.I. truck. Promptly at 09:30, they drove to the front of Colonel Rickards' office. The colonel was standing ready for a day in the country and was not sure of all that would happen.

Barney had drawn a rough map of the correct road leading out of the outskirts of the city. It would lead to the more-or-less wide path that would take them to their destination. In the front of the vehicle was the Japanese driver with Barney in the center and the colonel on the passenger side The one remaining worker was cramped in the back with the tractor, holding on as best as he could. The truck's gears moaned a little as the Japanese driver shifted from low into the next gear.

As they reached the countryside, Barney began to recognize some of the places that he had visited before the war ended, when he was nothing but an enemy in the enemy's land. They had driven for about an hour when they came to the site of the old farmer that had shared some of his fresh-killed pork with he and Myoko many months ago. Nothing had changed; it was just as he remembered it. As they approached, the old man was carefully removing weeds from his flower garden. Barney asked the driver to stop for a few moments. He and the colonel stepped out and Barney greeted the old man in his own language. At first, the old man was very taken aback. A white man with a very important-looking military officer stopping to say hello to him? — *Most unusual!* he thought.

Barney explained to that he had met the man some time ago, under different circumstances, and just wanted to say hello. Again the old man was more puzzled. In his mind, he could not match any of what Barney was referring to and questioned such a meeting. Barney did not want to linger any longer so he promised to stop another time and better explain. Shaking hands, both Barney and the colonel returned to the truck. They slowly moved on up the hill as the old man kept watch until they were out of sight.

As they traveled, Barney began to point out some of the vegetable paddies that he had "borrowed" food from during his unwelcome stay. "That paddy over there," he pointed, "I took about ten pounds of sweet potatoes, and the one down by the road was always good for an armful of cabbage. When I was growing up, I hated cabbage —but when hunger sets in, steamed cabbage becomes very tasty when served with some fresh fish to a very hungry appetite. They kept me from hunger most of the time before I found my friend." On they drove.

Just before they came to a low hill, Barney pointed and informed the colonel that, "just beyond the cluster of bamboo is a trail that goes down to the beach. Some 75 feet down the trail is the hole in the cliff that i made into my security place." The colonel immediately ordered the driver to stop. "Barney, I want to see everything that you experienced while you were here, so let's go down to the cave where you lived."

At the top of the cliff, the scene down to the beach was breathtaking all by itself. They stopped and again Barney pointed to the long beach and the rocks where he fished and further, where he and Myoko spent long evenings watching the close of special days. Down the trail, past a hillside bolder was the entrance to Barney's cave. As the two men looked inside, Barney commented, "Nothing has changed since the last time I was here. Myoko and I escaped to this place when we thought that she was going to be forced to become part of a civilian suicide group that planned to meet and try to destroy as many of our invading troops as they could. It was very close and we had little room so we just cuddled up close and talked about what the end of the war might bring to both of us. Even so, it was a happy time."

Retreating to the truck, Barney began to have a strong surge in his adrenalin system. Just over the hill were the three paddies.

As the truck came to the top of the hill, Barney became very quiet. Just barely on the crest of the hill he asked the driver to slow down and stop so that he could see down to the small valley below. The image spread out below them was one that Barney would never forget. There were the three-tiered gardens that looked almost artificial because of their well-kept, tender care. Rows of dark green cabbage, terraces of carpets of sweet potatoes and the last paddy full of near ripening rice. Standing in the last part of the sweet potato patch was a small bent-over figure of a little old man, just like Barney had first seen nearly a year ago. Barney could not help but release tears of joy as they welled up in his eyes and dimmed his vision. He knew who was standing in the paddies. His heart was beating fast, but in a very pleasant rhythm. He knew that he was home.

They sat at the top of the hill overlooking the peaceful and quiet picture below them. Barney began to explain to Rickards all that had happened just as it happened, where the bastard of a Japanese soldier was buried in one of the paddies, the path that led to the fishing village farther along the path and on down to the barely visible roof of Myoko's home. "Over there, Colonel, where you see the large stand of giant bamboo, that's where I hid and first noticed the little old man. I would sit by the hours and watch and admire just how carefully he tended his garden. Again, that trail alongside the paddies leads to the fishing village where I borrowed some fishing poles and hooks."

Barney had kept his eyes on the little old looking figure in the field carefully working the plants. The figure did not look up even though Barney knew that it was well aware of their presence. He continued to tell Rickards of all his past journeys in the area, more about the hut where his friend lived and the soaking tub on the back of the structure. Then Barney could not hold back any longer.

"Colonel, she is that little old-looking figure out there in the paddies, working like a man, caring for her farm. Remember, I was alone and very scared, more than scared to be seen by anyone, when I first knew that I was stranded in this place. I stayed hidden in the bamboo for a number of weeks watching what I was sure was an old man. That old man became my bond to some other person to whom I could, in my own way, communicate with. We had many "conversations" before I made myself known to him. It stayed that way until the damn Jap soldier came by and struck the old man in the face with his gun. I felt that the damned soldier had hurt my friend and the anger that went through me demanded that I get revenge." Barney related the act of killing the enemy soldier and even now, it made cold shivers charge through his body.

Barney did leave some of the more personal items out. They were only his and Myoko's.

Barney then asked the driver to go on down to the figure of the old man still bent over completely ignoring them. As the truck stopped, the figure lifted its head slightly to see who was spoiling the peace and quiet solitude of the chores. Barney could plainly see into the face mostly hidden by the peasant-looking hat. Not a smile, but the very beautiful face as he remembered it, slightly covered with beads of sweat and fine dust.

Following Colonel Rickards out of the truck, he slowly walked toward Myoko. She did not recognize the man in the neat looking civilian clothes. Even as Barney was just a few feet away, there was no recognition. Only when he spoke and called her name did she drop her hoe and cry out in a very soft voice, "You did come back! You did come back!" Streams of warm tears ran down both of their faces. Barney folded her small body into his arms and whispered, "It"s just as I told you it would be. I am back, Myoko, back forever, forever."

The End